WHERE
SHE
LIES

MICHAEL SCANLON

WHERE SHE LIES

bookouture

Published by Bookouture in 2019

An imprint of StoryFire Ltd.

Carmelite House
50 Victoria Embankment
London EC4Y 0DZ

www.bookouture.com

ISBN: 978-1-78681-744-0
eBook ISBN: 978-1-78681-743-3

This book is dedicated to Nuala, Eileen and Sarah.
Three generations of strong, powerful females,
without whom I'd be lost.

'He who follows the crow will be led to the corpses of dogs'
— *Moroccan saying*

CHAPTER ONE

She cursed herself for having agreed to meet him in the forest. Even if here was where it had all started, properly started, that is – fumbling about in the inky black of night, the sudden jolt as he pulled on the seat lever, the way the seat shot back, and how he'd been above her, his hot peppermint breath blowing all over her face.

She tugged on the collar of her pink polo-neck jumper, bringing it up over her mouth, creating a warm cocoon of air inside.

He had a nice car, with big leather seats, but he preferred it in amongst the trees, always worried that someone might come along and catch them. She didn't care. Not any more. She just wanted him. She wanted him more than ever.

She pulled her mobile phone from her back pocket, yanking on it a couple of times because her jeans were so tight. She checked the time: 10.17 p.m.

He was late. He was always late now. In the beginning it had been different. In the beginning, he had been the keen one. But lately that had started to change. He was becoming bored.

Maybe she should teach him a lesson this time? Walk away, head into town, now, before it got too late, before it got completely dark. That would teach him.

But she knew she would not do that. She would stay. She would wait. Because he did something for her. He made her feel special. Like a woman. Not a girl. Everyone treated her like a girl. But not him.

The light had dwindled before her very eyes as if someone had turned down a dimmer switch on the world. With it came sounds she had not noticed before – the yelping of a dog way off in the distance, the call of a bird high up in the trees – and although she liked to think that maybe her mind was playing tricks, she heard the breaking of branches and the snapping of twigs a little behind her. She looked over her shoulder, could see nothing but the dark caverns between the trees.

And ahead, when she looked again, through the treeline along the edge of the forest, the lights from across the river backlit the world like a movie theatre. In the distance, white orbs floated – headlights she knew – moving on the road over there.

But then, when she looked back, there was no sound but the whispering of the branches in the breeze: *swish, swish, swish.*

And then, it came again, unmistakable now, the sounds of twigs and branches snapping, coursing a slow, steady path in her direction. Her eyes, straining through the darkness, were just about able to discern the abstract shapes, the outline of trees and finally, the familiar profile…

'You scared the shit out of me. Why didn't you bring the fucking car? Just this bloody once. It's late, you know. D'ya know how late it is?'

There was no reply, just the steady snapping of twigs and branches as they broke underfoot and he crossed the final few feet to her.

CHAPTER TWO

Beck's eyes snapped open. He was lying on his bed, the sheets crumpled around him, the duvet a pile on the floor. He looked about, confused… then remembered. His dream. An image of a figure in a black soutane flittered from his mind and was gone. And with it his confusion returned.

There was a sound. He turned his head and saw it then, his mobile phone on the bedside locker, the screen illuminating each time it rang, as if angry at the delay in getting his attention. He swallowed twice, his throat dry, reached out and picked it up, brought it to his ear.

'Hello,' he said, his voice hoarse. He listened, and as he did, he knew that while he had slept a nightmare had come true. For a girl. A girl who would never wake again.

Beck looked down at the body, noted the clean, healthy sheen of the hair, the full cheeks, the clean clothes, the boots –Timberland. His niece had a pair just like those.

The victim was about the same age too, fifteen or sixteen, maybe seventeen tops.

He noted the ruffled top of the pink polo-neck sweater. There was nothing to indicate how she had died, or indeed, why. Her clothes had not been disturbed, her pockets not turned out. Beck discounted robbery as a motive, especially here. Robbers didn't usually lurk amongst trees in isolated woodlands waiting for a victim to just wander by. But he couldn't be certain, not yet. From a distance, it seemed as if she was resting, sleeping maybe. But up close, it was apparent she was dead, the skin a greenish-blue hue, eyes starting to sink into their sockets like pebbles into mud, the face stiff and angular in its death mask.

Had she somehow, by freak of nature, succumbed to something? Sudden cardiac arrest, perhaps? It happened. Because there was nothing – no blood, no bruising – to indicate how she might have died.

Still, there was no doubt. Beck knew in his bones that she had been murdered.

His eyes were drawn to the pink polo-neck again. He had read an article in the FBI International Bulletin on the garda portal recently, titled 'The Importance of Crime Scene Integrity'. He knew what he was about to do was bad practice. But he went ahead and did it anyway, squatted down onto his knees, took out a pen from the inside pocket of his parka jacket, nudged the tip into the collar of the jumper, pulled it down. And immediately saw the dark purple and yellow ring of bruising about the neck. He put the pen back into his pocket and stood again.

He turned, walked along the track through the trees and down the embankment to the pathway. Two ruddy-cheeked young guards in high-visibility jackets were standing at the bottom, part of the recent batch of graduates from the Garda College in Templemore, Beck knew. He could tell, by their wide-eyed, slightly confused expressions, that this was most certainly their first murder scene.

He nodded as he passed by.

Superintendent Andrew Wilde and Inspector Gerald O'Reilly stood a little further down the pathway. There was no cordon tape. Wilde didn't think one necessary, the location being so isolated. Beck disagreed. A rambler – anyone – could literally stumble across the body, although granted that wasn't likely. But still. And no one had been posted on watch. Hadn't anyone heard of foxes?

'We're waiting on forensics,' Wilde said, stating the obvious, and, as an afterthought: 'I hope you didn't go poking around up there, Beck.'

'No, boss.'

'Because,' Inspector O'Reilly added, 'you do as you are directed now. Nothing more. Nothing less. This is not your case.'

The superintendent looked at his watch. 'Yes, yes, Gerry, he knows all that.'

'They have to come from Dublin,' Beck said. 'Forensics. In a van.'

'Really, Beck?' O'Reilly said, arching his eyebrows. 'Do they now?'

'Just saying.'

'At least it's not raining.' It was Wilde. He looked at the ground, as if debating something. Looked up again, said to Beck, 'Now, we all know you've investigated your fair share of murders, Beck. Let's say it like it is. You're only here because of, well, no one really knows the reason for that, do they? The less said about that the better. So, what's your reading on all this?'

There was the sound of something moving in the gravel. Beck looked and saw the heel of O'Reilly's right foot grinding into the path.

'A bit early to tell, isn't it?' He caught O'Reilly's look, his eyebrows still arched as he stared at him.

'She's young,' Wilde said. 'Attractive, well dressed…'

'A boyfriend,' O'Reilly added, a little too quickly. 'A jilted boyfriend. Something along those lines, maybe.'

'Hmm,' said Wilde, and looked at Beck.

Now it was Beck's turn to raise his eyebrows.

'Maybe she killed herself,' he said, although he knew that wasn't true.

O'Reilly's boot heel ground into the gravel of the path again.

Beck glanced at the watery blue sky. The weather forecast was for high winds, possibly rain later. The trees should offer some protection. As crime scenes went, it was a good location for a body, if there was such a thing. He wanted to tell Wilde to at least set up a proper perimeter, have everybody signed in and out. But he didn't. Because that was no longer his place.

He wondered how long it took a van to get here from Dublin.

CHAPTER THREE

Cross Beg is a town of hills and alleyways, from a time long, long since passed, when those that clawed the rough scrubland about here gathered in the lee of the riverbank and bartered with one another to survive. The river water is made brown by the bog land through which it flows, and from this it gets its name: Brown Water River. An abbey followed, where the cathedral now stands, and people began to live within its walls, so that slowly the town of Cross Beg began to form, sprouting up like moss between barren stones.

Ned Donohue opened the door and craned his neck, looking up and down the street before finally stepping out, pulling the door shut behind him. Quickly, in that peculiar gait of his – head forward, feet angled outward like a wind-up duck – he moved down Plunkett Hill. He reached the first alley and fell into its shadows, stopped and leaned against the wall. He looked through the permanent grey twilight to the wedge of daylight at the other end, between the two black bookends that were the buildings on either side. The smell of piss from the gutters. The council came and cleaned the alley most days, ever since complaints had begun appearing in the letters page of the local newspaper, *The Connaughtman*. Except no one ever cleaned up the dog shite. That was everywhere.

He started walking towards the wedge, thinking of how best to cross the street outside to get to the next alley. He felt like a mouse being hunted by a cat – a cat he couldn't see and wasn't certain was even there. But a cat that he knew, when he least expected, could pounce.

He reached the end of the alley, paused before scurrying out onto the street and across the road, not stopping until he reached the sanctuary of the next alleyway.

CHAPTER FOUR

The big-panel van turned into the gravel car park, which had been newly laid – a sign the state forestry service, Coillte, would soon be coming to chop the wood. The lettering on the side was in Gaelic, '*An Biúró Teicniúil*', and beneath it, the English translation: 'Garda Technical Bureau'. Following it was a black Volvo S70, and sitting in the back, the state pathologist Dr Derek Gumbell. Beck took a last pull on his cigarette and stubbed it out under his shoe. He had wandered down here, frustrated with Wilde and O'Reilly's endless quotations from murder crime scene manuals. As a result, they weren't actually getting anything done. Beck had spent some time studying the newly laid surface, looking for fresh tyre marks, or footprints – anything – but finding nothing. The cigarette was his first of the day. He was pleased with that.

Beck and Gumbell went back a long way. Although the state pathologist liked fast cars and garish shirts, he was a balding, foul-mouthed, grumpy middle-aged man best suited to a profession dealing with the remains of the dead. Like Beck, he was unmarried, but had a daughter somewhere that no one knew anything about except that she lived with her mother.

Gumbell got out of the Volvo and stretched, glancing around. He did a double take when he spotted Beck.

'My God. Beck. Is that you? Well, fuck me. I heard you'd been sent somewhere or other. So here you are. Fucked up big time, didn't you?'

Subtle as ever, Beck thought. He walked across to join him.

'Superintendent Wilde,' Beck said, 'is the senior investigating officer, not me. I've no interest in investigating anything. My sole ambition is to get out of the backwater that is Cross Beg. Any interest in this case is purely one of curiosity.'

'That's quite a sermon, Beck. I know, you've been demoted. Sergeant now, isn't it? You'd need a parachute for a drop like that, ha ha.'

'Hmm.'

'Been demoted myself, in a sense. Dr Price, my deputy... you know her, don't you?'

'We've never actually met.'

'Well, anyway, urgent case of – she mightn't want me to say it, so I'd better not. Anyway, here I am instead. Wouldn't mind, but I had a round of bloody golf at four.'

'Yes, Beck, I'll look after this.' O'Reilly's voice from behind. 'The body is this way, doctor. When you're ready.'

Beck turned.

'Someone's been reported missing, at the station,' O'Reilly said. 'Go and check it out, will you? Let me know if there's anything in it... please.'

Beck felt the 'please' was added only because of the presence of the pathologist.

Gumbell called after him as he walked away. 'Your number still the same, Beck? I'm staying over. We must meet for lemonade and a chat later.'

Beck stopped, half turning. 'My number is still the same,' he answered.

'One hell of an investigator. You've heard of him, haven't you? I mean, he's one of the best,' Gumbell said.

O'Reilly forced a half-smile. 'I've heard of him,' he grunted.

CHAPTER FIVE

She was pacing the floor when he got back to the station. The duty sergeant had told him her name over the radio: Theresa Frazzali. Beck thought it rang a bell. Then it came to him. Frazzali's restaurant and takeaway in the centre of town.

She was a small woman, with shoulder-length blonde hair parted in the middle, black roots visible like a line had been drawn in marker pen down the centre of her head. She had large green eyes, and small tight lips that drooped in the corners, running into deep furrows on either side of her chin. She had a tissue in her hands, twisted into a hard knot.

He didn't know that she knew him, but once she saw him, she stepped in front so he would have to stop. 'Sergeant Beck.' It was a statement, not a query.

'Yes.'

'My name is Theresa Frazzali. Tanya, my daughter, didn't come home last night. I told the officer, over there…' She nodded her head in the direction of the public counter. 'This morning, that is, she didn't come home. I mean last night. God, I don't know. I haven't seen her since last night is what I'm trying to say. The officer told me to wait for you. Why would he do that? Is something wrong?'

She was on the verge of tears now, but holding back, waiting for reassurance, waiting for him to say, 'No, Mrs Frazzali, nothing is wrong. The officer asked me to see you because he wanted me to tell you not to worry – that's all, you know. This kind of thing, unfortunately, happens all the time. Your daughter will be home shortly, you'll see'.

But that was not what he said. What he said was: 'Your daughter. Can you describe her?'

Mrs Frazzali stared at him, her eyes widening. 'Why? What's wrong? Have you found someone?'

'Mrs Frazzali,' Beck said, 'if your daughter was missing, like you think she might be, then I'd need to know what she looks like, and also what she was wearing, wouldn't I? But that doesn't mean anything has happened to her.'

Mrs Frazzali relaxed. 'Of course. Yes, of course. You would. Wouldn't you? Let me see, Tanya's about five six, my height... Actually, she looks a lot like me, but a much younger version.'

'Do you remember what she was wearing, Mrs Frazzali?'

'What she was wearing? I didn't see her before she went out. I don't know what Tanya was wearing. I can't be sure.'

Beck said nothing for a moment, considering, then asked, 'Does she have, by any chance, a pink polo-neck jumper, and Timberland boots?'

Mrs Frazzali stared at Beck. He could see the confusion on her face.

'Why do you ask?'

He placed his hand gently on her elbow, guided her to the bench. They sat down.

She tried to twist the tissue in her hands, pressing her fingers into it, the tips white, but the tissue was so tightly knotted it couldn't move any further. She looked at him and lifted the corners of her lips into a faint, desperate smile, then reached into her handbag, took out her mobile phone, pressed a button, scrolled through it and offered it to him.

'It was taken two weeks ago. At her cousin's birthday. It's Tanya.'

Beck took the phone. The photograph of three girls, laughing, arms intertwined across each other's shoulders, was taken at close range, so Beck could clearly see their faces. He thought of the body in the forest, peeled away the death mask, gave colour to the flesh, reset the eyes, buffed up the hair. And saw her. The girl in the middle. Tanya.

He handed the phone back to Mrs Frazzali.

'Mrs Frazzali,' he began, but already she was holding her face in her hands, palms squeezing her cheeks as she stared at him, like she was trying to stop herself from falling apart.

CHAPTER SIX

'The body is that of Tanya Frazzali. Fifteen years old.'

'Really. How're you so sure?' O'Reilly's disembodied voice at the other end of the line.

'Her mother. I just spoke with her, at the station. She reported the girl missing.'

'I see. No doubt?'

'No doubt. She showed me a photograph, on her mobile phone. It's her.'

'We'll have to wait for an official identification, of course.'

'Yes, of course.'

'You still at the station?'

'Yes.'

'Stay there. There's a briefing in one hour.'

Beck put the phone in one of his pockets, reached into another for a pack of cigarettes, fished one out and lit up, leaning against the front red-brick wall of Cross Beg garda station. The building was, supposedly, a prime example of period architecture, circa 1890. The Office of Public Works hung flower baskets from its front wall each spring. It was October now, and they were overdue in coming to take these down again, the baskets still hanging there, the flowers all withered and dead.

He watched Mrs Frazzali walk along the pavement and turn into the car park of Crabby's supermarket at the end of the street. Beck had offered to have someone drive her home, but she'd refused. He gave instructions to the officer on desk duty to forward her name to victim support immediately.

CHAPTER SEVEN

The first forty-eight hours, Beck knew. The Window, they called it. Which came after The Golden Hour. Which came after the crime. Forty-eight hours. Then the window started to close, the investigation slowed, momentum was lost.

Forty-eight hours.

Beck sat at a desk in the deserted Ops Room. The weak October sunlight filtered through the high, narrow windows, and the old wrought iron radiators made a clicking noise as the water circulated inside them. The door to the public office was open. He could hear the desk officer out there, answering a phone that never seemed to stop ringing. As he listened, the clicking from the radiators appeared to grow louder and louder, and Beck remembered the sounds of the revolver chamber turning. *Click, click, click...*

The telephone rang in the public office again, a loud, shrill noise. It sounded twice before being answered: 'Hello, Cross Beg Garda Station...'

The Ops Room was filling, uniform and plainclothes officers arriving from outlying stations and districts. Beck sat listening to the jumbled sounds of their conversations.

A whiteboard was wheeled in at the top of the room, Superintendent Wilde and Inspector O'Reilly following, standing on either side of it. Wilde had a marker in his hand, holding it in the air like a conductor's baton. O'Reilly's hands were clasped in front of him, head bowed, as if deep in prayer.

'Quiet, people,' Superintendent Wilde said, waving the marker about as the room fell silent. He allowed the silence to percolate, then continued. 'First things first. For the duration of the investigation, briefings take place at 9 a.m. daily in this room. Understood? Good. Now, at 3.07 a.m. this morning, a 999 call was received in the Comms Room here at Cross Beg. The caller, male, reported finding a body in Cool Wood just outside the town, that of a young female. The call was made from a phone box in the square. The caller wouldn't give his name or any details, but he had a pronounced stutter. The officer who took it thinks it's Ned Donohue, or Neddy, as most people know him. And most of us here know him. When Neddy gets nervous, the stammer comes out. I've listened back to the tape myself, and I agree that it's likely him. A unit's been round to his house twice already, but he's not home. Now, yesterday was Monday, dole day here in Cross Beg, and Neddy likes to drink cider and get out of his head. He's known to wander about the place when he's like that, including Cool Wood. We need to find him as soon as possible. Anyone who doesn't know Ned, check the system – there's a photograph of him on there. Ned doesn't like the gardai, and can get very anxious when he has to deal with us. Due care and attention when dealing with him, please.'

Wilde turned to the whiteboard and wrote 'Ned Donohue' on it in a heavy scrawl. He went on: 'The victim is believed to be a local girl, Tanya Frazzali, fifteen years old. The body has not been formally identified, but we're confident that's who it is. Her family own the Frazzali restaurant on Main Street – been there over fifty years, very popular place, originally Italian, as the name suggests. The victim was a student at St Malachi's College… Sergeant Beck, you spoke with her mother. She reported her missing, correct?'

Beck cleared his throat and stood. 'Yes boss, that's correct. Mrs Theresa Frazzali came to the station earlier today. She was upset her daughter, Tanya, had not come home last night. From her description and a photograph of Tanya she showed me on her mobile phone, I'm satisfied the body is that of Tanya Frazzali.'

'Did anyone else agree with this opinion?' It was Inspector O'Reilly, raising his head now and staring at Beck. 'Did you ask?'

Beck said nothing.

'Well, did they?' O'Reilly pressed.

'I have no doubt,' Beck said. 'It's Tanya Frazzali.' Beck wanted to smile, because getting up someone's nose the way he seemed to be getting up O'Reilly's was a compliment of sorts.

O'Reilly gestured with his hand, as if brushing Beck away.

'Scene of Crime are still processing the scene,' Wilde went on. 'Likely to be there for the rest of the day, and tomorrow too. They haven't found a mobile phone, by the way. Whether the victim had one with her, of course, we don't know, not as yet. The cause of death, the state pathologist believes at this stage, is asphyxiation. The victim was strangled. This will not be officially confirmed until after the autopsy, which takes place tomorrow morning at the County Hospital.'

Wilde looked about the room.

'Suggestions, people,' he said. 'Who could have done this? I want to see some hands in the air... yes, you.'

'A boyfriend? It's usually the way, isn't it?'

'Anyone else?'

'I agree. In the woods and all – has to be a boyfriend, a lover.'

'And you?' Wilde pointed towards the back of the room.

'Maybe she wasn't killed in the woods at all. Maybe her body was dumped there.'

Wilde wrote 'family and friends' on the whiteboard, circled it twice. 'It appears she was murdered in the wood, by the way,' he said, and continued, 'Anyone's radar showing possibilities? I want names.'

'Anyone's capable of it. Especially the clients we deal with.' The same voice from the back of the room.

'Yes, yes, I know,' Wilde said. 'But specifically, does anyone come to mind? Come on now.'

The room fell silent again.

'How wide do you want to throw this net?' a female voice asked.

Wilde pursed his lips, thinking about that. 'For now, I'm talking about Cross Beg and the station's district.'

'That narrows things down considerably. You'd be the best judge of that yourself.'

Wilde looked a little uncomfortable now. His conversation was coming full circle.

'Okay,' he said, turning to the whiteboard. He began writing down names. 'Malcolm Nugent, Vincent Fletcher, Darren Murphy…'

'Don't forget Raymond "Nobby" Clarke.'

'How would I forget him?' Wilde said, writing the name down. 'I thought he was sectioned in the psych unit in Galway indefinitely.'

'He was released under supervision into a community-based programme,' someone said. 'The voices in his head have stopped, apparently.'

'Claire Somers.' It was O'Reilly. 'Claire, where are you?'

A hand rose. 'Over here.'

'Welcome back.'

'Thank you.'

'You're with Detective Sergeant Beck, okay? The man has a tendency to go solo. Not in Cross Beg. And Beck?'

'Yes?'

'The family of the deceased. The Frazzalis. Visit them. That should keep you out of trouble. And assure them we're doing everything we can. Don't let me keep you. Get on with it.'

That suited Beck fine. Going through the motions. Beck had no intention of doing anything other than tinkering around the edges of this if he could help it. It seemed O'Reilly was of the same mind.

CHAPTER EIGHT

Detective Garda Claire Somers had short blonde hair, was of stocky build, dressed in blue jeans, a grey NYU hoodie, white sneakers. They were standing in the hallway outside the Ops Room. She extended a hand and Beck took it. Her grip was firm, the flesh tough but soft at the same time.

'He doesn't like me running about on my own, seemingly,' Beck said. 'Did he tell you to report back on what I might get up to?'

A look flittered across her eyes.

'That's okay,' Beck said. 'He would do, wouldn't he?'

'If it's any help, I think he's an arsehole too.'

She went and got the keys to a car – a Ford Focus – and found it using the registration number on the key fob; it was double-parked by the main door of the station. The car chirped once as she pointed the remote and unlocked it.

'I haven't seen you about before,' Beck said as they got in.

'I've been away. Got married, actually. Travelled Europe for two months on my honeymoon. That would explain it.' She put the key in the ignition and turned it. 'The Frazzalis live on River Road. I should know the house.'

'You've had reason to visit there before?'

She did a U-turn and drove along Main Street. 'Yes. Mr Frazzali. He killed himself number of years ago. Went into the river – it's the method of choice locally.'

Beck thought about that. 'Into the river? How so certain? He could have just fallen in, couldn't he?'

'There was a witness. When they recovered the body, his hands were still in his trouser pockets. He didn't put up any fight... on the contrary.'

'Any suicide note?'

Claire changed gears as she took the Focus round a sharp bend. 'No, nothing. Seemingly most don't leave one. Not in Cross Beg, anyway. Unusual. Alcohol plays a part, increasingly drugs. Probably seems like a good idea at the time, I suppose.'

'And was Mr Frazzali under the influence of anything?'

'Antonio? No, no. Completely clean.'

Beck looked out the window. 'Any other children?'

'A son. Tony. A handsome lad. He manages the restaurant.'

'I see,' Beck said. 'On a lighter topic, who's the lucky man?'

'The lucky man?'

'Your new husband.'

'You mean lucky woman. That'd be me.'

'Yes, but your husband?'

She laughed. 'I don't have a husband. I have a wife. I married a woman.'

Beck said nothing for a moment, taken off guard. 'Oh,' he said then.

'"Oh" – I get that a lot.'

'I bet you do.'

'Are you shocked? Some people are.'

'Shocked? No. That's a strong word. If that shocked me, I'd spend every day shocked by something or other. Life would be one long shock.'

'Surprised?'

'Of course.'

'Have you got a problem with it?'

'I don't have a problem with it.'

'Just asking. Some do.'

'Things have changed, the referendum and all that… By the way, did you ever think I might be gay? Or are you just assuming that I'm not?'

'I'm not assuming anything. Are you?'

'No. I don't think so. Not so far, although I'd like to think I'd try anything once.'

They both laughed, the atmosphere lightening.

'So, your wife. Who's she, the lucky woman?'

'Lucy Grimes. Journalist with *The Connaughtman* in Galway.'

'Did she take your name? Or you hers?'

'We both kept our names. It's simpler.'

'No, I'm not shocked. I'm pleased.'

'Not everyone feels the same way, as I say. And you?'

'And me?'

'You married, or…?'

'No, I'm not married or…'

'Really? Never married?'

'No. You sound surprised.'

'I am. You're quite… presentable. I'm sure there was, or is, interest.'

Beck shifted in his seat. 'Yes,' he said vaguely, 'I'm sure there is.'

CHAPTER NINE

River Road twisted by the bottom of low hills at the edge of Cross Beg, the river on one side, the tops of prominent houses peering out over ivy-crusted walls on the other.

'Can we pull in somewhere?' Beck asked. 'I've just thought of something.'

'What, now?'

'Yes.'

She turned into an agricultural gateway a short distance ahead, a narrow track disappearing into a thick hedgerow on the other side of a galvanised steel gate. Claire cut the engine.

Beck got out of the car and stood, breathing in deep, looking over the gate along the track towards the field.

'Unless my sense of direction is completely off,' he said as Claire joined him, 'it should be possible to reach Cool Wood from here, from this road, shouldn't it? I mean, that field up there runs behind these houses.'

'It is possible. The field does run behind these houses. At the top is the town cemetery. Beside it, Cool Wood.'

Beck considered. Did he want to do this? No was the answer. But his damned cop's curiosity did.

'Fancy a walk?' he said.

'Not really.'

You heard her, she doesn't. Forget it. Go and talk to the Frazzalis. Like you're supposed to. Nothing more. Nothing less.

But Beck walked to the gate instead, placed a foot onto a lower cross bar and began to climb over. He waited on the other side while Claire followed.

They walked up the narrow track and into the field. It stretched all the way along the back of River Road to a point further ahead, where it dipped abruptly down into the Brown Water River. On the other side Beck could see the grey uniform drabness of a housing estate.

'Chapel Park?' he asked.

'The one and only,' she said, as if referring to an unruly child.

They walked to the top of the field, the ground rough and spongy beneath their feet. They stopped at a low stone wall; inside it, amid the high grass and weeds, old headstones stood like lopsided dirty teeth.

'This is the old section,' she said. She pointed off to the right. 'That's the town over there.' She swivelled her arm. 'And there's Cool Wood.'

Beck turned slowly in a half-circle, hands on hips, taking it all in. His view gave him a sense of perspective, the town spread before him like a tapestry, colours of sand and yellow, of white and blue, of grey and black. He hadn't expected so many colours. At the edges green curled round, tucking everything in, while in the middle the thick ribbon that was the river cut across, and everywhere wisps of smoke rose from chimneys like delicate embroidery. From a distance, Cross Beg looked almost pretty.

'It must be very different for you,' Claire said. 'Compared to Pearse Street, that is.'

Everyone knew there was a story to tell about Beck. Even Claire, on her first day back at work, knew that. He was a one-time hotshot, a detective inspector in the proven busiest station in the country, Pearse Street, the very heart of the action, dropped like a rock to the rank of detective sergeant in, of all places, Cross Beg.

Yes, there was a story to tell, but Beck, in his silence and in the way he set his jaw, was making it clear that he wasn't going to tell it.

He counted with his fingers. 'Four from the end, in that direction,' he said, ignoring the question. 'The Frazzalis, correct?'

'Um.' She worked it out too. 'Yes, you have it.'

'So, Tanya could have left her house and come this way to Cool Wood.'

He led the way to the wall and over it, careful not to dislodge any loose stones. The graves in the old section were completely overgrown. He was careful too as he walked not to trip on the rough edges hidden beneath the grass and weeds. The remnants of another stone wall marked the border between the old cemetery and the new, but it had mostly crumbled away. On the other side of it the grass was trim and the headstones laid out in neat symmetrical order. Beck walked between graves in the direction of Cool Wood, stopping at the high cement block wall running down the side of the cemetery and partially camouflaged by the overhanging branches. If Tanya had come this way, how had she got over that?

'There is a way in,' Claire said, reading his thoughts. 'This way.'

He followed her to a low section of the wall with steps.

Beck placed a foot onto the step and started over, Claire behind. On the other side they stood on a narrow strip of soft ground between the wall and the trees. He looked ahead. This was not a forest designed to have any recreational value. Its existence was purely for commercial reasons. The fast-growing pines would be ready for harvest within twenty years, a relatively quick turnaround for timber. But pine was not a native species, and within a forest like this nothing much lived – it was an eerie, silent, even forlorn place.

He noted the seemingly abstract tangle of branches and trees in front of him, like a confused drawing in heavy strokes of charcoal, flashes of green and brown mixed in. But gradually, a pattern began to emerge: the straight-line symmetry of the trees, a trench running down between each row where the ground had originally been scooped out to make the raised beds for the planting of seedlings. It was impossible to walk in these trenches now; the tangle of branches with their prickly wild hawthorns were better than any barbed wire.

'How did she get through all that?' Claire asked.

Still he looked, his mind trying to decipher the knotted tangle. Off to the left, little beads of a colour lighter than those surrounding it caught his eye. Beck approached, and the little beads meandered off into the forest. He identified them as the exposed pale bark of cut branches. Beck saw now that a tunnel had been carved through the branches and brambles, clearing a pathway through the trees, the discarded cuttings lying on the forest floor like a loosely knotted rope mat. This was probably one of many like it cut by the forestry service in preparation for the arrival of machines for harvesting.

'This is how,' Beck said, but more to himself than to Claire.

They walked to the entrance of the makeshift tunnel, spheres of weak light filtering through the branches. Beck thought of *The Lord of the Rings*. But who was the Dark Lord Sauron of this particular tale?

CHAPTER TEN

A Mercedes-Benz and two BMWs were parked side by side at the top of the tree-lined driveway to the Frazzali house. Standing next to the cars was a small knot of people, talking quietly to each other. They scarcely glanced over as Beck and Claire passed by. The front door was open. Beck and Claire stood before it, looking in at an open-plan reception area, a table in the centre, a vase with flowers on top, behind the table a chaise longue with carved wooden legs. It had the appearance more of a hotel than a private house. Beck was about to call out when a door opened and a young man emerged. He appeared not to have noticed them, began walking away in the opposite direction.

'That's Tony,' Claire said.

'Excuse me,' Beck called. His words came out much louder than he'd intended.

Tony stopped and turned, paused for a moment before walking over. He was dressed in a tight white T-shirt that showed off pumped biceps and a Mediterranean olive complexion. His features, both face and body, were in perfect proportion. Sad green eyes in a very handsome face stared back at Beck.

'Tony Frazzali,' Beck said. 'Detective Sergeant Finnegan Beck, and Detective Garda Claire Somers. I know this is a very difficult time. But could we have a word?'

Tony slowly moved aside and nodded for them to enter. They followed him to the chaise longue and he sat down at one end. Beck and Claire remained standing. Beck could feel a coldness in the air. It wasn't a physical coldness, but a coldness nonetheless, and he had felt it before, too many times. It came only with tragedy.

'Is your mother here?' Claire asked gently.

Tony sat back, his hands by his sides, staring ahead. 'My mother has been sedated. She's sleeping.'

His voice was gentle, soft, dreamlike, and yet in the acoustics of the open-plan room, it carried with it a powerful, precise clarity.

Beck looked at Claire.

'There's a lot of people working on this, Tony,' she said. 'Just so as you know. We won't stop. We called to let you know that.'

'Thank you,' he said. 'I appreciate it.'

'Tony,' she said, 'I hate to mention this, but we'll need to make a formal identification at some stage…' Her voice trailed off.

'Of course. I'll do it.'

'Thank you. Someone will be in touch with the details.'

Tony's eyes shifted now, taking in Beck.

'Someone told my mother about you. That's why she asked at the station – asked for you. You've done this before, isn't that right? Investigated…' The word seemed to stick in the back of his throat: 'Murders.'

'Yes,' Beck said. 'I have.'

Tony leaned forward suddenly and swallowed a couple of times. He raised his hands to his face and rubbed them across it briskly. 'She was only a girl, a girl… Ah, Jesus Christ.'

Beck sat down next to him, said softly, 'Do you know who might have done this? Can you think of anyone who might have wished your sister harm? I have to ask.'

Tony blinked, regaining his composure. 'No, nothing like that. Jesus Christ, no.' He wrapped his arms tightly around himself.

'What about friends? Did Tanya have many?'

Tony smiled. 'Oh yes. Loads. Her best is… oh God, *was*, Melanie. Melanie McBride. They went to St Malachi's College.'

Beck saw Claire with a notebook in her hand now, writing something down, presumably the name.

'Has Victim Support contacted you?' she asked.

'Not yet.'

'They will. Very soon. Have you got anyone with you, Tony? Family, a priest, anyone like that?'

'Some cousins outside. And our priest, Father Clifford, has said he'll visit when Mum wakes up.'

'Good,' she said.

'Did Tanya have a mobile phone?' Beck asked.

Beck saw Claire turn and look at him out of the corner of his eye.

'Of course.'

'They didn't find it, Tony,' Claire said.

'Didn't they? I was ringing it earlier, before we... Oh God, before we got the news.'

'Do you know where she might have kept it?' Beck asked. 'Here at home, that is?'

'She always had it with her. Always. She never bothered with an iPad. Just that.'

'Would you mind if we maybe looked in her bedroom?' Beck asked.

Claire shifted from one foot to the other.

Tony took a slow, deep breath, exhaled. 'Her bedroom.' He pointed to the stairs. 'Up there. The one with the pink sign on the door... I won't go with you though, if that's alright.'

'That's fine,' Beck said, standing. 'Thank you.'

They crossed to the staircase with its twisted wood spindles and went up the wide steps to the first floor. The door with the pink sign was midway along a thickly carpeted corridor opposite. A boy band with suitably brooding expressions stared down from a poster on the wall in Tanya's bedroom. Beck looked around – at the clutter of shoes and the clothes piled on the floor in a corner, the dresser by the window, its top a mixture of cuddly toys and make-up, a wardrobe door left open, brightly coloured clothes hanging haphazardly inside; bright colours, lots of pink. Everything was exactly as it had been when Tanya was here last, but everything had irrevocably changed now. The pink duvet on the bed, with its white lace trim, was crumpled as if Tanya had just been lying there and had left the room and would be back in a minute. But Tanya would not be back in a minute. Tanya would never be back again.

Beck noted everything.

He took the pair of latex gloves he always carried from a pocket, separated them, held one out to Claire.

She looked at it. 'This isn't a crime scene.'

'You don't know that. That's for forensics to decide. If and when they get here.'

Claire snatched the glove from him, pulled it on.

Beck used his mobile phone camera to take photographs of the room, in case these were needed later.

Claire started with the drawers – the places where intimate items might be kept – while Beck looked everywhere else.

There was no phone.

When they went back downstairs, Tony was gone. They found him outside, standing with his relatives, smoking a cigarette. There was a subtle similarity in the appearance of the group that Beck had not noted earlier. As he looked now, he could see it.

Traditionally, Beck knew, Italians in Ireland traced their origins to the province of Frosinone, pronounced *fros-e-no-knee,* which was south of Rome and north of Naples. They had come to the country during the 1950s, seeking opportunities following the war, and unlikely as it was, had found them. Italian restaurants, takeaways and ice cream parlours flourished.

'Thank you, Tony. We'll be in touch,' Claire said.

'Did you find it? The phone.'

'No. We did not.'

Tony drew on his cigarette and blew out a thick stream of smoke without inhaling. 'I rang it,' he said, 'while you were in the room, searching.'

'It didn't ring,' Claire said.

Tony's eyes widened. 'Yes, it did. It rang. I heard it.'

'It did?' Claire answered, looking at Beck, who was looking at her with the same expression of surprise.

'The phone,' Claire said as they walked back down the driveway from the house. 'Where is it?'

Beck took a moment to reply. 'The obvious answer,' he said, 'is that the killer has it. Maybe kept it as a trophy, a trinket. That changes things, and in a way I don't like.'

'How so?'

'Well... it brings a new perspective.'

'Yes,' Claire said, slightly irritated. 'In what way?'

'Certain types. Like... well, serial killers.'

'Did you say serial killers? You mean, like Ted Bundy? Aren't you running away with yourself a little there?'

'Certain types, I said. Anyway, it's just a thought – a suggestion. I think it would be a good idea to visit the school. Speak to this Melanie girl.' He checked his watch. 'We still have time.'

'I don't know. Shouldn't we run it by O'Reilly first, or someone? We'd need to give it a little time. The poor girl's body's just been found.'

'That's precisely why we need to do it now,' he said. 'We wallow in time until it runs out. And time is already running out. Anyway, if that's how you do things in Cross Beg, I don't want to waste my energy swimming against the tide. We can leave it. Play it safe. Run it by O'Reilly first, like you say.'

Nothing more. Nothing less.

They reached the car and Claire stood by the driver's door. As she was about to open it, a 1990-registration Toyota Crown pulled in from the road and parked in front of them. The big old car looked all of its twenty-nine years. Behind the wheel Beck could see a long-faced man with black hair. The white dog collar in his black shirt was stark against his sallow skin.

Father Clifford got out and bounded over. He seemed to be a man of excessive nervous energy. He smiled, a strained smile, the smile of a man who grappled with the big-ticket questions and knew he didn't have all the answers.

As he approached, he seemed to have to force himself to slow down. Beck tried to calculate his age, but his complexion was ageless, like an ecclesiastical Peter Pan. He introduced himself, his handshake firm.

'Are you family?' he asked.

'Cross Beg gardai,' Claire said.

'God be with you in your hunt for whoever is responsible,' he said, his accent imbued with the gentle west of Ireland lilt. 'It is the devil's work. No doubt about it. Shocking. Utterly shocking. I will pray that He helps you to quickly find this, this… animal.' The priest blessed himself. 'I find it very hard to be forgiving. Such an innocent child. How could this happen? How could it? All I know is that I must be here for them in their hour of need. Goodness knows how poor Theresa will deal with this. Forgive me, but I must go. If there is anything I can do, please let me know, won't you?'

'I will, Father,' Beck said. 'Thank you.'

The priest turned and walked quickly past them, turned right and disappeared into the house.

Claire looked at Beck. 'I've been thinking,' she said. 'What you said makes sense. We should go to the school after all.'

'You think?'

'I think.'

Beck sighed. 'Let's get on with it then.'

CHAPTER ELEVEN

St Malachi's College was a little out of Cross Beg, built on a low hill; it was a sombre, grey stone building with a slate roof and narrow windows. Every town in Ireland had a building like it, whether a school, convent, or old workhouse, a lingering reminder of a time when colour did not exist, when everything was either grey or black and white. The old part of the school was to the front, a newly built section at the back.

They climbed the wide steps to the open front door and went in, stood in an alcove on a coarse-haired mat, and Beck pushed down the gleaming handle on a second door. They stood for a moment in the eerie silence of a school in session, began walking down the chequerboard corridor, the walls on either side half panelled in wood, the grey above leading to a vaulted ceiling with thick wooden beams. At regular intervals pale rectangles stood out from the wall, reminders of frames that had once hung there.

At the end of the corridor a central rotunda separated the old building from the new, corridors running off it – gleaming blue linoleum floors, bare concrete block walls, banks of lockers, a couple of display cases with trophies inside next to a noticeboard. There were four doors side by side in the wall. A notice on the first door said 'School Secretary'. It was slightly open. Beck went to it and knocked.

'Come in.'

He pushed the door open and stepped into the room. She didn't look like a school secretary. She wore loose jeans, sandals and a multi-coloured patchwork top. She looked like someone who'd just strolled in off a 1960s San Francisco street. Her hair was white and tousled, but at the same time, Beck considered, a great deal of effort had gone into making it look that way: it appeared too carefully arranged, too brushed, to be simply haphazard. She had black, thick-framed round glasses and a necklace of brightly coloured beads.

Her smile disappeared as he said, 'I'm Detective Sergeant Finnegan Beck, and this is Detective Garda Claire Somers. We need to speak to the school principal, please.'

A nerve began to twitch beneath her right eye. 'To Mr O'Malley? Why? Is something wrong?'

'Tanya Frazzali. She was a student here, I believe.'

'Still is. You said "was".'

Beck was about to answer when the secretary asked, 'This has nothing to do with that body found in Cool Wood this morning, does it? I heard about it earlier. A young girl. Jesus, it's nothing to do with that – tell me that's not why you're here.'

Beck hesitated. Couldn't she just get on with it and go and get the principal?

'Oh, God,' she muttered. 'It is, isn't it?'

'If you could get Mr O'Malley, please.'

She said nothing for a moment, then, her voice dazed: 'I'll bring you to his office.'

'And something else,' Beck said. 'We'd like to speak with Melanie McBride. She's a student here too.'

The twitch beneath her right eye became even more pronounced. 'Melanie. Why do you want to speak to Melanie?'

Beck felt like shouting, telling her to mind her own bloody business and do as he'd asked. But he also knew that this was her business; this was everybody's business.

'I need to ask her some questions,' he said instead, 'that's all. She and Tanya Frazzali were friends, I believe. Best friends.'

'Melanie's parents will have to be present.' Her tone was suddenly professional. 'At least one of them will, anyway. I mean, this will be – this *is* such a shock... for everybody.'

'I understand that,' Beck said, 'but if it wasn't important, I wouldn't ask, believe me.'

'I'll ring Melanie's mother.'

'Thank you.'

'I'll show you to Mr O'Malley's office now, then. This way.'

It was two doors down. She knocked once and went in without waiting for a reply. The school principal was behind his desk, talking on the phone. He was clearly surprised to have people barge in. He glanced to Beck and Claire, said into the phone, 'I'll have to ring you back', and hung up.

'Mr O'Malley. It's the guards. About Tanya. Tanya Frazzali.'

Mr O'Malley observed them silently. He had the build of a child but the head – bald except for tufts of hair over each ear – of a sixty-year-old. Beck guessed he was probably in his early forties. Naturally raised eyebrows gave him a permanently surprised expression.

Still, he did not speak.

'I'm sorry to have to tell you this,' Beck began, 'but the body of Tanya Frazzali was found this morning in Cool Wood. She'd been strangled to death. We wanted to inform you officially, before you heard it anywhere else.'

The school secretary took a short intake of breath. Her voice came out as a whimper. 'My God. My God. Tanya.'

The principal was silent for a long time. Finally, he spoke. 'Inform the staff, Mrs Cunningham. Discreetly. And contact the school counsellor. We need her. Immediately.'

'One moment,' Beck said. 'We need to speak with Melanie McBride, Tanya's friend. I'm sure you can understand the urgency of this situation.'

'You need to speak to Melanie? What, right away?'

'Yes,' Beck said. 'Right away.'

'I'm about to ring her mother. I'll do that first, shall I?' Mrs Cunningham added.

Mr O'Malley sighed. 'I suppose so.'

CHAPTER TWELVE

Karen McBride was a tall, regal-looking woman with delicate features, dressed in a beige trouser suit, her neck and hands draped in jewellery and her skin glowing with what Beck was convinced was a well-applied professional fake tan.

When the school secretary brought Melanie in, the girl went immediately to her mother, who took hold of both her hands, nudged her into the seat beside her. She was a pretty girl, Melanie, with long, thick black hair and the same delicate features as her mother, though her build was a little on the heavier side.

'Mam. What's all this about?' She looked about the room, and her eyes settled on Beck and Claire. 'And who're they?'

Beck had assumed the school secretary would already have told her about the police who had come to speak to her. Obviously not. There were no other chairs in the room, so Beck and Claire remained standing, leaning against Mr O'Malley's desk.

'I'm Detective Sergeant Finnegan Beck, Melanie. This is my colleague, Detective Garda Claire Somers. I need to ask you some questions.'

Melanie considered this information and observed them both, her expression blank, said, 'Ya. I don't see any ID.'

Karen McBride glared at her daughter. 'Melanie!'

Beck reached into an inside jacket pocket, pulled out his wallet and opened it, displaying his ID card.

'You're right,' he said. 'My mistake. Sorry. I should have done this first.'

Melanie didn't even bother to look. She folded her arms as her shoulders slumped and she curled into her mother.

'That's alright, darling,' her mother said, putting her arms round her, pulling her close. She looked at Beck.

Beck wondered at Melanie's behaviour. After all, no one had told her the reason for this visit. So why the theatrics? Did she think they had come for her, maybe? He pushed the thought to the back of his mind.

'We'd like to ask you some questions, Melanie,' Claire said gently. 'In relation to Tanya Frazzali.'

There was silence for a moment. Melanie's head was buried in her mother's chest now.

'What? Tanya? Why?' the girl said, her voice a couple of octaves too high, clearly surprised. There was a sniffling noise, like she'd been crying. Melanie pulled away from her mother and looked at Claire. Her eyes were red-rimmed. Beck was curious about that too, but that was for another time, if ever.

'Melanie,' her mother said slowly. 'A body was found in Cool Wood. This morning. A young woman. That's why the detectives are here. They believe it's Tanya.'

'Tanya?' Melanie said, with curiosity more than anything. 'Are you saying that she's dead? In the woods? Is that what you're saying?'

'Yes, Melanie,' Beck said. 'That's what we're saying. So you see, any information you give us – like if she maybe had a boyfriend – could help us apprehend the person responsible.'

'Melanie,' her mother said, 'if there's anything you know, you've got to – you *must* – tell the detectives here.'

Melanie swept her head from right to left, like she was following the trail of an insect flying about the room. Then she stopped and turned her head to the ceiling.

She said, her voice low, 'There's nothing much to tell. She was seeing somebody. But I don't know who. She wouldn't say.' She paused. 'I mean, not that she wouldn't say who she was seeing, but she wouldn't even say she was seeing anybody in the first place. She wanted to keep it a secret. I didn't like that. We have no secrets, me and Tanya. But I knew she was seeing somebody. So I asked her. But she told me she wasn't. She lied. Why? Maybe it was somebody she shouldn't have been seeing. Some boys are off limits, y'know. They're going steady. But that don't stop them sneaking around behind their girlfriends' backs. Had to be something like that. Still, she could have told me. She could have told me anything. Unless he was like, old, or something, maybe, I don't know, or like, married. But I don't think Tanya was into any of that.'

'How are you so certain?' Claire asked. 'That she was seeing somebody, that is. I presume you mean romantically?'

'Romantically?' Melanie said, putting her head to one side, like a puppy dog hearing a sound for the first time.

'So. She was in a relationship?' Beck clarified. 'How did you know?'

'I just did. 'Cause I know Tanya better than anyone, that's how. And something wasn't right, like I say. Why make it a big secret if it isn't? She went beetroot one day when I asked her about it. I says, "Tanya, are you seeing someone?" I knew right then. She went beetroot. That was well suspect, that was. I mean, I felt hurt. We had no secrets, like I say.'

'You never saw her with him, did you?' Beck asked.

''Course not… well, not really.'

'Not really? What do you mean, "not really"?' It was Melanie's mother. She wasn't pleased with having to listen to any of this.

'What I mean is, I thought I saw her. A couple of months back. I was with you, Mum. We were driving by Cool Wood. It was evening time. I could swear it was her. She was with somebody. A man, I think. I couldn't get a good look, though. They ducked into the trees as we passed, but I didn't say nothing.'

'You didn't say "anything", Melanie, it's not "nothing".'

'We drove past,' Melanie went on, ignoring her mother. 'I remember thinking, "What's she doing out here at this hour?" That was well suspect, too. But she said it wasn't her, when I asked her in school next day. I remember she looked really tired. I started thinking it probably wasn't her after all.' Melanie paused, stretched out the fingers of one hand, and added, 'You know her dad died a couple of years ago? Her mother and brother run the restaurant now, so Tanya's at home on her own a lot. I always thought that was really cool. Now I'm not so sure.'

Her mother pulled Melanie close.

'Oh Mum,' the girl said, losing all her swagger and sounding like the child she really was. 'Oh Mum, poor Tanya...'

'I think that's enough,' Karen McBride said. 'Can we finish this now? By the way, does Gerry know you're here?'

'Gerry?' Beck said.

'Inspector O'Reilly. He's a good friend of the family. I don't think he'd appreciate your line of questioning either, by the way.'

'Don't you?'

'No. I don't.'

Beck nodded. 'I've asked everything I need to ask for the present. We can finish this now.'

CHAPTER THIRTEEN

The street lamps threw down cocoons of light along the old crooked streets of Cross Beg as Dr Gumbell walked through the door of The Hibernian, one of two hotels in Cross Beg. The other was The Brown Water Inn, a couple of miles outside town and considerably beyond even his own generous overnight allowance. His room had already been booked and paid for by his office in Dublin. He checked in without fuss, went to his room, showered and changed into fresh clothes and came down to the bar. Beck was already there waiting for him. Dr Gumbell sat on the stool next to him.

'My room smells of mould,' Gumbell said. 'Or maybe it's just the smell of death that permanently follows me.' He reached for a bar menu, perused it.

A pint of Guinness sat on the counter in front of Beck. He picked it up, took a long swallow, put the glass down again.

'Pint of stout?' Gumbell said. 'You're taking to this country caper better than I ever imagined... Are you eating, Beck?'

'Yes. The joint of the day, roast beef.'

'Good enough for me.'

They spoke little while they ate; silence was not something to be filled in for either of them. They knew each other too well for that.

'Dry as the sand of the Gobi Desert,' Gumbell grumbled when he'd finished and was pushing his plate away. He had cleared it all the same.

They ordered more drinks: Beck another Guinness, the pathologist another bottle of the strong local craft beer called 'The Final
Nail', which Beck thought apt, considering the occupation of the
person drinking it.

They moved from the counter to an alcove. There were perhaps
a dozen people in the bar – a few lone men at the counter and
mainly couples spread about at the tables. The curtains had not
been drawn, and the lights along Main Street glinted through the
windows. It was a place that was easy to hide in: large with corners
and alcoves lost to the shadows of the murky light.

'It's the most intimate of deaths, in my opinion,' Gumbell said.
'Strangulation. The killer has to get right in there, look his victim
in the face, press his hands around the neck, squeeze until the life
drains away before his very eyes and the victim is dead. A total of
four minutes, on average – a long time considering the intensity
of the procedure. The killer must be both very determined and
physically fit. Strong. It's not as easy as it appears in the movies,
Beck.'

'I'm well aware of that,' Beck said. 'But she was a girl, Tanya,
a slight girl. Would the killer still need to be so strong?'

'No, probably not. But he was, anyway. The amount of force
exerted was far in excess of that required. Most likely the killer is
naturally powerful, possibly works out. He also has large hands
– the marks on the neck are almost an inch wide, not consistent
with the use of a ligature or chokehold. His bare hands did the
work. He throttled her to death. And something else: blood under
the fingernails, minute particles of flesh. She scratched him, Beck.'
Gumbell picked up his glass and swirled the beer around, took a sip.

'DNA?'

'Yes,' Gumbell replied. 'But only of value if there's something
to match it to. Useless otherwise.'

Beck said nothing for a moment. Gumbell could treat people
as imbeciles sometimes.

'I know that,' Beck said.

'I need a chaser. How about it, Beck, you too?'

Beck thought about it. 'Why not? Two scotches?'

Gumbell looked about the room. 'I suppose it'd be too much to ask for table service in a place like this. No Beck, not scotch. Who do you think you are, James Bond? We're Irish, Beck, for God's sake. Two Jameson's, man.'

Beck got up. 'I'll look after it.'

Gumbell nodded towards his glass. 'And a pint of Guinness this time, instead of this hipster rubbish. When in Rome, and all that...'

'Have you presented this to Superintendent Wilde?' Beck asked when he came back with the drinks.

Gumbell nodded, knocking back his Jameson in one gulp. 'Yes. I was on the telephone to him before I came here. I told him I was meeting you.'

'Good. Because it wouldn't do if I was to hear about things first.'

'Oh, I see. Pecking order, is there?'

'Something like that. Any other injuries?'

'Not that I could see. The autopsy is tomorrow. But I suspect not.'

'Any evidence of sexual activity?'

'None. But there well could be. Again, the autopsy.'

'Time of death?'

'I'd put it at about midnight, give or take, last night.'

Beck stared into space, thinking. 'Could there be prints, fingerprints, on the neck?'

'Hmm. There might be a possibility, but lifting latent fingerprints is not simple, you know that. Anyway, it doesn't apply in this case. Because I'm pretty certain of one thing. The killer wore gloves. Leather. And not very good ones. The victim's sweat mixed with the black dye. The colour ran. It's just about visible.'

'Really, gloves? I hadn't thought of that. Does that mean he came prepared? Ties in with something I was thinking of earlier.'

'It always does,' Gumbell muttered. 'Don't look into it too much. It was a bloody cold night.'

'Her phone's missing,' Beck said, and added: 'I need a cigarette.'

They went outside and lit up, Gumbell sucking on his cigarette in that awkward way that occasional smokers do. They were standing in the doorway of a disused shop just down from the hotel. A light drizzle was falling, the wind picking up; an occasional car passed by.

'A movie set,' Gumbell said, spewing out cigarette smoke. 'An Irish version of, I don't know, *Magnum P.I.*' He gave a rare laugh. 'But you don't have a moustache, Beck, the top of your head is bald, you don't drive a Ferrari and this place is no fucking Hawaii.'

'You're talking shit,' Beck said.

'Isn't it great?' Gumbell replied. He held his cigarette by the filter, pointing it into the air, staring at it, turning it round and round. 'I can get drunk with you and not have to worry about it, Beck. Almost anyone else on the force I wouldn't feel comfortable with. You should feel privileged.'

Beck looked up Main Street, away from the hotel. Some shop windows still had their display lights on. The Supermac's near the corner was the brightest star in a dark galaxy. Beck could see shadows on the street outside as the people moved about behind its windows. Loud, slurred voices floated up the street through its open doors: 'Ya bollocks, Macky, I'll give ya a smack on the mouth so I will.'... 'Ah, fuck off.' ... 'Leave him alone, Tulip, will ya, leave him alone'... 'Make me. You want a smack too?'... 'Up Chapel Park. Up the Chapel Park, boys.'

Beck flicked the stub of his cigarette into the air, watched it tumble upward and then down again, like a shooting star, dying on the wet road.

'Come on, doc, let's go back inside,' he said.

CHAPTER FOURTEEN

The town slept. All shops and houses along Main Street and those off it were in darkness. The town appeared deserted. The only illumination came from the street lamps. Cross Beg was as it was a hundred, maybe two hundred years ago.

In Cool Wood, the motor of a portable lighting unit made a low grinding noise that carried off into the night. The SOC officer in charge had approved a night shift, concerned about the forecast for bad weather in the morning.

In a house emptier than it had been two days before, Tony Frazzali could not sleep. He sat staring with unfocused eyes at the fifty-two-inch TV, its sound muted, the stub of a thick spliff held between two fingers. His mother Theresa was two doors down from her son. She had finally woken from her drug-induced slumber and now lay staring at the ceiling of her bedroom, groggy and too numb to cry. Father Clifford had been at her bedside when she'd opened her eyes earlier. He'd said he'd been praying for her. He'd told her Tanya was in heaven, along with Antonio. Mrs Frazzali found such comfort in those words. And Father Clifford had said that one day they would all meet up in heaven, that nothing could ever separate them again. They would be together for all eternity. Father Clifford had given her such peace. She looked on it differently now. Tanya and Antonio were not dead. They were merely waiting.

Ned had finally gone home, creeping through the alleys, crossing the streets, scurrying up Plunkett Hill, and now he sat in his cold kitchen with a blanket wrapped around him, a blunt kitchen knife in his hand. He did not sleep. His eyes were closed but the lids flittered about, drool hanging from a corner of his mouth. He was waiting.

Melanie was in bed, but not asleep. The light from her phone washed her upper body in a dull glow as she texted furiously. Once the police had finished in the wood, they would gather and remember Tanya. They would have a party. That's what Tanya would have wanted. One hell of a party.

Tanya slept. The sleep of the dead, her body taken from Cool Wood in the back of a private ambulance with blacked-out windows. It lay now on a cold steel tray in a freezer at the mortuary of the County Hospital.

CHAPTER FIFTEEN

The morning light filtered through the curtains. Beck raised an arm, covered his eyes and moaned. He had been unconscious more than asleep, his nightmares silenced by the alcohol in his blood, banished to the wastelands of his mind. But now, as he began to wake, his tongue felt like a strip of sandpaper in his parched mouth, and his head pressed down on the pillow like a ship's anchor.

He'd gone and done it again. And what goes up must come down. His bladder was painful, as if someone was sitting on it inside his belly. Still, he did not move. Eventually, he reached out and fumbled on the bedside locker for his watch, before he noticed that it was on his wrist. He raised one heavy eyelid and peered at the time: 8.40 a.m. He cursed. The briefing was in less than a half hour. He pulled back the duvet and twisted his body and plonked two feet onto the cold floor. The room pitched, as if he were on a ship in a heavy swell. He closed his eyes and waited for it to pass, then opened them again. He got up and went into the shower, pushed the heat regulator all the way into the blue zone, and turned the water on. The shock of the cold water on his flesh instantly cleared his mind, peeling the hangover from him, temporarily at least.

Dark grey clouds hung over Cross Beg as he walked to the station. Every second shop seemed to have a 'For Sale' or 'To Let' sign in its window. He lit a cigarette but after a couple of pulls felt nauseous and threw it away again. The town was slowly waking, the lanky buildings along Main Street pressing in on either side, their facades weathered beneath moss-veined black-slate roofs. Most shops didn't open for business until 10 a.m. – there was little point. It struck Beck that above the stripes of colour that were the ground-floor shop units, like rouge on old whores, everything above the shop sign was neglected, paint peeling and mottled curtains stuck to dirty glass in old window frames. People didn't look up above the door lines, there was no need. A sharp wind stirred the air.

Images of the night before flittered about in his mind. He remembered leaving The Hibernian, but, as for anything else afterwards, there was nothing. He consoled himself that if anything of importance had happened, from experience he knew he would have remembered it.

And then, from the back of his mind, a memory stuck its tongue out at him, goading him, thumbs in ears, fingers wiggling. It brought with it a memory of him talking into his phone. Beck felt the first stirrings of fear inside him. He stopped and took the phone from his pocket. The blasted thing was dead; he'd failed to recharge it.

He continued to the station, went through the doors and was struck by the silence. He'd forgotten the security code for the keypad on the wall by the public counter. Then it came to him, and he punched it in. The door clicked and he pushed through onto the corridor on the other side and then took the first door to the left into the Ops Room.

The briefing had already begun, O'Reilly standing at the top of the room by the whiteboard, holding a sheet of paper in his hand. '… hopefully we can find out what happened. You've got the details. Look after it, you two.' He paused, looking at Beck. All heads turned. 'Thanks for joining us, Sergeant Beck. We haven't taken you away from anything urgent, I hope.'

A ripple of sycophantic laughter wafted through the room. Superintendent Wilde was absent, which meant there was no one to trim O'Reilly's sails. All seats were taken, so Beck joined those standing by the wall, like stragglers at the back of church during Sunday mass service. He realised he was sweating.

O'Reilly's eyes were still on him. 'Sergeant Beck. Now, as I have just said, Ned Donohue was brought in less than a half hour ago. Real results are achieved by a concerted, planned approach, not by freelance operators.' Again, a ripple of laughter, at what Beck had no idea. O'Reilly added, 'I could have suggested we simply write and request that he come in and merely help us with our enquiries. I heard they do that up in Dublin, would you believe that?'

Beck could taste stale cornflakes at the back of his throat. He swallowed quickly a couple of times.

O'Reilly paused for emphasis. 'Tell you what, Beck, I'd be interested. You come and join me in interviewing him after this briefing.' He paused again, looking about the room and smiling to his audience. 'We'll see how good you city boys are, huh? Coming down here trying to tell us how it's done. Well, we'll see.'

For the third time, laughter spread through the room, as predictable as a greasy breakfast in a roadside café.

O'Reilly pointed to the whiteboard. It was beginning to look a little cluttered. Then he looked at Beck once more. 'Something else,' he said. 'Don't be late for briefings again.' And, pointing down the room: 'Andy Grimes?'

'Boss.'

'The house-to-house. Throw up anything?'

'Nothing. No one heard a thing. The nearest house is a half-mile from the wood. Unlikely, anyway.'

'CCTV, who's looking after that?'

'Me. Tom Weir.'

'And?'

'Canvassed a number of places. By places I mean the creamery, the filling station and the council offices. I'm waiting on the creamery. I've collected other footage from businesses in the town.

I'm going through it. Nothing so far, but I'll need everything to spot any patterns. Going through it, like I say.'

'Who's looking after Nugent, Fletcher and Clarke? Someone speak to me.'

'That'd be me.'

O'Reilly looked down the room. 'Okay, Jackson, go ahead.'

'Nugent and Fletcher can be discounted. Nugent's moved to Cork – living with a girl down there…' A chorus of 'Aahh' went through the room. 'They have a baby, supposedly he's turned his life around. All I can say is God help her and the baby. As for Fletcher, he's in the university hospital in Galway, has been for a couple of months. I can't pronounce it, but I'm glad to report that what he has is terminal. So there's justice in this world after all. Nobby Clarke, however, is still outstanding. Nothing's changed with him from what I can gather, still hearing those voices in his head. Could bring him in for questioning, but I'd rather wait until we have something concrete, otherwise it'll just be a waste of time.'

O'Reilly looked at his watch. 'Okay, Jackson, but keep an eye on him. That goes for you all. We'll wrap this up. You have your lists. Beck and Somers, County Hospital, preliminary autopsy report should be ready. Think you can handle it, Beck, after we finish interviewing Ned, that is?'

Here it comes, Beck thought. And right on cue, the warbling twitter rippled through the room.

'Okay,' O'Reilly announced. 'Briefing over. Get on with it, everyone.'

The room began to clear. Beck saw Claire Somers talking with two uniformed officers on the other side, nodding at something one said. Then she turned and came over.

'I tried ringing you, Beck. Have you got your phone switched off?'

'It's dead.'

'Give it to me. I'll give it some charge while you're in there.'

'Oh...' He took it from his pocket and handed it to her. 'Thanks.'

'And here.' She gave him a mint. 'Your breath...'

He took it, popped it into his mouth. He realised that Claire Somers was a 'carer'. Beck had come across lots of carers in his time: mothers of wayward sons, spouses of violent alcoholics, collectors of lost pets and abandoned souls. And he knew being a carer brought with it its own problems.

Beck could see O'Reilly leaving the room and started to follow. In the hallway outside, the inspector was waiting for him.

'The way I see it, Beck, is you have a natural ability to fuck things up,' he said, his voice ugly. 'All by your lonesome, with no help from anyone else. You think you can fuck things up down here, too, don't you? It doesn't work like that, not in Cross Beg. Not on my patch.'

'You're safe enough,' Beck said. 'I plan on staying in Cross Beg only as long as I have to. I've no interest in this case beyond what I would call the affliction of curiosity that comes with being a police officer, which, despite everything, I still am. That aside, you stay out of my way, and I'll stay out of yours.'

O'Reilly smiled. 'Sensible man,' he said.

'You still want me in on this, or shall I go get myself a coffee? I think a coffee is a better idea.'

'No,' O'Reilly said, his tone curt. 'You're with me on this.'

CHAPTER SIXTEEN

Ned had moved his chair into a corner of the room, away from the interview table, and was sitting on it, arms folded tightly over his chest and his feet crossed beneath him. He had on an old frayed sports jacket that was a couple of sizes too big for him, a flat cap with a dirty frayed peak, red Nike runners and green trousers. If someone didn't know, they might have thought his dress style bohemian. The reality was he dressed in whatever he could find at the local charity shop. He looked at O'Reilly, kept his eyes on him, ignored Beck.

'Sit over here, Ned, like a good man,' O'Reilly said, pulling a chair back from the table, purposefully scraping it across the floor and sitting down.

Beck pulled out a chair and sat down next to him.

O'Reilly spoke again, louder. 'Get the fuck over here, Ned. Now. You don't want to upset me. You know what happens if you upset me.'

Ned looked at Beck for the first time. Beck met his eyes and held them, smiled.

'I'm Detective Sergeant Finnegan Beck, Ned. Come on. We'll turn on the video and voice recorder and everything will be fine.'

Ned shifted in his chair. He uncrossed his feet, but his arms remained folded across his chest. His expression changed, his features softening.

'He-he-here,' he said. 'Finnegan. Like in Ja-Ja-James Joyce?'

Beck nodded. 'Like in that, named for him, in fact. Yes, Ned.'

Ned smiled now, a big gormless smile, one front tooth missing. He got up, took his chair with him and came and sat on the other side of the table. He sat well back into it, his eyes wary, flicking from O'Reilly to Beck.

O'Reilly looked at his watch. 'Interview with Edward Donohue, better known as Ned or Neddy, suspect in the murder of Tanya Frazzali…'

'Here,' Ned squawked. 'I'm no sus-sus-suspect in anything. I towelled you…'

O'Reilly placed a palm in front of Ned's face and he fell quiet. O'Reilly went on '… Present Inspector Gerald O'Reilly and Detective Sergeant Finnegan Beck. Interview commencing now' – he glanced at the big white-faced clock on the wall – 'at 9.53 a.m. on 17 October 2018.'

'Here,' said Ned to Beck. 'Your mother must have been fi-fi-fierce smart to want to give you a name like that. Was sh-sh-she now?'

'Edward Donohue,' O'Reilly said. 'I put it to you that you made a 999 phone call to Cross Beg garda station in the early hours of Monday – that is, yesterday – reporting finding the body of a young female in Cool Wood, the identity of whom has been officially confirmed earlier today as that of Tanya Frazzali of Bridge Street, Cross Beg. Is that correct?'

'Yes, Inspector, co-co-correct,' Ned said.

'Why didn't you give your name to the operator when you called? You could have saved us time and effort if you had,' O'Reilly asked.

'No comment,' Ned said.

'No comment? What do you mean, no comment?'

Beck could see a vein begin to throb on the side of O'Reilly's head.

'I want me so-so-solicitor,' Ned said. 'No comment.'

O'Reilly turned off the recorder. He looked at Beck. 'It breaks down sometimes. I told them we need a new one. We're still waiting. Okay, Beck?'

Beck said nothing.

O'Reilly turned his attention back to Ned. 'Listen, you little prick. You don't need a fucking solicitor. You'll be walking out that door in five minutes if you answer my questions. If you don't answer them, you'll be carried out in twenty-four hours. Do you understand that now?'

Ned folded his arms again. 'I want a so-so-solicitor, I want a solicitor, I want a solicitor.'

A tearing sound as O'Reilly's chair scraped across the floor and he got to his feet. He leaned onto the desk. 'Jesus Christ! You're asking for it. By Christ, you're asking for it. Answer the fucking question.'

Ned covered his head with his hands as if expecting O'Reilly to strike him at any moment. Beck knew they were losing him.

'I wi-wi-will not,' Ned said, but it was more a whimper. 'I will not, I will not, I wi-wi-will not.'

O'Reilly towered over him like a snorting bull.

Beck sighed. He wasn't slow to use force himself sometimes. The difference was in knowing when and how to use it. He couldn't watch this any more.

'Ned,' Beck said gently. 'If you answer the questions, I'll give you €20. You can buy a few cans.'

Beck hoped O'Reilly wouldn't speak now. If he did, they could lose Ned completely. Beck saw the inspector turn towards him out of the corner of his eye. Beck thought: Keep your mouth shut.

Ned looked at Beck with the expression of a child, a child who'd been scolded but was now excited again at the prospect of being given a treat. 'Make it a €50 and I'll sing like a ca-ca-nary.' He pointed to O'Reilly. 'But I'm not talking with him here. Not him. I'll talk to you. But h-h-him, that man, he's a t-t-terror so he is, the whole town knows it.'

'First off,' Beck said before O'Reilly could say anything. 'It's twenty euro, Ned. Now, I can't promise anything else.' Beck looked at O'Reilly: Ball in your court.

O'Reilly was quiet, calculating, staring ahead at the wall. 'Okay, okay, whatever it takes. I'll send Somers in. You and Neddy boy here are good company for each other. Two misfits if ever I saw them.'

'I know you. You're not a bad s-s-skin,' Ned said when O'Reilly was gone and Claire Somers had sat down in the chair vacated by him. 'You were one of the ones following me for a wh-wh-while, weren't ya?'

'Following you?' Claire said.

'Aye. Following me. You were following me, weren't ya, the whole l-l-lot of ye? Youse been following me for years. Did ya think I'd not twig it? I often ca-ca-catch one of ye walking behind me. I'm not as thick as I look, y'know.'

'The guards aren't following you, Ned,' Beck said. 'Sorry to have to tell you this, but you're not important enough, although that might change after today. But if the guards were following you, for whatever reason, believe me, you'd be the last to know about it.' Beck pressed the button on the tape recorder. 'Interview with Edward Donohue recommenced at 10.06 a.m. Now, tell me, Ned, where were you last Sunday night into Monday morning...?'

Ned fumbled in the pockets of his jacket. Then he pulled at the top of his trousers. Then he rearranged his cap.

'Ned,' Claire said. 'We're waiting.'

'I know you're wa-wa-waiting. Everyone is waiting. God above is waiting. The whole world is wa-wa-waiting. They're waiting up at the railway station for the train to Dublin, so they are. Aye, and you're waiting. I seen him do it. I s-s-seen him kill the poor girl. I seen it. There was a moon, a big fat moon. I could s-s-see the North Star and the Milky Way, so I could. I know all o'dem stars. I s-s-saw everything, so I did. And it was horrible cruel what he done.' Ned fell silent. Then, his voice a whisper: 'I was there in the bushes, with me bag of ca-ca-cans. I musta had about ten. I was well on it, so I was, so I fell asleep. I woke up with the cur-

cur-curse of the cold on me. I didn't know what I was seeing at first. I thought I was having a nightmare.' He took a deep breath, calmer now. 'The young wan was standing no more than twenty yards away from me in the clearing. And he was standing in front of her. I thought he was t-t-trying to kiss her, he had his hands around her neck. But th-th-then when the legs began to buckle under her I-I-I knew what he was doing, I knew he was squeezing her to death – he was str-str-strangling the young wan.' Ned's voice rose, his eyes widening, and his hands began moving through the air as he emphasised his story. 'I called out, so I did, I said, "Le-le-leave the young wan alone. Clear off, you. Go on. Cl-cl-clear off." But he only turned and looked at me and I swe-swe-swear to God – but you know what he done next?' Ned looked at them both. 'Do you know what h-h-he done next?' he asked again.

'No,' Beck said.

'He started to la-la-ugh at me. Swear to God. Ah, here, the poor young wan was being killed and he was laughing at me. The strangest laugh ever, like a hyena.'

'Who?' Beck asked. 'Who did you see?'

Ned took a deep breath. He folded his arms again and sat back in his chair, as if trying to make himself disappear.

'I don't know who I seen. I don't know his name. '

'Who was it?' Beck realised he wasn't asking, he was demanding.

Ned bowed his head, said nothing.

'Tell me,' Beck said.

Still, Ned remained quiet.

'Ned…' It was Claire.

'Johnny Cash,' Ned said finally. 'The Man in Bl-bl-black. He's come back from the dead, so he has.'

'Are you trying to be smart now, Ned?' Beck asked, keeping his voice even.

Ned shook his head. 'Ta-ta-tall, he was, with black hair – dressed in black from head to foot. Johnny Cash.'

'Okay. So he *looked* like Johnny Cash.' It was Claire again.

'Ah, I dunno, I dunno,' Ned whimpered. 'I want to go home. Will ye lave me alone? Lave me alone, will ye? St-st-stupid auld Ned. That's it, isn't it, stupid auld Ned? I don't know what I seen. It was dark. Lave me alone! I want to go home. Lave me alone! Lave me alone! Lave me a-a-alone!'

'Ned,' Beck said. 'Calm down. You said there was a moon. You said you saw it all. You said that.'

'Sure – who'd believe me? Stupid auld Ned, simple, he is. You'd be stupid to believe a word out of his mouth.'

Beck sighed. This was going nowhere. He was starting to think the whole story might be nothing but a figment of a simple, deluded mind.

'And what did you do then?' Claire asked.

'I ran. I took off. I ran like the fox with the hounds on its tail. I know the paths through the tr-tr-trees like the back of me hands, so I do. I ran. I ran like I never ran before, and I didn't stop till I got to me house. I stayed awake the whole night and I haven't slept since. He-he-he'll come for me next, so he will.'

'He didn't try to follow?' Beck said, mock surprise in his voice. 'And when you took off, did you take your cans with you? Because there was nothing found up there.'

'No, he didn't try to follow. I had a pack of twelve. I only drank ten. I wasn't waitin' for him. Stupid auld Ned's not waiting round like an auld beast dow-dow-down at the slaughter house to be killed and strung up. Ah, no.'

'Ned, let me see your hands,' Beck said. 'Come on, put your hands on the table.'

Ned slowly placed his hands on the table. Beck looked at them, turning them over. They were small and bony, a heavily nicotine-stained index and middle finger on the right. He could tell that underneath that oversized jacket he had on there was the typical malnourished body of a chronic alcoholic. Ned barely had the strength to choke a cough.

'Will you lave me a-a-alone?' Ned whimpered.

'We will,' Beck said. 'We'll leave you alone.'

CHAPTER SEVENTEEN

The County Hospital was built in the grounds of the old work-house. The original perimeter stone wall still stood, and outside of that, what was once a muddy track was now the main Galway road. A bronze plaque embedded in the wall read: 'IN MEMORY OF ALL THE WRETCHED AND NAMELESS WHO PASSED FROM THIS LIFE AND LIE BENEATH HERE'.

The hospital car park was full, so Claire nudged onto the footpath near the door, across double yellow lines. They got out and were walking towards the hospital when a security guard with a pinched face came through the revolving doors wearing a hi-vis jacket, 'Hospital Security' emblazoned across the front.

'You can't park there.'

'Guards. We won't be long,' Beck growled. He was still smarting from the encounter with O'Reilly earlier.

'Guards? Where're you going?'

'The morgue,' Beck said, drawing level with him.

'It'd be quicker that way,' he said, smiling now, pointing back along the way they had come. 'Turn left there. Straight ahead. It has a separate door. You'll see the sign. You don't have to go through the hospital at all.'

'We still have to leave the car.'

'That's alright. I'll keep an eye on it.'

'Thanks,' Beck said.

They turned and walked along the path, went left and stopped before a door in the ivy-covered wall. Beck could see a sign through the leaves: MORGUE.

An orderly was stacking boxes in the hallway when they went inside. The air was cold and musty, smelt of bleach and antiseptic.

'Where's Dr Gumbell?' Beck asked.

The orderly looked at them. He recognised Claire, nodded his head. 'The guards,' he said, huffing, mumbling something to himself. 'I'll have to sign you in. Over here.' He led them to a cubicle, went inside and placed a ledger on the counter, a pen tucked underneath the clip. Beck signed and the orderly led them to an office, bare except for a metal table and some chairs. High on the wall was a small window. A light bulb inside a yellowed shade hung from the ceiling at the end of a long cord.

'I'll get him. A couple of minutes.' The orderly turned and left the room.

'This place gives me the creeps,' Claire said.

'Have you been here before?'

'No, surprisingly. There hasn't been a proper murder in this town for years. And Coroner's Court is held in The Hibernian when it's needed.' She looked around. 'This place, no. Thank God.'

Footsteps approached outside, stopped at the door. The old brass handle turned. Dr Gumbell came into the room, leaving the door open, a sheaf of papers pressed to his chest. He barely glanced at them as he walked around the desk and sat down. He placed the papers before him, the palms of his hands on the desk on either side, and looked over his glasses, first to Beck, then Claire.

'Preliminary results,' he announced. 'Yes, yes, what have we got here?' He sifted through the documents, took some out and set them to one side, scratched his nose.

Claire reached into her handbag and took out a notebook and pen. She opened the notebook and rested it on her knee, the pen held ready.

'Notes,' Gumbell said. 'I keep telling you to take them, Beck. You could learn from that girl. Now, on with the show. No surprises. Cause of death... erm, just before I deal with that, just to let you know, there were traces of Xanax and marijuana in the victim's body. She wasn't high at the time of death, but recently had been. Okay? Now, as I was saying, cause of death…'

'Question,' Beck asked. 'Was she a regular user? Of narcotics in general, that is?'

Gumbell sighed. 'If you want the greater details, Beck, then read the bloody report.'

'And is it in there? That detail?'

Gumbell pointed a finger, said in a fake American accent, 'You. You. You're good, you.' Beck recognised it as a line from Robert De Niro in the movie *Analyze This*. Gumbell became serious again. 'I would say she liked to smoke cannabis. As for anything else, I don't know. But she hadn't been smoking cannabis for very long, I would suggest. The reason I say this is that I scoped the trachea and observed signs of irritation, need I say separate to the blunt force injuries caused by the compression of the strangulation itself. There was also mucus culmination, and there's slight bronchial inflammation to the lungs. But for anything more definitive we'll have to conduct a hair follicle test. Classic symptoms of novice cannabis usage, I would argue. These symptoms dissipate and disappear over time with continued use. But she didn't pass this stage. The conclusion is that she was either a very irregular user, or had recently taken up the habit. I would say the latter. May we move on now?'

Beck nodded.

'Cause of death: manual strangulation. The use of hands, or throttling, to use the older, what I consider more brutal, expression. The time of death, as I said: midnight. Thereabouts. She'd had sexual intercourse before she died. The act appears to have been consensual. There's no bruising or any signs of force; the vaginal lining is normal. A pubic hair that is not from the victim was found in the crotch area along with traces of fluid, both taken for DNA analysis. Fragments of grass and dirt were on the underside of the clothes, but not much – not as much as you'd expect if she'd simply laid down on the ground. My guess is a blanket, or something of that nature, was used. But there was nothing found at the scene, no blankets or anything like it, by Scene of Crime. What happened I imagine is the victim and her lover arranged to meet, one of them brought along something to lie on, they met, had sex – not a romp by the way, this was organised – and afterwards she fixed herself up. They'd done this before, this was their place.'

'How do you know all that?' Beck asked. 'And what defines a romp, by the way?'

Gumbell shook his head, gave Beck a wry smile. 'You think I have a crystal ball? I don't know. It's my intuition, my instinct, that's all. Because, figuratively speaking, the bed was made and the room was tidied. Neat. Not a romp. Which to me translates as energetic, maybe even rough, sex. This doesn't appear to be any of those. The victim had even brushed her hair. I could be wrong. Yes indeed. But that is the – unofficial – opinion of the state pathologist, based on little more than this.' He tapped his belly a couple of times. 'Oh, and a little thing called experience, in this case twenty-five years. Happy?'

'It doesn't make sense,' Claire interrupted. 'I don't know how or why it doesn't make sense, it just doesn't.'

Gumbell looked at Claire, then at Beck. 'It never does, my dear. It's not supposed to make sense, any of it. To kill someone, in the flower of their youth, no, of course that doesn't make sense. Beck, you'll catch him, won't you? That may sound like a question, but it's not, it's a statement. Made with great certainty. By the way, how are you this morning?'

'I won't be catching anybody. This is not my case. I already told you that. I'm strictly working to order. Nothing more. Nothing less. I'm okay... and you?'

'And me? Why, I'm wonderful. And why wouldn't I be?' He took a deep breath. 'The smell of formaldehyde in the morning makes a man feel young. By the way, I'm staying over again tonight. Same time and place, my man – okay by you?'

'Let me get back to you on that,' Beck said.

'Nonsense,' Gumbell said. 'I'm looking forward to it already.'

Claire looked at Beck with a knowing expression.

'As I was saying, there was no sign of force,' Gumbell continued, 'except for, of course, the quietus, the final act, the coup de grâce, the death – call it what you will. Quite straightforward, no theatrics. The killer simply placed large powerful hands around her neck and squeezed until there was no life left. He was facing her.'

'What?' Claire asked.

'He was facing her,' Gumbell repeated. 'Sometimes a killer might come from behind, you know, for purposes of expediency, but mostly because he doesn't want to have to look his victim in the face. But this was from the front. He wanted to see her, and her to see him; he wanted to watch her die. You find cases like that sometimes in domestic violence. A husband will strangle a wife half to death in a fit of rage, from the front, but they usually stop, give up just before it's too late, their rage spent by the whole effort of it all. If that weren't the case, there'd be many more wives and partners lost to strangulation in this fair land of ours, that's for sure. But that's not the case here. His rage was measured and controlled, carefully calculated. He squeezed and squeezed with brutal determination until there was no doubt that she was dead. An ice man cometh, Beck. Oh, and another thing.'

'Yes? What's that?'

'The layered effect of the bruising indicates that the pressure was not consistent. That he relaxed at times, just a little, before applying pressure again. He played with her, is what I'm saying.'

'You mean, like hovered her between life and death?'

'Exactly. What about lunch?' Gumbell said.

'Lunch. I can't think of lunch right now,' said Claire.

Beck looked at his watch. It was already two o'clock.

'Why are you looking at your watch?' Gumbell asked. 'Time is a manufactured state of mind, Beck. People once lived by the sun and they did perfectly fine.'

'Did they?' Beck asked.

'I'm hungry,' Gumbell said. 'Let's eat. Jack! Jack!'

Gumbell gathered up his papers, shuffling them into a neat brick. The orderly came into the room. Gumbell said, 'Take these up to the girl in the office, Jack. Soon as you can, good man.'

The orderly crossed the room and picked up the papers. As he was turning again to leave, Beck saw him raise his eyes heavenward and mouth something to himself, what seemed like the word 'gobshite'.

CHAPTER EIGHTEEN

The name was written over the door in Irish: 'O'Ceallacháin'. The pub was near the river, on the corner of Bridge and Clifden Streets. A little further on and it would have had a view of the water through its large front windows. As it was, it looked out on nothing but the row of buildings opposite. The pub was like a good whiskey: aged and full of character. The barman was in his mid-fifties, heavyset but not fat, wearing a white shirt with a red tie and a white apron. The apron struck Beck. He'd only ever seen those worn by bartenders on a visit to New York City once. Pretentious, was the word he'd use for it.

The barman ran his eyes over them, taking them in, deciding whether or not to smile.

'Lunch?' Gumbell said in his best booming courtroom voice.

A stubby finger pointed in the direction of the menu board, fixed to a pillar by the counter.

'What do you recommend?' Gumbell pressed.

The barman picked up on the refined diction and made his mind up. Smiling now, he said, 'The fish pie, with cod, salmon and smoked haddock in a creamy béchamel sauce.' Then, looking at Claire: 'Don't I know you?'

'It's possible,' she replied.

'Aha, yes, I've seen you about… You all gardai, then?'

'He's not,' Beck said, pointing. 'He's the state pathologist.'

'Well now, is he indeed? You're welcome to O'Callaghan's', he said, beaming, using the English version of the name. He leaned on the counter and extended a hand. 'Michael O'Callaghan, grandson of the original Michael who first established this great institution.'

Gumbell spoke to him in Irish. '*Sin go hiontach, nach bhfuil an tádh ort?*'

O'Callaghan smiled sheepishly. 'You caught me. I can't speak a word myself, I'm afraid.'

Gumbell grinned. 'It means, "That's great, aren't you lucky?"'

'Does it now?' O'Callaghan said, not certain if it was meant as a compliment or an insult.

They ordered three fish pies – no alcohol, just water – and went and sat at a table. But then Gumbell got up and went back to the counter. When he returned he was holding a small glass in each hand, quarter-filled with amber liquid. He sat down, pushed one across to Beck.

'You can blame me, Beck. It's not your fault. I bought them. Peer pressure. You wouldn't have bothered if it weren't for me. Drink up quick before you can think about it and change your mind. I know you'd do the same for me. Come on, bottoms up.'

The double whiskey burned and caressed the back of Beck's throat all at the same time, and instantly he felt it begin to spread through his bloodstream, the warmth of a glowing sun. *Oh shit*, he thought.

Claire sipped from her water. She looked at the empty glass Beck put down on the table.

Gumbell spoke. 'Get the pints in, Beck. We have to have a chaser.'

'I thought it was the other way round,' Claire said, with an edge of sarcasm in her tone. 'The shot was the chaser.'

'Does it matter?' Gumbell asked, picking up on it. 'Does it fucking matter? This is all merely a ritual, young lady. It doesn't matter, none of it. Why do you keep asking questions that don't matter?'

Beck stood. 'I will have to pace myself.'

'Beck,' Claire said. 'Sorry to spoil the party, but aren't you making trouble for yourself? O'Reilly and everything...'

Beck gave a wary smile. 'I will have to avoid him then. Don't worry, Claire, it would be unfair of you to worry if I'm not.'

She gave a resigned shrug of her shoulders.

Beck ordered two pints of Guinness at the counter. O'Callaghan was businesslike, not engaging in conversation. And there was no conversation between Gumbell and Claire when he went back with the drinks and set them down on the table.

Beck looked around. 'I've never seen so many suits.'

'This is where the suits come,' Claire said. 'Business types. Everyone in Cross Beg who's someone comes here. Big fish in a small pond. It has a reputation.'

'Really?'

'Yes. Really. You see the way he looked at us? When we came in. There's a pecking order. Guards below the rank of inspector don't quite fit in it.'

Beck laughed. 'Yes. But the doctor here does.'

Gumbell scowled, raised his glass and took a long swig. When he put the glass down again, it was almost empty. Without a word, he got up and went to the bar to order another round of drinks.

Beck clapped his hands. Claire shot him a look.

'Fish pies?' the young waitress announced.

The plates were placed on the table before them, hot and steaming. Beck took his knife and cut into the delicately layered mashed potato. He heaped some onto his fork and placed it in his mouth. It was very, very good.

When she'd finished, Claire pushed her empty plate away. 'I'll be leaving. I'll take the autopsy report with me, shall I?'

'Yes. Good idea.'

'I presume you're not coming?'

'The doctor wants to discuss some things with me. Strictly in the interests of the case, mind.'

'It's not even your case.'

'It doesn't stop him discussing it with me, does it?' Gumbell snapped.

Claire stood. 'I'll pay for my lunch on the way out.'

'It's okay. I'll look after it,' Beck said.

'No. Why should you? I'll get it myself.'

Beck watched her as she walked away. As he did, he became aware of a conversation at a nearby table. He glanced over, saw two men – one young, with gelled-back hair, the other older, wearing a tweed jacket.

'... twenty K should do it,' the younger one said.

'You think so?' the older man replied.

'Oh ya, no more. Put another twenty K in and it's making money for you.'

'You really think so?'

'It's all about costs, Vinnie. Keeping those down, I mean – get a youngster working for you, sixteen or thereabouts. No requirement to pay full minimum wage at that age, it's a little over six euro an hour. You're saving what? Maybe a hundred a day, between everyone.'

'That's a big saving for sure.'

Beck thought of the waitress, who looked no more than sixteen herself.

Gumbell peered at him over the rim of his glass.

'Christ,' Beck said. 'You're drinking like a camel at an oasis today.'

'After it's been in the desert for six months,' Gumbell added, allowing himself a wonky laugh.

CHAPTER NINETEEN

Blackness. Utter and complete blackness. Lost within it, floating, no sound, no sight. Beck snored, a loud, stuttered explosion of noise through his mouth that seemed impossible would not wake him up. He had not drawn the curtains, and so the room itself was not completely dark, the light from the street outside turning the night a shade of sepia.

But there was noise. Other than his snoring, that was. A loud rapping on the front door, with it the hoarse croaking of the buzzer. The noise would stop for a few seconds, then start again: bang, bang, bang, croak, croak, croak.

Beck moved, shifting from his back onto his side. The snoring stopped. For a moment there was silence. Then it came again: bang, bang, bang, croak, croak, croak. This time his eyes partially opened. Bang, bang, bang, croak, croak, croak. His lids fully lifted and he stared ahead into the washed darkness.

Beck didn't know what had woken him. Time slowed. In an instant his brain spluttered and churned with a multitude of images – the final moments of a drowning man, his life played out before his eyes. He attempted to put order and sequence to the images, to play them back as if in a movie, to make them coherent. But it was impossible. All he had was a beginning.

The feeling inside him, like something was squirming about, it caused his chest to tighten, his breathing to become shallow and rapid. And with it a fear, a terrible fear, as he held up the pieces of his shattered memory and tried to understand. The walk from

O'Callaghan's, clear and focused, pints, in quick succession, in a couple of anonymous pubs, the familiarity of The Hibernian Hotel, the image hazy and vague, then gone. Nothing but that blackness.

Bang, bang, bang, croak, croak, croak.

The realisation that someone was at his front door brought him fully into the moment. He stood, wobbling slightly, and he knew he wasn't quite sober. And then, on the bedside locker, he saw it, an empty half-pint bottle of Jameson. The sight of it brought some relief, because it meant he had not gone over the edge in full public spectacle in a pub or somewhere; he had done it here, in his bedroom. He realised something else, too: that he was still dressed, fully dressed. He even had his shoes on.

'Christ,' he said aloud. He went to the window and looked out.

There was a woman there. He could see her profile, but nothing else. Was it Claire? He couldn't really see. It looked like her – the build did, or was it just similar? He decided that it had to be her. Who else could possibly be calling – he looked at the time: 11.15 p.m. – at this hour? Natalia, maybe? His heart quickened. Could it be? He could hardly believe that it might. He ran a hand through his hair and went down to answer the door.

It wasn't Claire.

It wasn't Natalia.

'Mr Beck, are you alright?'

'What?'

'Are you alright, Mr Beck?' she repeated.

It was a woman named Sheila, although he never referred to his landlady by her Christian name.

'Mrs Claxton,' he said.

What the hell's she doing here, at this hour?

Beck owned his own house in Dublin, which he didn't plan to sell; his sojourn in Cross Beg would be as short as he could make it. He'd never thought that having a landlady living next door would be a problem, until now.

Her eyes were wide with concern. 'I thought you were dead,' she said, and he wasn't certain that she was relieved he wasn't.

'Dead?' he said, confused. He felt woozy, like he might collapse. 'I have to sit down, sorry,' he said.

He went into the kitchen and she followed. The kitchen was tidy only because he rarely came in here. He lived for the most part in the living room, where he watched nature programmes on TV and read books and newspapers. That was, when Gumbell wasn't about, or it wasn't a Friday night, or a Sunday night, or a Saturday night, or maybe a Monday night too, sometimes.

He sat at the kitchen table. He was sweating again, he felt hot, but Mrs Claxton had her coat buttoned and her hands in her pockets. She glanced about the room, at its 1970s fittings, stopping to stare at the orange curtains, still gathered in their ties by the windows in the way only a woman can gather them. Beck had never once closed them.

'I'll be honest, Mr Beck. I saw you come in a couple of hours ago. You were in a state, is all I can say. I'm not making a comment about it, mind. My late husband could get like that too sometimes. No, that's not what worried me. I heard an awful banging noise and I had images of you lying on the floor maybe choking to death on your own vomit or something. That kind of thing happens to people when they're… you know, like you were. I went to bed and I slept for a little while but then I woke up and I heard the noise again. I kept worrying that something had happened to you. I imagined you lying on the floor gasping for breath. I couldn't live with myself if anything happened, so I had to come round. But I can see you're well enough, thank God. And as I'm here, shall I put the kettle on, make us a cup of tea? I need one after all this.'

He would really have liked a drink, but he knew that what he liked was not always what he needed. And a drink was the last thing he needed right now.

'What?' she said.

'What?' Beck said in return.

'You just said, "No, no, no".'

'Did I?'

'Yes. You did. Did you fall? Perhaps you have concussion? Really.'

'I don't know,' Beck said. 'But I'm sorry to have disturbed you.'

She went to the sink and turned on the tap, put the electric kettle spout into the flow of water and went and switched the kettle on, then stood with her arms folded, looking at the curtains. Finally making her mind up, she leaned across the sink, took the curtains from their ties and pulled them shut.

'I'm going to put on the central heating too, Mr Beck, if you have no objections? And set it to come on in the morning and evening. I left you a full tank of oil when you moved in. And you've never used it. I know you've never used it. I would have heard. It needs to be used, Mr Beck, otherwise the condensation gets in, ruins the oil after a while. Can you not feel the cold?'

'Not really, Mrs Claxton. No. But turn it on, yes.'

They talked generally; Mrs Claxton had no difficulty making chit-chat, she left no blank spaces for him to fill. Beck drifted off into himself, half listening, coming out every so often to say something like 'Really', 'Yes', 'No' or 'I didn't know that', and once, 'It's no weather for ducks', with no clue as to what they were talking about except that winter weather had formed part of it. What he was really thinking about was tomorrow. He expected to be suspended from duty.

The fun part of the previous night, or what had made it seem like fun – the alcohol – was leaving his system now. Left behind was the residue, which would linger, every drop of merriment wrung from it, nothing left but the thoughts of doom and gloom fanned by the bellows of fear and anxiety. He would have to take a couple of Dr Gumbell's magic little pills later. He had no particular inclination to acquire a drug as well as a drink habit, so took the yellow happy pills rarely, only during those times when he felt particularly rattled, which he felt certain was only a matter of time as the alcohol slowly drained from his system.

When he looked at the kitchen clock it was gone midnight and he thought: why is she still here? It was then that his addled brain realised that something else was taking place here other than Mrs Claxton's concern for his welfare. He noticed that she'd taken off her coat. It was draped over the back of her chair. She wore a jumper, a pink jumper, of a very thin fabric – he could see through to what she had on underneath. She was sitting a little back from the table, her legs crossed. He could see that underneath the jumper she wore something bright and red, that it extended down from the line of the bottom of the jumper for a short distance, a very short distance. It was a red satin, or silk, nightie. He could see that her nipples were prominent, pushing through the cloth like thimbles.

He looked away, embarrassed, warmth spreading from his ears and across his cheeks. Mrs Claxton, whom he'd never seen in anything other than high-neck blouses and long, dour skirts or trousers. But he reminded himself the woman had rushed over here thinking she might find him dead on the floor. She had come here to help. The fact that she was wearing a short red nightie was not something to be read into.

He knew he needed to go to bed and try and get some sleep. He forced a yawn.

'It's getting late,' he said. 'Thank you for coming to check on me, it was very kind. But I need to get some sleep now, or at least try to.'

She smiled. She had a nice smile; it lit up her face. He saw she was wearing make-up: mascara, lipstick, a touch of colour on her cheeks. Her hair was black, thick, tumbling about her face to her shoulders. She was an attractive woman. Not young, but not old either. A bit like himself, really.

'How long have you been here now?' she asked.

Beck couldn't think straight. 'Here in this house?'

She nodded.

'A few weeks.'

'Soon it will be six. You liked it as soon as you saw it, didn't you? You remarked on the red brick and the granite cornerstones. You said they were pretty. My husband liked those too. Did you know I knew my husband little more than three weeks before he asked me to marry him? I miss him. It's why I don't live in this house any more. Too many memories. You remind me of him, Mr Beck. My husband. I miss him. I miss his touch. Do you know what I mean?'

She stood there, his normally formal landlady, thick-thighed, a grin now playing on her lips, one hand resting on a hip, the other hanging loose by her side. He said nothing. What could he say, other than perhaps: 'Mrs Claxton, I might be crazy here, which is completely possible, because my brain is fried and I'm not thinking straight as I've had enough alcohol in the last forty-eight hours to kill a horse, or at least a donkey, and my neurotransmitters are sparking and misfiring and giving me a distorted image of the world, so I don't know what's what, but are you coming on to me?'

He didn't say that, of course. He remained silent. She stepped over to him, ran a hand slowly and gently along his cheek.

'You're a handsome man,' she said. 'I don't think you realise it. And there's a quiet strength about you, a sense of sadness, too, and loss. I'd like to hear about that, that sadness and loss, sometime, if you wouldn't mind telling me.'

And he detected, because she was so close to him, the aroma of alcohol on her own breath. Gin, he guessed. She giggled softly, turning.

'I'll say good night, Mr Beck.' She gave an exaggerated playful swivel of her hips. 'And leave you wondering about it all.'

And then she was gone, and Beck was standing alone in his kitchen with something he hadn't had in a long while. It was an erection.

CHAPTER TWENTY

'You're early, Beck,' Claire Somers said, standing behind the counter in the public office. 'Amazing.'

Beck hadn't seen her there. His head felt like it had a nest of insects inside, all scurrying about behind his eyes. He stopped and turned, walked across the foyer to the counter.

'Prepare yourself, Beck,' she said. 'Wilde wants you in his office. Immediately.'

Beck tried to think of an answer to that but couldn't. What he thought was that he should have stayed in bed and rung in sick. That seemed like a very good idea right now, but it was too late. An acrid taste crawled up from the back of his throat into his mouth. He swallowed it back down quickly.

'I tried to cover for you,' Claire went on. 'Wilde wanted to know where you were, when I got back to the station yesterday. I couldn't outright lie.'

'Is he…' Beck began, but his voice caught in his throat, making a hollow sound, like one speaker of a two-speaker sound system. He cleared his throat, added, '… in his office now?'

'Yes.'

Beck nodded.

'Sorry, Beck.'

'Don't be. Don't take any responsibility. This is my stuff. Can you buzz me in, please? I've forgotten the security code again.'

When he stepped into the hallway on the other side of the door, he popped a tablet, the 'little yellow saviours' as Gumbell called them, proceeded up the stairs to the first floor. Superintendent Wilde's office door was open. The room looked like it belonged in a museum – old lacquered wooden floorboards, antique desk with a glass shaded lamp on either side on its top, creaky wooden chairs. Wilde himself sat behind his desk in an enormous modern leather swivel chair that to Beck appeared almost vulgar in its august surroundings.

He looked up when Beck appeared in the doorway, squeezing his lower lip gently between a thumb and index finger. His expression gave nothing away. He pointed to the hard wooden chair in front of his desk.

Beck crossed to it and sat down.

'Where were you yesterday afternoon, Beck?'

'I was with Dr Gumbell, sir, the state pathologist.'

'I'm well aware of who he is. What you do in your time is your business, but when it infringes into your working time, then it becomes my business.'

'I know that.'

'Do you still want to be a police officer, Beck?'

'I ask myself that same question.'

'And did you give yourself an answer? Because all it would take is a letter in your best joined-up handwriting.'

'I know that, too. But there's the matter of my pension. My present rank is sergeant; any lump sum would be considerably less than if I were still an inspector. I can't afford it, is what I'm saying.'

'I don't know, I don't know,' Wilde said, as if to himself. 'Your record speaks for itself. In the report I received on you... You look surprised.'

'I didn't know anyone went to the trouble of writing a report on me.'

'I requested it, Beck. I needed to know what I was dealing with. But the report said your work for the last period while at Pearse Street was marked by a consistent and profound apathy.

You probably feel hard done by. Anyway, Beck, could you please hold it together? No more problems. Can you do that?'

Beck nodded. 'Yes.'

'Darren Murphy, whose name came up at the briefing on Monday?'

Beck nodded again.

'Has a history of violence towards women. Yesterday morning he reported being assaulted on his way home from The Noose pub on Sunday night. The same night our victim was murdered. The County Hospital confirmed he presented at A&E with marks to his face but left before receiving treatment.'

Wilde looked down at a written statement. 'Section Three, namely a golf club. He's a local drug dealer. Check Pulse for details, and keep me informed. Get on to it immediately, will you? Skip the briefing, anything you need to know you can find out later.' He glanced down at the statement again. 'I'm getting a headache, Beck. Get on with it. And don't give me any more grief, please.'

'You think he might have something to do with the murder?' Beck asked.

'Why do you ask? Of course he might have had something to do with the murder. He might be the person responsible. Beck…?'

'Inspector Reilly tolerates me on this case at best. Which suits me fine. I consider myself only passing through Cross Beg.'

'Jesus. Did you really just say that? Only passing through. You know I could suspend you, right now, for what happened yesterday? So tell me, what do you think would be a good move on your part right now?'

Beck got to his feet. 'I'll get on to it, boss.'

'Yes,' Superintendent Wilde said, 'you do that.'

Beck went back to the public office. He could see through the safety glass into the Ops Room, filling now with uniforms and detectives.

'Why are you in here, anyway?' he asked Claire.

'O'Rourke, the duty officer, went to get some breakfast. He should be back in a minute.'

They checked the Pulse system. In his statement, Murphy said there had been three attackers, one of whom had been armed with a golf club and had repeatedly struck him about the head and body. That made it a Section 3, assault with a weapon. He'd received stitches to his head as a result. Other injuries were minor, including bruising and minor lacerations to his face and right leg.

'Superintendent Wilde said Murphy left the hospital before receiving treatment,' Beck added.

Claire brought up a picture onto the screen. 'There. Darren Murphy.'

Beck leaned forward. Murphy's mug shot stared back: shaved head, narrow, close-set eyes, pug nose, wide mouth and chin. He reminded Beck of a pit bull terrier. There were eighty-six incidents listed in his catalogue, too many to go into now. Beck knew that the true number was at least double that; these were merely the incidents for which he'd actually been arrested. Murphy would be twenty-three on his next birthday – his first incident was recorded when he was nine, for shoplifting. He had been below the age of criminal consent back then, but the incident was recorded anyway. There were other shoplifting incidents, but by far the bulk of his criminal activity was drugs-related, simple possession and possession for sale and supply incidents. Darren Murphy was a drug dealer, and being hit over the head with a golf club was an occupational hazard.

Claire was reaching for her coat.

'Let's go,' she said. 'O'Rourke's taking the piss.'

CHAPTER TWENTY-ONE

They stopped at a chemist's shop on the way. Beck needed something for the growing pain in the centre of his head. Blake's Chemists still had its original facade: two large bay windows framed in red wood, black marble over the door, the word 'Chemist' written in extravagant lettering across it. There was a small hollow between the windows with the entrance door at its end, the walkway laid in marble.

Beck opened the door, and the bell above it sounded. At the counter, he waited. A man emerged from the door to the dispensary at the back of the shop and approached.

'Rebecca,' he called. 'Rebecca. Where is that girl? Are you being served?'

'Something for a headache?' Beck asked.

The man picked up a green and blue coloured box from a shelf next to him and placed it on the counter in front of Beck.

'Should do that trick. Four ninety nine please.'

'What is it?'

'Paracetamol. Essentially.'

Beck gave him €10 and waited for his change.

'Any closer to finding who killed that girl?' the man asked.

'And you are?' Beck said.

'Norman Blake. I know you're a detective. I've seen you about.' He handed Beck his change.

'Have you now?' Beck said.

'It's a small town, after all.'

'So it is,' Beck said, turning. 'Thank you for these.'

As Beck left, he could feel the man's eyes boring into his back. He hadn't answered his question.

The door to number 27 Chapel Park was painted canary yellow. Beck gave it three business knocks. He could sense someone looking out at him through the peephole. There was the sound of a bolt sliding back, and the door slowly opened.

Darren Murphy was standing there, a crutch pressed tight into his right armpit, dressed in a spotless white T-shirt, black tracksuit bottoms and *Despicable Me* slippers. The top of his head was swathed in a beige bandage; there was bruising beneath his right eye and a series of small cuts to his right cheek. Beck tried not to stare at those cuts, considering if someone's fingernails – specifically Tanya Frazzali's – could have inflicted the wounds. Apart from this, Darren looked exactly as he did in his mug shot, except now he had a smirk. Beck saw that both his arms were heavily tattooed. On the side of his neck was a tattoo in Chinese script, something Beck felt confident Murphy hadn't a clue as to the meaning of.

They say a person's appearance can mirror who they are: an accountant will look like an accountant; a banker will look like a banker. Darren Murphy – well, he looked exactly like what he was: a thug.

'Hello, officer,' he said in mock formality, running a hand over his face. 'You're up early.'

'It's not that early, Darren,' Claire said.

'Can we come in?' asked Beck.

'Urgent, is it?'

'Lippy as ever, I see,' Claire said. 'Yes, it is urgent.'

'How urgent? Is it, like, just urgent, or is it, like, really urgent, or is it, like, really, really, urgent? That might do it.'

'Do you want me to arrest you?'

'For wha'?'

'I'll find something, believe me,' Claire said.

'You'd better come in.'

Darren stepped aside and Beck and Claire entered. They followed him as he hobbled down the thickly carpeted hallway to the kitchen. The floor here was marble-tiled, the kitchen appliances gleaming, the place remarkably clean. There was nothing standard-local-authority-issue about any of it. Outwardly, the life of a middle-ranking drug dealer was the polar opposite to that of his customers.

'Home alone, are you?' Claire asked, standing in the middle of the room.

Darren sat down on a leather button-back high stool at the breakfast island, hanging his crutch from the back of it. He didn't offer either of them a seat. A half-eaten roll of some description was on the counter in front of him. Darren was looking over Beck's shoulder. Beck turned. A flat-screen TV was mounted on the kitchen wall, the sound muted. It was hard to decipher what was on; it seemed to be night-time in whatever programme Darren was watching.

'Who's yer man?' Darren asked, looking at Beck, picking up his bread roll.

'Detective Sergeant Finnegan Beck,' Beck said.

'Finnegan Beck. What kind of a fucking name is that?'

'Less lip, sunshine,' Claire said. 'We're here in the service of the State. Otherwise we wouldn't be here at all. But in the State's eyes, all men are equal and all that nonsense. Though we know better than that, don't we, Darren?'

'I already made me statement,' Darren said. 'Yer should be off looking for that headcase what murdered Tanya.'

'How do you know we're not?' Beck asked. 'Did you know her, Darren?'

Murphy belched, dropped the bread roll back onto the counter. 'Ya, I knew her.'

'Professionally?' Claire asked.

'What's that mean? I'm unemployed. Actively lookin' for employment, I am. I'm professionally unemployed, if that's what yer mean?'

'I'll tell you something, Darren…' Beck said.

'Will you now?'

'It'll really get your attention. Not a lot of people know this.'

'Comedian, are you?'

'No, Darren. I don't think you'll find this funny at all. It's this. There was blood found under Tanya's fingernails. She'd scratched someone, Darren. And guess who I'm looking at who has marks on his face?'

'Ah, for fuck sake. No way. Jesus, you can't… No fuckin' way, man. Yer supposed to be here investigating da scumbags jumped me the udder night and did this.' He pointed to his head. 'Look. This. And now you're wha'? Blood under the poor girl's fingernails. Wha'? I can't believe yer tinkin that I did it. I didn't. I never killed Tanya. Don't go there. Don't.'

If Darren was lying, he was making a good job of it. Enough to fool Beck. And that would be a first.

'Tell me about Tanya,' Beck said. 'I'm not going to make an issue of small stuff, understand?'

Darren looked pale. 'Let me put it like this. She wasn't doin' nothing that no other young wan in this town wasn't doing. Plenty are doin' more than she ever did, a lot more, believe me.'

'What's that supposed to mean?' Claire asked. 'Was she taking drugs?'

'Naa, not drugs, drugs.'

'Strictly soft, then,' Beck said. 'Like weed.'

'Ya,' Murphy said. 'Like weed. Something like that.'

'What about the others?' Beck asked. 'You said they were doing a lot more than Tanya was.'

'Ah ya, y'know.'

'No, I don't,' Beck said.

'What rhymes with y'know?'

Beck thought about it. 'You mean, for money? Hoe?'

'For wha'ever they can get,' Murphy said. 'But Tanya didn't do that, she didn't spread it about. She had her sugar daddy, so she had. She was strictly for his eyes only.'

'How do you know all this?'

'Everybody knows all this.'

'Who was he?' Beck asked. 'This sugar daddy.'

'Except that part, that is,' Murphy said. 'She kept that strictly, strictly to herself.'

'Where exactly did this happen?' Beck asked.

'Everywhere, you gotta keep your eyes peeled.'

'No,' Beck said. 'Your assault. Where exactly did it happen?'

'Um, right. Church Hill. Halfway up. There's a big tree behind the wall, the branches hang out over the street. Right there. That's where I was ping-powed.'

'Ping-powed?'

'D'ya never hear of that? It's street slang, man.'

'I'll take your word for it,' Beck said. 'Any witnesses?'

'Ya, the three bastards who done it, that's who.'

'They came from behind and you said you never saw them,' Claire said. 'That's what you said in your statement.'

'Ya, that's right. I never saw them.'

'Then how do you know there were three of them?' Beck asked. 'If you didn't see them, that is.'

'Mister, I wasn't looking at nobody. I was tryin' to protect myself from a hidin' that could have killed me. That's wha' I was doing. But I knew there were three because I heard them mouthin' off, okay?'

'They were talking,' said Claire. 'What were they saying?'

Murphy placed a hand on the top of his head. 'This really hurts, y'know. Ouch. I don't know what they were saying. I wasn't paying too much attention at the time. Like I say, I had other priorities – like saving me skin.'

'Steady on there, Darren,' Claire said. 'Aren't you being a bit melodramatic now?'

'No. I'm not. That's what happened. If you don't believe me, tough. But you probably wouldn't believe a word out of anyone's mouth from Chapel Park, would ya? Your mind's already made up.'

Deflection, Beck thought. 'What about your face? Where'd you get those marks?'

'When I hit the gravel,' Darren replied. 'Those little stones are like shotgun pellets, so they are.'

'What do you know about shotgun pellets?' Beck said.

'I got a bellyful couple of years back. No one was ever caught for that either.'

'We'll let you know how the investigation progresses,' Beck said, nodding to Claire that it was time to leave.

Walking back to the car, he said, 'We'll need to check the DNA database. See if there's a match to the blood sample taken from the victim. I doubt it. Even if he did do it, he'd hardly advertise it by reporting he was assaulted. Doesn't make sense. Another thing, if you'd just had stitches put into the top of your head, would you put a hand on it?'

'No,' Claire said, 'I wouldn't.'

'Neither would I,' Beck said.

CHAPTER TWENTY-TWO

'Have you been in here before? You look familiar.' The top of the barman's lip was lost to a thick moustache.

Beck shook his head. 'No. I'd remember if I had,' he lied.

'Seamie Doherty, you still alive?'

'Good to see you too, Garda Somers,' Seamie said. His voice was high-pitched like a girl's, the flesh on his bony face tight as a drum's skin. He sat on a stool, crouching forward onto the counter. He reminded Beck of a stray cat he'd found curled up on his Dublin doorstep one time. It had been in a bad way. By the time he'd fetched a glass of milk from the fridge and gone back to feed it, the cat had died, lying on the ground like a discarded child's toy.

Seamie was one of a handful of punters sitting along the counter, the rest having scarpered when Beck and Claire came in.

'You're new,' Claire said to the barman. 'Here, do you mind turning down that television? The FTSE 100 doesn't interest anyone in here, does it? Hope I'm not being politically incorrect when I say that, not stereotyping anybody?'

'You are,' the barman said. 'And I don't work here, not as such. I'm doing a favour for Christy. He's my brother-in-law.'

'And what's your name?'

'Richie.'

'That's nice of you, Richie,' Claire said, not sounding like she believed him, and to Beck: 'Christy owns the place.'

The pub smelt of piss and bleach. The carpet was mostly threadbare and pockmarked with cigarette burns. The place was small and poky, the roof low, red imitation-leather bench seats against the wall, a line of grime on the torn wallpaper from where people's heads had rested against it. Between the counter and the wall were a few small wooden tables with cushion-top stools. At the end of the bar were two tatty wooden doors; a sign on one said 'Ladies', the other 'Gents'. Beside the gents was a dartboard. Beck was at a loss as to how the board could be used. It was above a bench seat and any dart thrown would have to go over the head of the person sitting underneath it. Maybe that was the whole point? It depended on who was sitting there.

The barman stood with his back against the cash register and folded his arms. A sign pinned to the shelf beside him said, 'If You're Rich, I'm Single'.

'Darren Murphy was in here Sunday night,' Claire said.

Beck was impressed with her confident and mildly aggressive approach. He liked that, and was happy to take a back seat.

'Sooo?' the barman said.

'Sooo,' Claire mimicked him. 'He only got his head caved in on his way home. Who was in here that evening? You have CCTV?'

The barman scoffed. 'CCTV. You think anyone'd drink in here if we had CCTV? No CCTV, darling. Anyway, why aren't you off looking for the killer of that poor girl? Everyone in the town's terrified.'

'That's what Murphy wanted to know too. Your concern is noted. By the way, you don't look too terrified to me. And I'm not your darling.' Claire looked up and down the bar. 'Any of you gentlemen in here Sunday night?'

'Aye, but I saw nuthin,' Seamie said.

'What about you, sunshine? Jimmy Doherty, isn't it?'

Doherty had his back to them, watching the muted TV, doing his best to be ignored. He looked at Claire now. Beck guessed he was in his mid-twenties. He had a facial tic, his eyes repeatedly blinking. Beck found it hard to look at him without feeling the need to blink himself.

'I wasn't here Sunday night. I was workin'.'

'Working?'

'Don't sound so surprised. Check if you want. The Hibernian. In the kitchen. I'm a porter, kitchen porter. Not proud, me. Work is work. Do anythin', I will. Go and ask if you don't believe me. They'll tell you.'

'I will,' Claire said. 'Don't be in any doubt about that.'

'And you?' Claire said to an old codger with a quarter pint of Guinness in front of him. It was obvious by the colour of the residue along the side of the glass it had been there for quite a time.

'Wha' d'ya think?' the old codger asked.

'I think you were home in bed,' Claire said.

'With me girlfriend,' the old codger said. The remark took some of the tension from the room, like air from a balloon. The bar laughed, including Beck and Claire.

'Tell me,' Beck asked no one in particular. 'When Darren Murphy was leaving here Sunday night, did he have anything with him?'

No one spoke. Beck caught a glance exchanged between the barman and Seamie.

'It's not an incriminating question,' Beck said. 'It's straightforward. Did he have a bag with him or not?'

The barman said, after a brief pause, 'I don't know if he had a bag. If he did, I didn't see it.'

And Beck knew right off that he was lying. He could see it: the change in intonation, the shift in body language, the arms folding tighter.

Claire watched Beck with a curious expression.

'I see,' Beck said. 'As I say, it has no particular relevance. That's the last question. We'll be on our way now. See, that wasn't so bad, was it?'

The barman unfolded his arms. 'Don't be in any hurry back, will you?'

'Don't worry,' Beck replied. 'I won't.'

'Why did you ask if he had a bag?' Claire asked when they were outside.

'Because I think he's covering. I think he had something. And he *lost* it.'

'Like what?'

'A drugs consignment,' Beck said. 'Which he wanted to keep. Maybe Richie even gave it to him. I don't know. Anyway, he says he *lost* it. Or was robbed of it. Whatever.'

'But that's just a guess.'

'Of course it's just a guess. But it happens. To drug dealers. A lot. Church Hill, Claire. Let's get up there. Have a look around.'

On one side of Church Hill was a low stone wall, open ground on the other with a few houses, mainly bungalows, fronting the road. At the top of the hill, a right turn led down to Chapel Park. Claire pulled the Focus onto the pavement next to where the branches of a tree – as described by Murphy – overhung the pavement.

Beck got out of the car. He lit a cigarette and drew in deeply, feeling the kick at the back of his throat.

'When you say Murphy lost something, why didn't he mention it to us?' Claire asked as she joined him.

'Because drug dealers lose things all the time, comes with the territory.'

'Well, you've lost *me* now,' Claire replied.

He walked to the wall and peered across it. 'You've been in Cross Beg too long,' he said.

On the other side was a field of weeds and wild grass. He stood there thinking, smoking his cigarette. He flicked the stub into the field and climbed across.

'Where're you going?' Claire called, leaning over, but making no attempt to follow.

'Give me a minute.'

Beck moved from left to right, walking along by the wall on either side of the tree and out into the field. He came back and climbed over again, stood beside Claire and looked along the pavement.

'It didn't rain last couple of nights,' Beck said. 'And anyway, it's sheltered here under the branches. So if he was assaulted like he says he was, there should still be blood here. He'd have lost quite a bit of it, by the way he described things.'

'I see where you're going with this,' Claire said.

'Drive me back to Murphy's place.'

CHAPTER TWENTY-THREE

Murphy looked like he was going somewhere. He wore a lime-green anorak with yellow imitation fur surrounding the hood.

'Going out?' Beck asked when he opened the door.

'What d'ya want now?' His demeanour had changed. He had not expected Beck and Claire to call a second time.

'Just a word,' Claire said. 'We won't keep you. A couple of minutes, that's it, then we'll be gone. Alright, sunshine?'

Murphy turned. 'Alright. But it better be quick.'

He brought them into a sitting room, small and clean like the kitchen, and expensively furnished.

'By the way,' Beck said. 'I never asked. You live alone?'

'Why ya want to know that for?' Murphy hobbled to an armchair and sat down on the arm.

'No reason.'

'His mother,' Claire said. 'Darren lives with his mother, don't you, son? Who's at work now, by the way, cleaning offices on the industrial estate. Works hard, your mother, doesn't she, Darren?'

There was a prolonged silence as Murphy stared at Claire. Intimidation some might call it, but not a very good attempt, Beck considered.

'There's no easy way of doing this,' Beck said, pointing. 'Could you look at that, please?'

Murphy turned his head to follow Beck's outstretched arm. Beck took his opportunity, pushed him from behind onto the settee, pinning him down so he couldn't move. Murphy roared.

Beck felt about for a bandage clip, but couldn't find one. Instead he found a couple of safety pins, the type hospitals had stopped using over thirty years ago. Murphy jiggled like a fish, shaking his head from side to side. Beck fumbled to get hold of a pin and open it. He had to force Murphy's head down into a cushion to do it. He finally got a pin and unclipped it – the tip went into Murphy's head and he squealed like a pig, shouting about garda brutality, that he'd sue the lot of them, that they'd all lose their jobs, that the four horsemen of the apocalypse would run them down and send them all to hell, that the story would be on the front page of every newspaper in the country by morning. Beck unfurled the bandage, round and round, until eventually he pulled it from Murphy's head, and Murphy fell silent, stopped his thrashing about and the only sound was that of his panting. Beck looked closely at the top of his head, at the dark stubble sprouting like young grass because it hadn't been shaved in a couple of days. But other than that, his head was as smooth as a baby's arse, with not a mark or a stitch in sight.

'You were saying?' Beck said. 'Something about garda brutality.'

'Ah, fuck off,' Murphy said.

CHAPTER TWENTY-FOUR

Murphy sat at the same interview desk as Ned Donohue had the day before, giving off an air of defiant indifference, but Beck could tell he was worried.

'When's this interview startin'?' He forced a yawn. 'I'm getting bored.'

'We're expecting the senior investigating officers, Darren. Once they heard we had a suspect for the murder of Tanya Frazzali, well, they dropped everything to get down here as quickly as they could. Won't be much longer.'

Darren's face crumpled into shocked surprise. 'Whatever,' he sighed, trying to recover his composure, but his shaky voice gave him away.

There followed a silence, and Beck hoped it was heavy for Darren, that it pressed down onto his shoulders. Beck allowed that silence to linger, like seasoning on a steak, softening Murphy up.

'I think we'll just get on with it,' Beck said. 'What you think, Darren? Unless you want to wait for them? It's up to you.'

Darren turned his close-set eyes onto Beck. He was no longer able to hide his panic.

'Ya, ya,' he blurted, 'let's get on with it.'

Beck had lied.

He was not waiting for Wilde or O'Reilly, although he had rung Wilde and told him Murphy was in custody, but nothing more.

Beck was about to press the red button on the recorder when Darren spoke.

'Before you do that,' he said.

Beck threw a glance at Claire.

'Yes?' Claire said to Murphy.

'I was thinking…'

'You were thinking,' Beck said.

Darren looked at Beck's finger, poised above the red record button. 'I want to have a word with Garda Somers here. Privately.'

'You can't have a word with me privately. We have rules and regulations about that sort of thing.'

'You didn't heed the rules when you held me down and took the bandage off my fuckin' head, did ya?'

'I don't know what you're talking about, Darren,' Claire said. 'Now say it out loud. What is it?'

'I didn't kill Tanya Frazzali, okay?'

'You said that already,' Beck said.

'The DNA won't be a match. You'll see. And I was in The Noose. You already checked. And then I was in the hospital soon after. I didn't have time to kill anybody.'

'You a detective now, Darren?' Claire said. 'You left the hospital before receiving treatment. Did you think we wouldn't check? Just accept your name was on the patient register and not question it? We're not that thick, Darren.'

'I shouldn't be here,' he responded, ignoring the remark.

Beck knew everything Darren had just said was probably true.

'But you are here, Darren, and will be until this time tomorrow. Then, if everything works out like you think it will, no problem, you're out of here, except, that is, for the small matter of the false reporting of a robbery. In the meantime…'

'In the meantime?'

'For starters, we search your home,' Beck said. 'From top to bottom.'

'I want to talk. Off the record.'

'Off the record,' Beck said.

'Off the record.'

'Talk. I'll decide if it's off the record or not.'

Darren fell silent, thinking. Then, 'Suppose someone has a grow factory. I mean, a big fucking grow factory. Maybe a hundred plants, ya.'

'What about it?' Claire said. 'Is that what you're telling us, Darren?'

'Give the man a chance,' Beck said, flashing a smile of reassurance to the drug dealer that said, 'See, I'm not all bad, play your cards right and I could be your friend'.

'Go on, Darren.'

'I can give you a name and address, ya. They're worth about fifty thousand euro.'

'Give us the name and address,' Beck said.

Darren looked at Beck, and that smirk of his reappeared. 'You think I'm stupid? You have to let me go first.'

There was an edge to Beck's tone now. 'You think *I'm* stupid, Darren? I didn't come down in the last shower. You're trying to get another dealer out of the way, while you get to keep whatever it is you're hiding in your house. Clever. But stupid at the same time. Look, you probably made up that cock and bull story about being assaulted, right? Because you're telling other certain people the same thing. That you were robbed. But there's consequences for telling people like that lies like those, isn't there, Darren? Unless you can convince them that you *really* were robbed. But that's the stupid part. Because it won't make any difference. And I couldn't give a flying fuck about any of it, Darren, so you read me wrong on that. I'm trying to find the sick fucker who killed a young girl. That's the part that I'm interested in, to hell with the rest.'

Darren laid his hand on the table, said matter-of-factly, 'Okay. What about this? I do actually know who Tanya Frazzali was seeing.'

Beck felt his breath catch at the back of his throat.

'If I can walk out that door – and my house isn't searched, that is – I'll tell you.'

CHAPTER TWENTY-FIVE

Superintendent Wilde shook his head and stuck his hands into his pockets. 'He's a lying toerag, gets away with murder, maybe literally in this case.'

He was standing by one of the high windows in his office. When Beck had appeared in the open doorway he'd been leaning over a filing cabinet, flicking through some files. He looked out the window now. 'Murphy can't be trusted to lie straight in a bed.' He began chewing on a corner of his lip. 'He's a lying toerag.'

Beck walked into the centre of the room. Suddenly he didn't feel so good. 'Mind if I sit down, boss?'

Wilde turned and looked at him. 'Not feeling so good? No surprises there. No need to sit down, Beck. Go back and tell Murphy he can fuck off. Search his house immediately. The DNA comparison will take hours anyway. He's going nowhere.'

Beck felt like throwing up. He took a deep breath.

'The assault didn't happen,' he said. 'It's a cover, for what I don't know. He pocketed a delivery maybe, something I don't particularly care about.'

'Neither do I, not right now anyway. You can tell him that, too, that we're not wasting any more time on him. And no deals. But still, if you can wrangle the information about the grow house out of him, tell him what he wants to hear, whatever it takes, that'd be great. Inspector O'Reilly can look after it.' Wilde winked. 'Should get a feather in his cap for that one – put a smile onto that crinkly face of his.'

Beck turned and started for the door. 'I'll get on with it.'

He went to the bathroom at the end of the corridor, sat quietly on a closed toilet bowl in a cubicle, gathering himself. When he felt better, he got up and went out to the sinks, ran a cold water tap, splashed some onto his face. Then he headed back to the interview room.

Murphy was leaning his forehead on the table, arms outstretched on either side of his head. He sat up when Beck came in. He didn't speak. Beck glanced at Claire and sat in the chair beside her again.

'Give me the name, Darren,' Beck said.

'So we have a deal then?'

We have a deal. Beck hated that term.

'We have an arrangement, Darren, yes.'

'If I give you the name, I can walk?'

I can walk. Jesus.

'Yes, Darren,' Beck lied.

'You better be telling the truth.' There was a cut to Darren's voice, like a threat, a glimpse into his nasty side.

'I haven't got all day, Darren,' Beck said. 'Name.'

'Drum roll,' Darren said, cockiness seeping in now.

'Last chance,' Beck said.

'His name…' Darren began.

And finally he said it.

Claire's voice squawked. 'What?'

'You'd need to be careful, people,' Murphy said. 'He's good friends with your boss, so he is.'

'Which one?' Claire asked.

'Yer man, Inspector O'Reilly. That prick.'

'Steady,' Beck said. 'That name. It rings a bell.'

Murphy said it again.

'Christ,' Claire said. 'It should.'

CHAPTER TWENTY-SIX

The trees murmured to each other, soft sighs and whispers, the gentle wind soothing them, carrying their leaves in a slow but persistent culling. Devoid of leaves, the branches were like clawed hands, stark against the grey sky. He remembered when he was five years old, or thereabouts. Yes, he could remember back that far. Waking in his mother's arms. To find her staring at him. Silent. Still. Just... staring. He had started to cry. But it made no difference. And in that moment, something changed. Forever. In that moment he became aware. That his mother was alive. But so too was she dead. It was those eyes. He could never forget them.

The trees were entering their winter twilight world now, caught between life and death. What was it like, he wondered, to be like that, neither dead nor alive? He thought about it all the time. He thought about all those who suffered, like him, walking the ungodly paths through a world corrupted.

That's when it had started. On his mother's lap. Soon after, there was that episode with the cat. Not that he'd wanted to kill it; no, just merely deny it sufficient oxygen so it would pass out. He'd wanted to experiment on its unconscious body. He'd wanted to know if pain could only be felt when the body was conscious. He'd wanted to know that if he tortured the animal long enough, would it wake up?

The cat was a bad idea, though; it squirmed about in his hands, spitting at him, lashing out with its claws. He hadn't thought of it doing anything like that. It cut him almost immediately, four identical parallel lies of smudged blood on his right arm. He dropped the animal, stifling a scream for fear his mother would hear.

It was two weeks later before he got another chance. Walking home from school one day, a neighbourhood friend's puppy wandered out onto the street in front of him… He had prayed for forgiveness that time. But it had been necessary to do it. It was something that had to be done.

Because he was fascinated by the vortex, the black hole, that existed between life and death.

To be neither dead nor alive.

To be neither dead. Nor alive.

He waited, though. He'd been waiting quite a while. He could almost smell it: the decaying twigs mixed with moss and herbs. It was everywhere.

CHAPTER TWENTY-SEVEN

Ned had worked his way through town and ended up more or less back where he had started. He cursed Cross Beg for not being any bigger, for not having more alleyways for him to slink along and hide in. Cursing, he turned, and with his peculiar duck walk even more pronounced now because of his frustration, he went from Plunkett Hill onto Bridge Street. He crossed here, oblivious to the traffic. Someone blew a car horn, unusual for Cross Beg.

On the other side of the street, he went through a gap in the low wall and down the steps to the muddy riverbank. It hadn't rained in the last couple of days, and the edge of the bank by the wall was dry. He went along here, following the trail worn into the soil by the feet of fishermen. He walked until the trail ended in high, wild, dead grass. He stopped and turned around, looking back at the town. He could see the first bridge and the buildings on either side, the spire of the cathedral. No matter where you went, the spire followed you like a bad conscience. He sat down, felt the dampness through the thin fabric of his trousers. The wind was enough to stir white tops on the fast-flowing water, high in tide now, speeding its way to the wide estuary where the Brown Water met the Atlantic.

Ned had a couple of cans in each pocket.

He lay down and looked at the sky, black puffy smokes of cloud here and there. He could feel the sharp edge of cold in the air. There was a storm coming. He knew what he had to do. Survive it, that's what he had to do. Survive the storm.

There was a sound, lost again on the wind.

Ned sat up. He heard it a second time. It was his name.

A coldness crept through him, but it was a coldness not caused by the weather. He turned his head in the direction of that sound. And saw him.

'Ned, I've been looking everywhere for you.'

There was nothing Ned could do but bless himself.

CHAPTER TWENTY-EIGHT

Beck was brooding. They were sitting at a corner table in a café a little down from the station. He stirred his overpriced lukewarm coffee in its fancy blue mug. Superintendent Wilde had refused permission to arrest for the purposes of securing a DNA sample. Without it, there was no way to prove if Murphy's accusations were true.

'Wilde never gave his consent for any deal with Murphy, did he?' Claire said. 'You lied to me.'

'What? Oh, I'm afraid not,' Beck said. 'The means justify the ends, you know.'

Her empty plastic water bottle was on the table in front of her. In anger she flicked it with the back of her hand harder than she'd intended and it flew from the table onto the floor. A couple at the next table turned to look. She reached out and picked it up again.

'It's the way you do things, isn't it?' Her voice was like escaping steam. 'Off the books. You want to put us all in danger?'

'I squared it with him.'

'With who?'

'Murphy.'

'How?'

'I don't think you want to know.'

'Tell me.'

'I don't think you want to know.'

'Tell me, Beck.'

So he told her that, as he was returning Murphy to his cell after questioning, he gave him his phone and allowed him to make a call while he waited outside. There would be nothing found when his house was searched later.

'The means justify the ends, do they, huh?' she said.

'Lesser of two evils. The drugs search in Sligo will yield significantly more.'

Claire fell silent, thinking. Beck sipped from his coffee, which was now cold.

'Why are we waiting? We should lift him immediately, shouldn't we?'

'We can't,' Beck said. 'I spoke to the Skipper. He's adamant. Evidence first. Something other than the word of a convicted drug dealer. Something that's not going to be a key to a money vault for a litigation lawyer. His words: "Things work differently in Cross Beg". He mentioned the man is friendly with O'Reilly, too, by the way. I think that might have something to do with it.' Beck pushed his coffee cup away. 'I didn't even want to get into this.'

'You're in it. What do we do now?'

'I don't know, I'm thinking.'

They both fell silent. Both thinking.

CHAPTER TWENTY-NINE

They walked back to the station in silence, the clouds that had been drifting in from the north all morning concentrating into a mass of deep black that stretched across the sky.

Beck sat at a desk in the Ops Room. A detective collating notes from door-to-door enquiries the previous day informed him that O'Reilly had left for Sligo in a hurry a half hour before. Beck smiled, drumming his fingers on the desk. It wasn't his desk. He didn't have one. But being desk-less suited him fine.

'Sergeant Beck.'

The uniformed officer was standing by the desk. He looked familiar. Beck tried to remember where he'd seen him before. Then it came to him: he'd been one of the two at the bottom of the embankment on Monday as he walked back from the body of Tanya Frazzali.

'Yes?'

'Something you might be interested in.'

Beck closed his eyes and ran a hand over his face.

'Okay,' he said, opening them again. 'What's your name, by the way?'

'Dempsey. Fergal Dempsey.'

'So, what is it, Dempsey?'

Dempsey looked uncertain. 'It's probably nothing.'

'Get on with it,' Beck said, and immediately regretted the irritation in his voice.

'A couple of weeks ago we got a shout, myself and my partner. A female reported being attacked on the footbridge at the back of the hospital. It's a shortcut into town. About eleven o'clock at night. Said someone tried to strangle her. She had marks on her neck.'

'I didn't know about this.'

'We went to her address. She declined to make a statement. We didn't record it as an assault.'

'Did you record it at all?'

Officer Dempsey looked sheepish. 'No. The inspector doesn't want us recording incidents unless a statement is forthcoming.'

'You have this person's details?'

'Yes. In my notebook. Right here.'

'Give them to me, please. Write them down.'

Dempsey opened his notebook, tore off a page, came to the desk and wrote down the details, handed the page to Beck. 'She's a Russian national, by the way. Works in the catering section at the hospital. First name's Nina, surname Sokolov.'

Beck took the piece of paper, looked at it. 'Thanks, Dempsey. Anything else?'

'No.'

'Okay then.'

Dempsey nodded once, turned and left the Ops Room.

CHAPTER THIRTY

First things first, Beck considered, putting his thoughts in order. He needed to speak to Nina Sokolov. But before that, and indeed before they pursued the man who Murphy had claimed was Tanya's boyfriend, Beck had to get firm confirmation Murphy himself wasn't involved.

He picked up the desk phone. He didn't have a number for blood analysis, so he dialled Garda HQ and asked to be put through to the lab instead. When he was connected, he spoke to a female. She whispered, 'Hello, blood analysis.'

Beck could hardly hear her. He stuck a finger in his other ear, told her who he was and asked if Morgan Ryan still worked in the section, and if so, could he speak to him.

'Morgan's busy,' she replied in a whisper.

'I'm finding it hard to hear you,' Beck said. 'Are you whispering?'

She raised her voice just enough for him to hear. 'Yes, sorry. The Commissioner is on a visit. That's why he's busy. Morgan.'

'And who are you?'

'Debra Anne Burke. I'm an analyst here.'

'Debra Anne. I need the results of a blood sample taken from the body of a murder victim in Cross Beg, Co. Galway.'

'I heard about that case. Young girl. Terrible.'

'Yes. It is terrible. Could you give them to me, the results?'

She paused, then: 'Um, I don't know. Morgan is the senior analyst. I think it's best if you wait for him, if you don't mind.'

'I don't really have time,' Beck said, keeping his voice calm. 'The superintendent here is waiting on them.'

'The superintendent?'

'Yes, the superintendent.'

'Um, well. Let me see. I'm right at my computer… Referred by Dr Gumbell. I can… There, I have the file right here. Yes, it's been processed, just finished in the last half hour. Yes, it's here.'

Beck turned his eyes heavenward. 'And what does it say?'

'The system did not return a match. DNA was extracted from the sample, but it will be some time before we have full results. However, it's O-positive, by the way, the sample. The victim's blood was O-negative, which is fairly rare. The O-positive, on the other hand, is fairly common.'

'No match,' Beck repeated, the flicker of hope that there might be a result extinguished. 'Okay, thank you, Debra Anne.' He hung up.

Beck stood and walked across to Claire's desk.

'Do me a favour. Tell Darren Murphy to go home. There was no match. I'm not surprised, as far as he's concerned anyway. It's not his blood.'

CHAPTER THIRTY-ONE

Back at his desk, Beck dialled Nina Sokolov's number. It rang for a long time before it was answered. '*Da*,' she said in Russian, sounding like she had just woken up and wasn't happy about it. Beck told her he was a policeman and did not speak or understand Russian. She said in English, 'Policeman,' and Beck immediately heard the suspicion in her voice. 'I work nights,' she said.

'Sorry. Did I wake you?'

'Yes. You did. I leave my bloody phone on.'

'I'm very sorry. I believe you reported an assault recently. I need to speak with you about that.'

'Why? I already talk to policemans. Everything okay now. Thank you. No problems. Everything okay now. Thank you.'

'Ms Sokolov. I need to speak with you. Just a few questions. It won't take long.'

'I speak now. I talk with you now. I work later. No come to police station.'

'I could come to you, at a time that's convenient – tomorrow, maybe.'

'No, no. Now. I speak now. Or I no speak. Please.'

Beck took a slow breath. 'Okay, Nina, we can talk now.'

He could hear a fumbling sound, followed by the clicking of a lighter as she lit a cigarette. The sound of a deep inhale. Beck suddenly felt like a cigarette himself.

'It happened at night, Nina. Eleven o'clock. Is that right?'

'Yes. Eleven o'clock. I was going to work. I was late for my shift.'

'Did you see your attacker?'

'No see. He have mask. I punch him in the balls. Motherfucker. Then I run off. I brown belt karate. Train for something happens like this. It happens before to me. In Moscow. I was raped.'

Her bluntness took Beck by surprise, made him a little uncomfortable. 'This time, Nina, were you injured?'

The sound of an exhale. '*Nyet*. No. Nothing. Mark to my arm, and a little to my neck, that is all.'

'Did he try to strangle you?'

'Motherfucker put hand to my neck, yes. And arm, yes. I think he want to drag me from bridge. Maybe he like to strangle me. He no strangle me. Russians tough peoples. Tougher than this motherfucker, yes.'

'His build, Nina, what did he look like?'

'He big fucker. Six foot, maybe more.'

'Thin?'

'Tin, what's this?'

'Thin, his build – slim, thin, you know? Or fat?'

'Yes, I see. I mean no. He build wide. How you say? Like shite house wall.'

Beck grinned. 'But you didn't make a statement. Why not, Nina?'

'Why not? Why, why not? No statement. Anyway, it okay now, I don't use that bridge no more.'

'Yes, but others do. We need to catch him.'

'You catch him then, yes. No need me. Your job, yes. Not mine. You catch him, yes. Motherfucker.'

Beck paused. He wasn't going to get any further here.

Then the line went dead.

Beck replaced the phone onto its cradle. He got up and went into the public office, stood in the doorway. Dempsey was leaning on the counter, filling in a form.

'Was there CCTV?' Beck asked. 'Of the attack on the Russian girl, Nina, from the bridge.'

Dempsey turned; he had the same sheepish look as before.

'Did you even go to the scene, Dempsey?'

'She didn't make a statement, so there was no point. That's what we thought at the time.'

'Can you do that now, first chance you get? Check for CCTV. And get it to me as soon as you can.'

Dempsey nodded.

'And Dempsey, just something to think about. If you ever come across a person with, say, a hatchet sticking out of the back of their head, which is something, by the way, that can only happen if someone else puts it there, what do you do then? Wait until they decide to make a statement before you act? No. I don't think so either.'

He left Dempsey to ponder that.

CHAPTER THIRTY-TWO

The crows stood on the rooftops and the disused old chimney stacks of the buildings along Main Street. Darkness was falling, and their time to roost had come. They were restless, cawing incessantly and baring their open beaks at one another. They sensed things that people could not. And something was not right.

Were they trying to tell him something?

Beck made his way quickly along the street.

'Mr Beck.'

He turned. For a moment he didn't recognise the figure wrapped up in a bubble jacket and a woolly hat pulled down over her ears. Melanie McBride was standing at the side of the street, just inside the doorway to an old office building. On the wall next to her was an unpolished bronze plaque inscribed with 'GRATTAN SOLICITORS AND COMMISSIONERS FOR OATHS, FIRST FLOOR'.

Beck stopped. There was a musty smell, tinged with something like vinegar, and it was hard to tell if it came from Melanie or the hallway behind her; a single light bulb was hanging from the ceiling, throwing her into shadow.

'Hello, Melanie.'

'We're going to have a gathering. Soon. In memory of Tanya.'

'In the wood?'

'Maybe.'

'I see,' Beck said, wondering why she was telling him this.

'Yes, in the wood, when this is all over. We have a special place, by the water's edge. I couldn't really talk, the other day, when you visited the school. My mother and everything.'

'Is there something you want to say now? If you want to speak to me, your mother should really be present.'

'Mr Sweetman, the English and Geography teacher at St Malachi's College. You should talk to him, that's all I'm saying. He always seemed very friendly with Tanya. I mean, *very* friendly.'

Melanie moved past him onto the street and quickly walked away. With it went that musty smell. It reminded him of methamphetamine. Beck hoped it wasn't.

He continued, his thoughts all rattling around inside him like an old threshing machine. More than once he was tempted to disappear into one of the pubs he passed. They offered such a simple, uncomplicated solution, even if one that was strictly transitory and always came with consequences.

He walked on. The forty-eight-hour window on the investigation had now closed.

Tanya's image would not leave his mind. Whatever the circumstances, she was a child, a child who had been abused and ultimately, killed. He knew he was too far into this to let go now. This had become his investigation.

Beck sat in the back garden, on the sturdy metal bench by the open kitchen door, smoking a cigarette. Mrs Claxton had told him the bench was an antique, over a hundred years old. It was dark now, and in the backs of houses along the next street over, lights were appearing in windows and curtains were being pulled shut. Each window, he knew, held its own story.

He thought of Natalia, imagining her voice on the night air. She had been ringing him lately. He knew it was her, even if the number had been blocked. He had not answered. He might have, had the phone rung long enough for him to convince himself that it was a good idea to do so. But it never did ring long enough for that, so he guessed she grappled with a dilemma similar to his own.

That last time he and Natalia had met was in Bewley's on Grafton Street, the busiest coffee shop in Dublin, the maxim being that when there was something to hide – like an illicit relationship, for example – it was always best to do it in plain sight as a means of avoiding arousing suspicion. That had been her idea, but he didn't care. She was going to give her marriage another try, she'd told him. She didn't want to break up with Jim. Their youngest child – she had three, she reminded him – was still in his early teens and needed her. When she told him, she misread his reaction. 'It'll be okay,' she said. 'You'll get over me. It'll just take time.' The truth was, Beck was relieved. His interest was only so strong as to the degree of her unavailability. If she was to leave her husband and come to him, his interest, he knew, would evaporate. And that, even Beck had to admit, was pretty messed up. Now that she was definitely unavailable, he wanted her again, more than ever. Seemingly, if the unanswered anonymous calls were anything to go by, so did she.

The wind stirred; the sky was pitch black. He took a last pull on his cigarette and flicked the end away, watching it tumble through the air before spiralling down to earth again. It landed somewhere in the grass. He could see its faint glow quickly fading before disappearing completely.

He could hear a sound wafting through the house and out into the night air. It was the croaking noise of the front doorbell. He stood, walked back in to answer it.

She was clutching a casserole dish, the smell of perfume and hairspray mixed with beef, vegetables and tangy sauce.

'Hi.' A big smile, well-cared-for teeth but a couple of gaps towards the back where she thought no one could see them.

'Mrs Claxton,' he said, surprised.

'I hope you don't mind my calling. I made far too much of this… Okay, the truth is, I made extra with the idea of bringing you some over. Can I come in?'

He moved aside.

She passed him, into the hall, and he followed her into the kitchen. She set the dish down onto the cooker and turned, both hands behind her, resting on the oven handle.

'Mr Beck. I want to apologise for the other evening. I think you might have got the wrong impression of me.'

Beck smiled. He thought of situations he'd been in during his illicit relationship with Natalia. 'Don't worry about it. You're talking to the master of regretful behaviour.'

She was silent, her expression thoughtful. 'I didn't say I regretted it, did I?' She looked into his eyes, then laughed, leaving him to wonder if she'd been serious or not. 'I won't delay, I'm meeting a couple of friends later. I can collect the dish tomorrow. I'll leave it to you.' She passed him on her way out again. 'Enjoy.'

A moment later, the front door closed. Beck went to the cooker, placed a hand onto the casserole dish lid to see if it was still hot. It was. He picked it up, along with a fork from the worktop by the cooker, and went to the table, sat down and removed the lid, began eating straight out of the dish.

Sleep came instantly, carrying him down, way down, into the subterranean labyrinth of his subconscious. Where they waited for him, greeting Beck with their shrill yelps and laughter. The Old Duffer, that mocking, vile inner demon, a caricature of every horror movie character Beck had ever seen. A small fat man, as Beck imagined him. With small eyes. The human equivalent of a mole. Pacing the floor, back and forth, biding his time. Others shimmied about; the faces that had gone before. There were so many, stretching back along the corridors of his mind, a macabre line-up of the dead. Some he would never forget, like the face of the victim in his first murder investigation. In life she had been beautiful, they said. But he had never seen her in life. She was smiling at him now, a portion of her head missing. She seemed unperturbed about it, one eye dangling from its socket on a sinewy string of muscle. Her husband had done that to her. What did he use again? A jigsaw? Yes, that was it. He had taken a jigsaw to his wife's head, the mother of his children. Merely killing her had not been enough.

Beck could hear what sounded like flowing water, and he wondered where and what it was. He stared past the line-up of the dead into the darkness. The sound was coming from below. He looked down, and as he watched, he saw movement, like the darkness itself was shifting, undulating, and he realised he was looking at water, flowing water, and Tanya Frazzali's body was floating in it, staring at him as she floated past, her pale dead skin stark against the black water. The sounds of the Old Duffer grew louder, scurrying about below. There was a sloshing sound as he entered the water too. He was laughing. Beck went to the water's edge. He could see himself in three-dimensional form, pacing back and forth, too afraid to enter. He didn't want Tanya to be taken, not by him. And then a new sound, louder than anything else. He froze, transfixed. It was that noise again: click, click, click. The turning of the revolver chamber. But what was it doing here? Now, at this time?

Beck woke with a start, his breathing rapid and shallow. He could hear the howling wind and the rain outside the windows like a furious animal. The whole room seemed to shake with the violence of the storm. He felt something press against his back, could feel it begin to wrap itself around him, begin to try and crush him. He pushed it away and sat upright. Mrs Claxton smiled at him. He saw her neck, long and thin, extending from her body.

With a sense of revulsion, he realised she had the body of a snake. She flicked out a forked tongue that touched his face, and though it was fleeting, he could still feel its scorching heat like an ember from the fires of hell.

His eyes snapped open and he sat bolt upright, his body bathed in warm, clammy sweat. Beck fumbled about for the bedside light in panic, pressed it, then flopped back onto the bed, the reptilian image of Mrs Claxton vivid in his mind. His breathing slowed and he was soothed by the relief of knowing that it had all been a nightmare.

CHAPTER THIRTY-THREE

A pale, bleary-eyed face stared back at Beck as he looked in the bathroom mirror the next morning. Cold turkey was a necessary evil in avoiding the permanency of a hopelessly drunken state; in other words, the misery-go-round world of the chronic alcoholic. One day he might give in to that, that attraction of rolling in the gutter, but right now he had no desire to. He hoped he never would. In the kitchen he drank a mug of instant coffee and ate the thick crust from a loaf of bread – all that was left. The living room had been warmed by the timer-controlled central heating and he sat in an armchair by the empty fireplace, scrolled through the contacts list of his mobile phone, stopped when he found the name he wanted and pressed 'call'.

The phone was answered on the fifth ring.

'Beck.' The voice was surprised and had the expected agitation of a busy person preparing for a busy day.

'Assistant Commissioner Sullivan, thank you for taking my call.'

'I was tempted not to, but…'

'Yes?'

'Do you know what time it is, Beck?'

'Sorry, sir, I apologise. I wasn't going to call, to tell the truth.'

'And I wasn't going to answer, to tell the truth. Someone was supposed to contact you. In due course. Did they?'

Beck thought: Due course? What does that mean? An hour, a day, a month, a year, what? 'No, they didn't.'

'Righteo, then. They will do.'

'For what reason?'

'I thought you knew. That's why you rang... Beck, why did you ring?'

'Something. I thought of something.'

'Something? What, Beck, for Christ's sake?'

'The revolver.'

'Yes, what about it?'

'Before I went in. I heard it.'

Silence.

'That came to you just now, did it?'

'Well... last night, actually. Yes, it did.'

'And...'

'You're not surprised, are you? You knew already?'

'I know it now.'

'What? Because I told you?'

'Spare me, Beck. They're looking into it again. That's how I know.'

Silence.

'Someone will be in touch, Beck. Okay?'

The line went dead.

CHAPTER THIRTY-FOUR

'Inspector Andy Mahony, Technical Bureau.' The inspector, a small thin man with epaulettes that appeared oversized and heavy on such narrow, round shoulders, stood at the top of the Ops Room, hands on hips, attempting to portray a sense of presence that wasn't there. 'We found nothing of evidential value, despite conducting a thorough search of the area... I have to say, matters weren't helped by it being such an open and isolated crime scene.' He glanced at O'Reilly next to him. 'Nor by the absence of a crime scene tent. And the ground up there is very porous. Footprints or tracks, anything like that, will simply disappear because it quickly reverts back to its natural contour.' The technical officer paused, looked at the floor and up again. He didn't add anything further.

'For the record,' O'Reilly said, his tone peremptory. 'We didn't have a crime scene tent because Ballinasloe took ours and haven't given it back yet. Moving on. We're spinning in the mud here. We need this investigation to move forward. Yesterday' – he paused as a self-congratulatory smiled crossed his face – 'from information received, I was able to coordinate an important drugs raid on a grow house in Sligo town. You may have heard about it. Fifty thousand euro worth of cannabis plants taken off the market. It coincided with a search of Darren Murphy's house here in Cross Beg. Unfortunately, that yielded nothing. Negative. We were surprised at that.'

Beck waited for a remark from O'Reilly, or a glance in his direction. None came. O'Reilly had no clue.

'That,' O'Reilly went on, 'is how you do it. That is what I'm talking about here. Results. Results. Re-sults. Do I need to say it again? Over and over? Come on, it's not good enough, people. Call yourselves policemen? We're getting nowhere here. You, Weir – where are you with that CCTV collection of yours?'

'Have everything that's available,' Weir said. 'Twenty-four different sets. Practically every camera there is in and about the town. We're going through it all. Takes a little time.'

'And what have you found so far?'

'A couple of cars have popped up across multiple locations, travelling from town within the relevant time frame, heading in the general direction of Cool Wood. We have partial registrations – going through the National Vehicle Database as we speak, trying to narrow it down. Will hopefully have more information by the end of the morning.'

'You. Beck. Murphy has been discounted, that right?'

'Yes, Murphy has been discounted.'

O'Reilly's eyes narrowed. 'Was there something else to do with that gouger? Do you need to tell the team anything?'

A knowing look crossed O'Reilly's face.

Beck cursed under his breath, taken by surprise. A murmur went through the room, people shifting in their chairs to look at him.

He didn't want to mention anything. Not just yet. A small town like Cross Beg, where everybody knew everybody, it was only a matter of time before the word got out.

'He gave a name,' Beck said. 'Of the person he says Tanya Frazzali was sleeping with.'

That got people's attention. All eyes were on him. No one spoke.

'Well, spit it out, man,' O'Reilly said.

Beck glanced at O'Reilly, then around the room. Said nothing, because he'd seen it too many times. While at Pearse Street. The Blue Sieve, they called it. Classified information sprinkled about like flour. In a big city such as Dublin, that might not be so bad. But in a small town like Cross Beg...

Finally, Beck said the name that Darren Murphy had given him, and the room erupted with loud voices.

'Quiet,' O'Reilly commanded. He looked at Beck: this was personal. 'You're on dangerous territory. Our local Pablo Escobar. The lying toerag. What were you planning to do with this information, anyway?'

'I know what I'd like to do.'

'Which is?'

'Arrest him.'

'You'd need more than that.'

Someone coughed, but there was no other sound.

O'Reilly gave a twisted smile. 'Enough rope,' he said. 'That's all you need. Enough rope.'

'I don't want this information getting out,' Beck said. 'It stays within these four walls. If anyone…'

The door to the public office burst open. A uniform rushed into the room.

'Ned Donohue,' he announced. 'His body's just been found. In the river.'

CHAPTER THIRTY-FIVE

His hands were not in his pockets; one was clenched, purple and rigid, the other tangled in the foliage just above the waterline of the riverbank. It was obvious the body had been there all night at least. He had on the same oversized jacket he'd worn when Beck had interviewed him, trapped air causing it to balloon above his back. His head was face down in the water, the thin, sparse hair on it like whiskers, his flesh a deep grey colour. He looked like a very large water turtle. More than a dozen officers crowded along the bank, churning the dead grass into mud beneath their feet. Beck and Somers stood to the side of them. O'Reilly was at the water's edge, directly above the body, peering down. In the distance, Beck could hear the familiar staccato sound of a fire engine approaching.

The firemen took his body from the water with the ease and ceremony of removing a dead pony. The big jacket helped, the grappling hook catching it with ease. They pulled the body ashore, lay it on its back on the bank. Ned's eyes were wide and staring; it was hard to tell whether in surprise or fright. There was a childlike quality to his face, even in death. Beck felt an almost overpowering sense of sadness. He closed his eyes and felt the emotion, then opened them again and let it go. He noted the arm with its bloodied hand stretched backward. Beck could see cuts to the flesh. The arm was at an angle, the fingers touching the ground and the elbow joint rotated so that it was raised slightly. It was an odd angle, and would prove difficult when placing the body into a coffin.

'He must have changed his mind, the poor bastard,' Claire said.

'Yes. He must.' It was O'Reilly, with his reappearing-from-nowhere act. 'Looks like guilt got the better of him, I'd say.'

Beck thought about that. 'Guilt?'

'Yes. For what he'd done.'

'What? The murder of Tanya Frazzali, you mean?'

'Why else would he throw himself in the river? It points to him. Ned Donohue killed Tanya Frazzali.'

'You'll be searching his house then? Ordering a DNA test?' Beck said.

O'Reilly looked surprised. 'Not yet. Soon. Let's get things sorted first.'

Beck bit his lower lip, enough to feel the intense sharp pain, enough to stop himself from yelling at this imbecile.

'Would you mind if I looked through Ned's house?' Beck kept his voice calm.

It was then that he saw the man standing in the high grass across from him.

'Who's that?'

O'Reilly turned. 'Oh, him. He reported it. Have a word with him, will you? I've changed my mind, search the bloomin' house if you want to. At least it'll get you out of my hair for a while.'

'What's his name?' Beck nodded towards the man.

O'Reilly furrowed his brow. 'I don't know. I've forgotten. I'm sure you can work it out.'

O'Reilly walked away with an exaggerated rolling gait, shoulders back. Cock-a-hoop was the term for it.

'Don't let him get to you,' Claire said.

'The only good thing about his ineptitude,' Beck replied, 'is that it compels me to work harder and try to do better. He's awoken me from my slumber. Thank you, Inspector O'Reilly.'

The man was wearing a frayed pinstripe suit jacket, brown corduroy pants and a flat cap. He was in his late sixties, Beck guessed, sucking on a roll-up cigarette.

Beck introduced himself, offered his hand. They shook. Claire said, 'You found the body, Mr…'

'Loughlin. Gus.' His voice held the slight tremor of a person suffering from emotional shock. 'Terrible, isn't it?'

'Do you mind if we just…?' Beck took a few paces to the right, swinging round so that he was facing the body. Gus had his back to it. 'I think that's better. Now, Mr Loughlin, can you tell us how you found the body, please? Exactly, if you could.'

Gus turned his head slightly, as if fighting an urge to look back over his shoulder again.

'Mr Loughlin? Gus,' Beck prompted.

Gus looked at Beck. 'I were just out for a walk. I don't have a dog any more. I used to have a dog, y'know. Name was Billy. But you don't need to have a dog to walk. That's what my friend…'

'Mr Loughlin,' Claire said. 'I know this is difficult. But if you could just answer the sergeant's question.'

'I were answering it, love. My way. I'm trying to get me head around it, see. The man here, the sergeant, said 'exactly', that's what he said, 'exactly'. I'm telling it exactly… d'ya want to hear it or not?' Gus brought his hand to his mouth and sucked on the roll-up. But it was gone, smoked down to nothing. He released his fingers and the ash disintegrated on the breeze and blew away. Beck could smell the rough cut of the tobacco. 'Billy died last month. But I still come here. I were thinking of Billy when I saw him… the body in the water. Just lying there, it was, or floating I should say, still and quiet as anything. Took me a moment to realise what I were looking at. It's a terrible thing. That's it. I just saw him there, in the water. That's it. Exactly. One minute I were thinking of Billy, the next I were looking at a body. And then I were wondering why he hadn't just climbed out of the water if he hadn't wanted to drown. I could see that he had tried. That's what it looked like to me. Maybe it were just too late. The water's not deep along the bank – you could stand up in it if you wanted to, even when the tide's in. Strange. He must have got tangled in the rushes and weeds, couldn't get out. That must'a been it. Panicked, like. He's dead anyway, the poor bugger.'

'Did you see anyone else about?' Claire asked. 'Maybe pass somebody while you were walking?'

Gus shook his head. 'No one comes down here much. It's too awkward – the slippery steps an' all. They've been talking about making it into a walkway since before I went away. Never did, did they?'

'Away? Where did you go away to?' Claire asked.

'Leeds, love. Over forty years. Came back only two years ago, retired, like.'

And Beck realised now where the slight inflection to his accent was coming from – the North of England, but not enough to make it immediately noticeable.

'Did you know Ned?' Beck asked.

Gus nodded. 'I knew him. Everybody knew him. But I *knew* him. We went to school together, the Christian Brothers – they gave myself and Ned a terrible hard time, y'know. It were an awful thing for any young lad to have to go through. That's all changed, though, about time too.'

'I'll need your address and phone number,' Beck said. 'We'll want to speak to you again at some stage.'

When Claire had written down his details in her notebook, Gus showed no signs of going anywhere. He planted his hands firmly into his jacket pockets and turned around and stood there, staring at Ned's body.

'Will you be alright?' Claire asked. 'Do you need someone to give you a lift home?'

'I'll be alright, love,' Gus said softly. 'Just need to get me head around this is all, if that's alright.'

And Beck thought *as do we all*. He could see a figure striding towards them along the trail next to the wall, clutching a medical bag.

'Dr Michael Anderson,' Claire said.

Dr Anderson was tall and gangly and loped along like a giraffe. He paid them no attention as he strode past. Inspector O'Reilly was waiting, close to the body, and the doctor joined him now. They began talking, O'Reilly emphasising words with animated gestures of his hands. Beck wondered what the odds were of the doctor signing off on a suicide.

He became aware of a low buzzing sound from somewhere. He realised then that it was his telephone ringing from the depths of a pocket. He searched and found it.

'Sergeant Beck,' he said.

'It's Garda Farrell here at the station. I have a call for you. Stand by, putting it through now.'

A clicking sound, then, 'Sergeant Beck?'

Beck recognised the voice immediately: Tony Frazzali. 'Yes, Tony, it's me.'

'Sergeant. I found something.'

'You found something? What?'

'Photographs. Of Tanya.'

'I see.'

'They're… revealing. I can't look at them.'

'Where are you now?'

'At home.'

'We'll be right over.'

CHAPTER THIRTY-SIX

The door was opened by a woman, dressed in blue trousers and a tunic uniform. A name tag gave her name as Rosa Torres. She smiled and led them into the large and spacious living room: high ceiling, bay windows, wooden floor covered by intricately woven rugs. At the end was an enormous fireplace with a black granite surround, two fabric settees in front. Tony was lying on one settee, his head on the armrest, one arm covering his eyes. He hadn't heard them come in.

'Tony, sir,' the woman said, as she led them across the room. Beck guessed by appearance and accent that she was Filipino.

Tony sat up. 'Wha', what is it?'

He was pale, his eyes red-rimmed and wide, his hair tousled. He was wearing what looked like the same tight T-shirt he'd worn when they'd first called, except that it was wrinkled now and dotted with what looked like coffee stains. Beck could smell stale sweat and a body gone too long between showers. There was also something else: the unmistakable aroma of marijuana.

'Sergeant Beck,' Tony said, getting to his feet, his voice deep and tired. 'Garda Somers.' Up close, Beck could see the pupils of his eyes were dilated.

'Hello, Tony.'

'I found them in a drawer,' Tony said. 'I was looking for her Taylor Swift CD. Someone gave it to Tanya last Christmas. She thought it was a bit naff, a CD, because she streamed everything. I wanted to listen to it, to be...' he blinked back tears, '... close to her. That's how I found them. They were at the bottom of the drawer, underneath everything. They're over here.'

Tony crossed to a dresser.

'How is your mother?' Claire asked.

'As well as can be expected.' The voice was not Tony's. It was Theresa Frazzali, who had just walked into the room. She crossed to the settee where Tony had been sitting and sat down. Her face was pale and gaunt, and she seemed to have aged considerably since this tragedy had all begun. In fact, Beck was shocked at the deterioration in her appearance since first meeting her at the station.

'I hired a carer,' she said. 'I have a friend, runs the agency. She insisted. I'm in no fit state, as you can see.' She lowered her voice. 'Neither is Tony. The funeral's on Friday at the cathedral. Our priest, Father Clifford, is organising it. Do you believe in heaven, Sergeant Beck?'

The question took Beck by surprise.

'I'm sure there is,' he lied, offering her reassurance. 'Yes, I'm sure there is a heaven. I mean, what's the point if there's not?' Beck didn't think there was a point anyway.

'I believe in heaven,' she said with finality. 'For Tanya's sake, I mean. Not my own…' Her voice quivered. 'Because she's too young, too young to…' She trailed off, unable to bring herself to say the words.

Tony walked over and handed Beck an envelope.

'You'll find them in there,' he said, his voice low. 'Mum doesn't want to see them either. You can burn them if you want.'

Tony went to the settee and sat beside his mother. She reached for her son and held him close.

Beck looked down at the envelope in his hands.

'Thank you for this,' he said. 'We'll let ourselves out.'

CHAPTER THIRTY-SEVEN

They parked on Plunkett Hill. An ominous creaking noise from underneath the car warned them that the handbrake was struggling to keep 2,900 lbs of metal stationary on the steep incline. Claire turned the steering wheel towards the kerb, released the brake, allowing the car to gently coast next to it.

'What you're telling me…' Claire said, pausing as she played back in her mind what Beck had just said. 'It's crazy. A sample from his gall bladder. I mean, how's that possible?'

'I thought it was worth a try. Because everyone gets ill. Some go to hospital. Some have samples taken. Maybe he was one of them. So I asked somebody I know. To check. And bingo, he'd had his gall bladder removed last year. The hospital kept a tissue sample. It's routine. They can keep it for up to ten years. I got it. Temporarily, that is.'

'How'd you get it?'

'I got it.'

'Your friend? The pathologist?'

Beck was quiet.

'Unbelievable.'

'Not really. I've done it before. It resides in the DNA and biology laboratory at HQ now.'

'Christ, you've outdone yourself this time. What about the legal implications of all this?'

'What about them?'

'It's not fucking legal, Beck…' She scrunched up her face. 'Is it?'

'It is. Permission is not required to obtain a DNA sample if the case is of sufficient gravity. Murder and statutory rape are of sufficient gravity, I would say, wouldn't you? I've rooted around in more than my fair share of dustbins in my time to know that. I got the sample, that's what counts. Twenty-four hours minimum for results. If I push it. And I'm pushing it. If it's not a match, no one is any the wiser.'

'It has to be an infringement of something or other.'

'No more than rooting around in someone's bin, everything being relative, when you think about it.'

'I'm thinking about it. I don't get the link, Beck.'

'It's a question of opinion.'

Claire stared ahead.

'Open the envelope,' she said.

Beck opened the envelope Tony had given him and withdrew the photographs. There were a half-dozen. The quality indicated they had likely been produced on a home printer. Beck went through each in turn. The first was of Tanya sitting on a chair wearing just a short skirt with her legs open, revealing her underwear. Beck turned it over and looked at the back. 'Wouldn't you prefer to come home to this?' it said in neat script. The next was of Tanya with a banana held to her mouth, and on the back: 'What man could ever get bored with this?' Another, Tanya lying on her bed in underwear. 'How long do I have to wait?' it asked. All the photographs were titillatingly similar.

'Why would she actually have photographed herself?' Claire asked. 'Is it possible to be so desperate?'

Beck replaced the photos in the envelope. 'Because,' he said, 'she didn't take the photographs herself. That's my guess. He did.'

Claire shook her head slowly. 'To think, at her age… I hadn't even been kissed, by the way, by boy or girl.'

'Anyway,' Beck said, handing her the envelope, 'I don't know what value these hold for us. Except as a depressing sentiment, maybe. Itemise them when we get back to the station. Now, we have a house to search.'

CHAPTER THIRTY-EIGHT

They got out of the car and stood looking at the row of houses on one side of the hill. Opposite was another row, but most of the houses here were derelict, windows and doors bricked up. There was also an open yard, a street sign announcing 'Hand Car Wash €6'. All of the houses on both sides were small and hunched together, but on the 'good' side, only one was in ill repair.

'That's the one,' Claire said, pointing. It was unpainted, moss sprouting from its eaves and the single ground-floor window by its front door cracked.

Beck wondered if the dereliction disease was spreading from one side of the street to the other.

He considered how they might gain access as he walked towards it. He stopped in front and looked at the door. It wouldn't take much to force it open.

'Is he in trouble again?' A small birdlike woman appeared in the doorway of the house next door. She stepped out onto the street now, looking at them.

'Unfortunately,' Claire said, 'Ned is dead. He drowned in the river. His body was discovered this morning.'

'The poor craythur,' the woman said, but didn't seem all that surprised. 'To tell the truth, I've been waiting for something like this to happen to Ned for years. Do you need to get into it, the house?'

'Yes,' Beck said.

'It's not locked. Just walk in.'

'Not locked?' Claire said.

'No. Ned never locked it. He had nothing to steal.'

Beck went to the door. The handle on it was loose. He nudged it down with the palm of his hand and pushed it open.

'One more thing,' Beck said. 'Did you see Ned recently? Did you notice anything odd about him, maybe?'

'Odd? Ned was already odd. But he got an awful shock finding that girl's body in the wood. It had a terrible effect on him, the poor craythur. Ned didn't kill her, if that's what you're thinking. He wouldn't kill a fly. No matter what anyone says. You talked to him. I know you did.' She shook her head. 'Still, killing himself. He hated water, y'know. He loved sitting and looking at it, but he was frightened of it. So why would he do that? Throw himself into the river? I don't know any more. I really don't know any more. But I think he's better off now.' She shook her head again, stepped back into her house and closed the door.

'Right,' Beck said. 'Let's get on with it. You got gloves, Claire?'

'Of course.'

Beck stepped into the hallway. It was narrow and short; at the end was an open doorway, another door leading off before that. Beck pulled on his gloves and flicked the light switch on the wall next to him. Nothing.

He walked slowly along the hall, immediately aware of the smell: a heavy, acrid stench, like a mixture of paint and burnt wool. He opened the first door, pressed the light switch inside on the wall. Again, nothing. Beck stepped into the room, covering his mouth. He'd found the source of the smell. In the fireplace were the remnants of burnt traffic cones, a single intact black base still in the grate, the residue of the burning plastic that had cooled around it now looking like hard lava.

'The poor fucker,' Claire said. 'Burning traffic cones to keep himself warm.'

They looked about the room. The floor was bare concrete, empty cider cans scattered across it. An old armchair was next to the fireplace, a couple of blankets strewn across the back. There was no other furniture. Presumably, any furniture that had been here, Ned had already burned.

'The next room,' Beck said to Claire, moving towards the door.

This was the kitchen. They knew it was the kitchen because there was a cooker in it, a remarkably clean cooker with the appearance of hardly ever having been used. There was a fridge too, but without a door. In it, of all things, was a used tea bag, sitting in a small puddle of coloured water. The sad poignancy of it was not lost on either of them. In the sink was a mug, the inside crusted brown. Against the wall in a corner was a mound of empty cider cans. Beck could smell the stale sweetness of them, sanding down the rough edges of the scent of burnt plastic.

There was nothing in this house but sad desperation and a handful of letters, all from the Department of Social Welfare in Galway. Beck looked at one of them: an enquiry into the efforts Ned was making in trying to secure gainful employment. Beck realised that Ned did not have a life. He had an existence. Throwing himself into the river would have been a release for him. Except, that was, that he didn't like water.

They went upstairs and into a bedroom – nothing in it but a bed with a filthy mattress on it. The next room was bare except for a cardboard box containing some odd socks. The last room was the bathroom, a bar of soap on its grimy sink and some old newspapers torn into strips on the floor next to the brown toilet bowl.

'There is nothing in this place,' Beck said.

They left the house and stood on the street outside. Beck lit a cigarette, took a long, deep pull.

'We need to organise to have that front door secured,' Beck said.

Claire nodded. 'I'll contact the council.'

As they walked back to the car, Claire said, 'I'm meeting Lucy for lunch. Want to join us?'

'Lucy, your wife?'

'The one and only.'

'Something I have to do first. Can I meet you there?'

'Of course. It's McCarthy's,' she said, and gave him directions.

Beck fell behind and reached for his mobile phone. He noted he was almost out of charge. He punched in the number and listened as it rang out. He was about to give up when finally the state pathologist answered.

'Yes?'

'It's Beck.'

'Yes, I know it's you, Beck.'

Beck could hear the sound of an engine in the background. 'You on your way somewhere?'

'What, old boy? Can you speak up?'

'Are you on your… never mind. DNA results. I need your help.'

'DNA. I have nothing to do with DNA. Not directly, old boy, you know that. Barking up the wrong tree.'

'Yes, I know all that,' Beck said. 'But I also know a telephone call from you can speed most things along. I need these results as quickly as possible.'

'My pet hate, Beck,' Gumbell said, 'as you well know, are those officers who ring up my department, or any other department for that matter, and take up valuable staff time trying to hurry things along. A right pain in the arse. Everyone is in a hurry. I mean, have you seen the way people drive? No one has patience any more. Things take time, Beck. You should know that.'

'That's a no then, is it?'

Gumbell sighed. 'The girl in the forest?'

'Yes,' Beck said. 'We got DNA comparisons to the samples you took from the body. The quicker I can have the results…'

'Don't let emotion get in the way of objectivity, old boy,' Gumbell said. 'Not like you.'

'That's alright for you to say, sitting in the back of a chauffeur-driven car. I'm looking up from way below, on the second-to-last rung of a very long ladder to nowhere. You should try it sometime.'

'You should have been a poet, Beck. But don't forget, justice is on your side, I have no doubt. The words of Edmund Burke: "The only thing necessary for the triumph of evil is for good men to do nothing". Now, I have to go, we're stopping for something to eat. Do you need any more of those little yellow saviours, to pull you through, my man? I'm concerned for you, you know... Yes driver, right here, park round the back.'

'About the DNA? Will you look after it?'

'Yes, old boy, of course I will. Anything for you, a fellow traveller along the Lonesome Highway – that's the title of a Hank Williams song, by the way. I'll send my size nine and a half boot up somebody's arse. Oh, by the way, are you really going to retire?'

'What do you mean?'

'You were adamant the other evening, said that you'd had enough, you were going to retire and move to – I can't remember the name of the place, sounded very exotic. Spain or somewhere, you described it beautifully. So beautifully, in fact, I thought I might retire there myself.'

Beck had no recollection.

'You can't remember, can you?' Gumbell said. 'I would suggest an MRI of your head, Beck. Your inability to remember anything after one drink is worrisome.'

'On that note, by the way.'

'Yes.'

'The other day, when we left O'Callaghans – the pub.'

'Yes, what about it? Don't tell me you don't even remember that, do you?'

'Yes, I remember leaving it. But after, I don't remember very much.'

Gumbell laughed. He never outwardly showed any drinker's remorse, not even to Beck. But the little yellow pills he took, Beck knew, were testimony to a type of angst that he felt all the same.

'We got hammered,' Gumbell said. 'But no one would ever think it. We were paragons of upstanding, if inebriated, citizenry. I did worry about you when you left The Hibernian, though. You were mumbling at that stage. You tottered off into the night. But nothing happened.'

'Thank you,' Beck said. 'And about those little yellow…'
Silence.

Beck took the phone from his ear and looked at it: dead.

CHAPTER THIRTY-NINE

It said 'McCarthy's Restaurant, Vegetarian a Speciality' on the glass panel of the door; Beck pushed against it and entered. The restaurant was long and narrow, with tables on either side of a walkway down its centre. Paintings hung from the walls, discreet price tags pinned beneath. A handwritten sign in cursive script announced, 'McCarthy's, Supporting Local Artists'.

Claire waved to him from a table. She was sitting with a petite blonde woman wearing scarlet lipstick and a low-cut, tight black top. As he sat his eyes studiously avoided the display of ample cleavage. He was embarrassed as to what he was thinking, which was that lesbians weren't supposed to look this good. He smiled broadly, camouflaging his discomfort.

'This is him, Lucy. Sergeant Finnegan Beck.'

'I don't know how to take that,' Beck said. 'What's she been saying?' He extended his hand. 'Pleasure to meet you, Lucy.'

She observed him with her warm, large blue eyes. She had a ready smile and her handshake was firm. She was also drop-dead gorgeous.

'Don't worry,' Lucy said. 'It was all good, once she finished telling me about all the bad, that is.' She laughed. 'How're you finding Cross Beg? You're not long here, are you?' She glanced at Claire. 'It's okay, darling, I'm not going to pry, I promise. She warned me not to, you know. But I'm a reporter, what can I do?'

'No,' Beck said. 'I'm not here that long.'

'So, where did you come from?'

Beck reached for the menu. 'From my mother, if that's what you mean?'

There was an awkward silence, then Lucy laughed. 'Point taken.'

'Actually, I'm joking,' Beck said. 'Pearse Street. I've been transferred from Pearse Street.'

'Hmm, Dublin South Central, a busy place.' But she didn't pry any further.

'And you?' he asked. '*The Connaughtman*, I believe?'

'Yes, that's right. It won't win me a Pulitzer Prize, but it pays the bills.'

'And are you running a story on the murder? Is that why you're here in Cross Beg today?'

'No. Actually I'm covering the district court in Ballinasloe. Life goes on. Thought I'd take a detour to see my baby.' She looked at Claire, closed her eyes and smiled. Beck thought it all looked a little over the top to him. 'Do you know,' she added, 'the story, the murder of that poor girl, doesn't seem to have generated much coverage, in the national papers that is. A sign of the times, unfortunately, I suppose.'

'Are you ready to order?'

The waitress was in her late twenties, with freckled skin, a mass of curly hair and a nose ring. She placed a jug of water on the table along with glasses.

Beck didn't find anything on the menu appealing. Claire told him to try the stuffed pasta shells.

They gave their orders, and as they sipped water, Beck noted Claire looking at Lucy, who had turned her head towards the front of the restaurant. Beck followed her gaze, saw a woman sitting at a table inside the front window looking back at her, smiling.

'I'm such a flirt, aren't I, Claire?' Lucy said, turning back again.

Beck rearranged his cutlery.

'Christ, Lucy,' Claire said.

'Oh come on, just because we're hitched doesn't mean we can't look.'

'You're embarrassing Beck here, is what I mean.'

'Am I?' She turned to him. 'Can I refer to you as Beck…?'

He nodded.

'We love each other very much, really. I just enjoy being mischievous, that's all.'

'Such a bloody drama queen,' Claire said.

'The district court?' Beck asked, changing the subject. 'Anything interesting?'

Lucy thought about it for a moment. 'A pretty standard list,' she said. 'There's one story I'm particularly interested in. Listen to this – it may sound like a joke, but it's not, it's true, honest to God: guy goes into a filling station riding a horse – well, he crossed the forecourt on the horse, but leaves it at the door while he goes in and holds the place up with a knife. True story. He was arrested soon after, nearby. You can't get very far on a horse after all. But you'll never guess his name?'

'I agree,' Beck said. 'I'll never guess.'

'George Cassidy.'

Beck gave a blank stare.

'The real name of Butch Cassidy, you know, as in *Butch Cassidy and the Sundance Kid*. What a headline: "Butch Cassidy holds up Ballinasloe Filling Station".' Lucy threw her head back and laughed. As she did, Beck felt her leg press against his under the table. He glanced at her, saw that she was staring at him now, a playful grin on her face. Beck tucked his legs beneath his chair.

They talked easily about a range of topics as they ate – politics, the weather, everything except the investigation into Tanya Frazzali's murder. But now, as they finished their meals, Lucy brought the subject up.

'Because I'm a journalist,' she said, 'a journalist who's married to a police officer, I have to be extra-special careful. I can't have anything that could get Claire here into trouble, be accused of leaking information. Everything has to be on the record. If it's not, people'll think she's the source. So I'm going to ask a pretty standard, innocuous question, and it's this: is this case any closer to being solved? Anything you'd like to say?'

Beck wiped his mouth with a napkin. 'Nothing I'd like to say,' he said, 'and that's a pretty standard, innocuous answer.'

Claire stood. 'I'm going to the bathroom. Can we drop the shop talk?'

'You were brushing against my leg earlier,' Beck said when she left.

'Was I?'

'Yes, you were.'

'I didn't notice.'

'I think you did,' Beck said.

'And are you complaining?'

'You're just married. What about Claire? How would she feel?'

'Our secret, then.'

'Christ,' Beck said, sitting back in his chair.

When they were making their way from the restaurant back to the car, Claire said, 'She's just a drama queen, completely, she doesn't mean any harm. Did she feel your leg under the table, by the way?'

Beck spluttered. 'Yes. She did. You knew?'

'She's always doing it. She must think you're married. She only does it to married men. Wants to test their reaction. Most rub her back, by the way.'

'What's she do, then, when they do that?'

'Oh, stops immediately, point made, writes them off as lecherous bastards.'

'A dangerous game.'

'I thought she'd change her ways after we married.'

Beck laughed.

'What?' Claire asked.

'Where did I hear that before? Tell me, do you know if St Malachi's College is open today?'

'The school? Why?'

'Because the girl, Melanie McBride, stopped me in the street yesterday. Told me, as she put it, to look at a Mr Sweetman. He's a teacher there. Said he and Tanya were very friendly. She emphasised the "very friendly".'

'Really?'

'Yes, really.'

'Ken Sweetman,' Claire said. 'I know him. Not personally. Just to see. The school was closed for a day on Tuesday. The funeral is Friday. Today it should be open. Don't we need evidence here too? Doesn't his reputation matter?'

'Oh, his reputation matters alright. I think Melanie knows that very well. And she knows child protection laws are strict. We have to speak to him. Immediately. If Mr Sweetman is up to something and we do wait, we could find ourselves up at Garda HQ manning the gate barriers. Here's the thing. I don't think I believe her. There's something about that girl. So we need to be discreet.'

'But you believe Murphy?'

'I didn't say that. But why would he lie? He knows he's going to get caught out if he does. Wouldn't make sense.'

She checked her watch. 'We could go there later, wait outside. For him to finish. Be about another hour and a half.'

Beck nodded. 'We can do it that way.'

CHAPTER FORTY

It was just gone four when they turned into the car park of St Malachi's College. Students were streaming out through the front doors and the gates beside them that led to the sports fields and the new school building compound behind.

They sat watching the school for twenty minutes or so, the stream of students emerging reduced to a trickle. Various teachers followed. Beck spotted Father Clifford, who was carrying a battered briefcase. Presumably he had been teaching RE. Most of the cars in the car park had gone, and they were about to give up when—

'There he is,' Claire said, pointing to a figure rounding the side of the school, pushing a bike, a leather satchel slung by his side.

They moved quickly, got out of the Focus and crossed the small hedge separating the car park from the roadway, blocking Sweetman's path as he was about to cycle off.

'Ken Sweetman?' Claire said.

Sweetman was underneath the glare of a street lamp. He looked towards them, balancing on the saddle of his bike. Beck and Claire moved into the pool of light.

'Yes,' Sweetman said, 'that's me.'

'I'm Detective Garda Claire Somers, and this is Detective Sergeant Finnegan Beck. We'd like a word.'

'A word? With me? Why? I'm in bit of a hurry – on my way to give a private tutorial, actually.'

'We waited for you,' Beck said. 'When we could have made our lives a whole lot easier by simply going in and taking you out from your class. But we didn't. We'd like *a word*.'

Sweetman got off his bike and leaned it against the wall. He was dressed in drainpipe jeans and a North Face jacket with a red zipper and collar. He pulled on the strap of his satchel and moved it so it was resting against his back.

'Sit with us in our car for a minute,' Beck said, and Claire led the way to the Focus.

Sweetman sat in the back and was clearly nervous. He had large dark eyes and was handsome, with a long, prominent chin softened by a goatee beard. He held the satchel across his chest like a protective shield. It was an expensive-looking satchel with thick metal buckles and was embossed with what looked to be an Italian designer name.

Beck twisted in the front passenger seat to look back at him.

'Mr Sweetman. We're investigating the murder of Tanya…'

'Yes, I know. Is that why you want to speak to me? Tanya, God. I had nothing to do with that. You hardly think…'

'Mr Sweetman,' Beck said, more insistent now. 'If you could listen, please.'

'Sorry.'

'In an investigation of this nature,' Beck went on, 'the public contact us with lots of information, most of it useless, but we must look into it – we must look into everything.'

The teacher looked past Beck, out through the windscreen. 'So what you're saying is that someone gave you my name?'

'Yes,' Claire said, 'that's what we're saying. Someone gave us your name.'

Sweetman fell silent and pulled the satchel closer to him. 'I see,' he said.

'Why would they do that?' Beck asked.

'I don't know. I have no idea why anyone would do that. What did they say, can I ask?'

'That you and Tanya were close,' Beck said.

The teacher gave a loud sigh and rested his head back onto the headrest, looking at the ceiling now. He was perfectly still. In the grey light, he had the appearance of a painting.

'I was close to Tanya, yes, if that's the term you want to use. She was a very sensitive girl, liked to sing. Did you know that? Did anyone know that?'

Beck shook his head.

'Most people never did either. Her voice was very beautiful, a subtle vibrato, very sweet. I play guitar, and one day she sang that song covered by Alison Krauss, "Down to the River to Pray", in my classroom after school. Does that make us close? What's wrong with that if it does?'

'Nothing,' Beck said after a pause. 'So why do *you* think your name was mentioned to us?'

'It depends on who did the mentioning. I have an opinion on that.'

'We'd like to hear it,' Claire said.

The teacher's brow furrowed.

'Was the person who spoke to you Melanie McBride, by any chance?' he asked.

'Why would you think that?' Beck answered.

'Because her name jumps to mind, that's all.'

'And there must be a reason for that,' Claire said.

Sweetman suddenly released the satchel and pushed it to the floor of the car, resting it against his feet. He leaned forward.

'I've been teaching nine years, five of those at St Malachi's College. Girls – how can I put this? – you have to understand them… That sounds really sexist, I don't mean it like that. What I mean is…'

'That Melanie was coming on to you?' Beck said.

The teacher fell silent, looking at him. 'How did you guess?'

'She was, then?'

'It happens from time to time,' Sweetman said. 'A teacher has to be very careful how he, or indeed she, handles it. You could crush budding emotions, feelings, that sort of thing, feelings that maybe have never been experienced before, and might not come again for a long time if you handle it incorrectly. A very delicate situation for everybody concerned.'

The teacher's choice of words brought to mind Gumbell's remark: 'You should have been a poet, Beck'. But he also considered that Melanie herself had not displayed any delicate budding emotions herself that he had noticed.

'Everybody concerned?' Claire said. 'Like who?'

'School policy is that the principal must be informed.'

'And was he?' Beck asked.

The teacher said nothing, just shook his head.

'I see,' Beck said. 'Why not?'

'I meant to. I just didn't get round to it. But I meant to. I did speak with Melanie, though. I explained to her. I thought that might be the end of it. To be honest, I put off speaking with the principal and then just, well, let it go.'

'When you say you explained to Melanie,' Claire said, 'what did you explain to Melanie exactly? What did you tell her?'

'The truth.'

'Which is?' Beck asked.

'That I'm gay. It's not something I advertise, but I don't hide it either.'

'I see,' Beck said. 'And did that put an end to it?'

'Not really. She didn't believe me.'

'Didn't she?' It was Claire, surprised.

'No. It all got a little crazy after that. She threatened she'd go to the principal, tell him I was seeing Tanya. I literally became ill for a time because of it. How would it look? I hadn't gone to the principal myself. It would look like I had something to hide. It left me in an extremely vulnerable position, I can tell you. And still does. She reported me to you, didn't she? I know you can't say that she did.' He sat back, ran a hand over his goatee beard and added, almost in a whisper, 'There's another reason why Tanya and I were friendly.'

Beck and Claire did not speak, allowing the teacher time.

'Myself and Tony, her brother, were involved. Had been for a long time. Tanya knew about it. She had no problem. But Tony wanted it kept secret. He hasn't told his mother he's gay, you see. He said he would, but something was stopping him. I think it's because he's an only son. Also his mother used to nag him about why it was taking so long for him to find a nice girl and settle down, said she wanted grandchildren and everything. Looking back, I think that was her way of getting him to open up about it. She's his mother, after all – she knew, I think, she had to. But Tony didn't want to discuss it. It's the main reason why we broke up, actually. That was just over a year ago now.'

'How did you find Tanya after that?' Beck asked. 'Did she seem the same to you?'

'I didn't see that much of her. I don't teach third year. But the little I did see of her, no, she didn't seem the same. There was something that seemed to have changed with her, something weighing on her mind. She wasn't herself. What's the word? She was never present, is the way I'd put it. That's it – she was never present, her mind was always somewhere else. I put it down to teenage angst. It's a really shitty time, if you ask me.'

'Can you still make your tutorial?' Beck asked. 'If you go now.'

The teacher looked at his watch.

'If I move fast. Maybe.'

'You're free to go, Mr Sweetman. Thank you for your help.'

As the teacher got out of the car and crossed to the wall to retrieve his bicycle, Beck muttered, 'Little Melanie is not all that she appears, is she? Some piece of work, eh?'

'Neither,' said Claire, 'was Tanya. With what was found in her blood. Xanax and marijuana. Screwing around with some older guy. Not that I'm taking any moral high ground here. I'm not.'

She made the sign of the cross.

'What was that for?' Beck asked.

'Guilt,' Claire said. 'Don't ask why. Gained from a lifetime of stifling, overbearing Catholicism. It just works every time, that's all I know.'

CHAPTER FORTY-ONE

Beck sat at his unofficial desk back at the station and checked Pulse. He saw that a post-mortem was due to be held on Ned's body that night at the County Hospital. By morning there would be indications if not a certainty as to the coroner's conclusion: suicide or foul play.

His mobile phone rang on the desk by his elbow. He picked it up, looking at the screen. A Dublin number, one he knew by the first three digits to be the Garda HQ. He pressed the green button. 'Hello.'

'Detective Sergeant Finnegan Beck?' the female voice asked.

'Yes.'

'The Office of the Assistant Commissioner An Garda Síochána, Maria Mulcahy speaking. You are requested to attend a meeting of the Incident Investigative Committee, reference number 5463, tomorrow morning at 9 a.m. at Garda HQ. Can you attend?'

Beck glanced at the clock on the Ops Room wall.

'Tomorrow? At 9 a.m.?'

'Yes, that's correct. Can you be there?'

Beck took a breath. 'Um, of course.'

It was raining. Beck hurried along Main Street, the lights in the shop windows displaying their wares like a tacky version of an Arabian bazaar. A man, small and round, behind the window of a jeweller's – Tuohill's, it said over the door – was removing a tray of rings. He smiled as Beck passed, a smile as false as the claim on the tray in his hands that said 'Pure Gold. Amazing Savings'. Beck nodded in return. He continued, passing the pub with a front window made up of different-coloured dimpled glass panels. He stopped to look at it. *What do you call a window like that?* Beck wondered. For some reason he decided he really wanted to know the answer to that question right now, so he went in.

There were few people inside: three people sitting on stools along the counter, a woman in a blue nylon house coat standing behind it, staring at the door, a TV blaring in the corner. Beck didn't care about finding the answer to that question now, saw it for what it was, an excuse. He turned and went back out again, continued along the street and went into the Centra supermarket at the end near the bridge. There he picked up a bottle of Spanish brandy for €19.99. Once home, he took a glass from the kitchen and sat in the sitting room, turned on the lamp on the low table beside him, opened the brandy and half filled the glass. He sipped.

Spanish brandy retained a unique flavour, he had learned. Hues of sherry from the sherry casks it was aged in. To be fully appreciated it demanded time, and should never be rushed. In this way, the full flavour and the strength of its Iberian character came through. Or so it said on the back of the bottle. Beck drank the contents of the glass in one swallow.

He needed to book a taxi to the railway station for the morning. He also needed to get a good night's rest. In the meantime, he'd have one more drink. Only the one, mind, he told himself. He poured more brandy into the glass, filling it three quarters full this time. He drank slower now, taking two gulps instead of one to finish it.

And then he felt the magic carpet slide beneath him, felt the lightness of his body as it raised him up. But there it hovered, not getting any higher, something holding it back. Beck refilled the glass, halfway this time, took a long gulp, finished it, but still he did not move. Instead the waves of memory washed over him, brittle and cold...

The balmy July evening offered a false sense of calm, a sense that all was well with the world. Summers in Dublin were usually warm, sometimes dry, occasionally sunny, but rarely all three. They were parked along side streets in nine unmarked cars, a total of twenty-seven officers, all armed. Temple Bar was a heaving cauldron of bodies along its cobbled streets, every bar, restaurant and club packed to the rafters, every language under the sun spoken within a two-square-mile radius. It was Rio de Janeiro at carnival time, Mardi Gras in New Orleans, a typical Saturday night in Dublin's party quarter.

Beck was anxious. He wanted this to be over with as quickly as possible. He wanted the celebration, an acceptable reason for him to get shitfaced.

They waited. And waited. At 11.30 p.m., the voice of Chief Superintendent Cavanagh, Special Operations, came over the radio: 'Thirty minutes remaining. If there's no movement, the operation terminates at midnight, all crews to return to base. Stand by.'

Beck thought of the choice of words – 'no movement' sounded like something bowel-related to him. Continuing with that analogy, he knew that what often followed on from periods of constipation were bowel movements of a sudden and violent ferocity.

And so it proved to be.

'Be advised: target emerging from working men's club, moving on to Essex Street East, in the company of a female,' the radio crackled.

The target was Jake 'Razor' Byrne: drug addict, dealer, armed robber and scumbag, vicious and unpredictable, the subject of discussion in the Irish houses of parliament no less.

They moved.

In hindsight, Beck should never have drunk that Polish beer. Polish beer was always strong, six of them certainly enough to impair judgement for most people. But Beck didn't feel impaired, he felt empowered. His real mistake was in leaving the empty bottles in the unmarked patrol car's boot.

As they moved they lost sight of the target. He had disappeared into a doorway, leaving his female companion outside on the street. Beck's radio erupted into life, a dozen different voices all shouting at the same time, all saying something different, forcing Beck to hold the radio to his ear, trying to decipher any meaning from the garbled words. And then the chant, as if at a football game: 'FBI. FBI. FBI.' The stag party had spotted him. They looked Scandinavian; big blond men wearing silly plastic Viking hats. They were also pissed, and the more Beck requested them to quieten down, the louder they became, jumping and pointing towards him. 'FBI. FBI. FBI...'

He was thinking that the whole operation was going pear-shaped when the first shot rang out, a loud, vicious crack that had no place on such a beautiful evening, a sound that temporarily silenced everyone, even the stag party. And two more shots followed, with it a chaos in direct proportion to the meticulously detailed planning that had gone into the operation. People screamed and ran in every direction. The teams stormed building after building looking for the shooter, the sight of the plainclothes officers with their firearms drawn adding to the bedlam.

As Beck led the way in through another doorway – it had a glitzy neon sign on the wall next to it: 'Dublin's Number One Thai Restaurant, First Floor' – he saw the body of Garda Jason Geraghty sprawled on the stairs, washed in the purple glow of the stripe lights running along the banisters on either side. His head lay in a pool of blood, the blood dripping slowly down onto the step below. Beck knew immediately that he was dead, because the pool was still, with no heartbeat to push more blood in to disturb it. Jason Geraghty, nickname Dynamo, who always joked he'd make it to Commissioner one day. The thing was, no one had thought it was a joke – they thought he'd make it. Jason Geraghty, who'd only joined the Serious Crime Unit six months before. Jason Geraghty, who was now dead.

Beck stopped at the bottom of the stairs, Jason Geraghty staring down at him, his eyes wide and unblinking and dead, a small red hole at the side of his forehead.

'… Mr Beck, are you alright? I was knocking at the door. It wasn't locked.'

'What?'

Beck turned. It took him a moment to realise that someone was standing in the doorway of the living room.

'Mrs Claxton?' he said finally.

She stepped into the room. 'Yes, it's me.'

Her eyes moved to take in the bottle on the table beside him. He looked at it too. It was half-empty… or half-full, whichever way you chose to consider it. He liked to think of it as being half-full, for now anyway.

'To what do I owe this pleasure?'

'It's an acceptable time to visit, I hope. It's not very late. No reason,' she said.

Beck laughed. 'An unaccompanied lady visiting a single gentleman in his lodgings, the very landlady no less. What will people say?'

She looked at him without expression. 'I'll make us a cup of tea, shall I?'

'Go right ahead,' Beck said.

She went into the kitchen. A short while later, when she came back into the room, a steaming mug in each hand, she noticed the bottle was empty now. She placed a mug next to it, sat opposite him on the settee. For a long time neither of them spoke.

'You don't look drunk,' she said.

'Don't I? But I'm floating above the thermals, believe me. I had to eventually.'

'Oh, I believe you alright.'

Beck stood. 'I'm going for a cigarette.'

'You can smoke in here, I don't mind.'

'I like it out back, sitting on that bench of yours, that antique thing.'

'I need to do something with that antique thing, as you call it. It's quite valuable, you know.'

Beck smoked his cigarette, imagining his mind as a chamber, opening the doors, allowing his thoughts free. With each exhale of breath he imagined pushing them out, until eventually the chamber was empty.

He could feel the cold air on his face, hear the traffic in the distance, the *tic tac* of what sounded like high heels on a street somewhere, someone laughing. And between those sounds, he could hear the very air itself, an almost imperceptible static, like a radio not tuned properly to any station. He sucked on the last of his cigarette and went back inside, stood in front of the empty fireplace, clasped his hands behind his back.

'I have an early start in the morning,' he said. 'I'm anxious to get to my bed.'

'Well, don't let me keep you,' Mrs Claxton said, getting to her feet and sounding a little put out.

She looked about for somewhere to put her mug, suddenly deciding she wasn't going to wash it. She nearly dropped it when she heard what Beck said next.

'Want to come with me? To bed, that is.'

CHAPTER FORTY-TWO

It was during the early hours of the morning when Beck awoke. It was still very dark. He was not completely sober. Mrs Claxton lay beside him. He couldn't be certain she was sleeping; the sound of her breathing was gentle but erratic. He thought of the bottle of Spanish brandy he had drunk, remembered everything up to the point when he had finished it and asked her to come to bed with him.

'Are you awake?' The voice so soft he wondered if someone had really spoken at all.

'I am,' he said.

'Nothing happened, between us I mean, we just slept,' she said, the words spoken quickly as if anxious for him to understand.

How did she assume he didn't know that already? Not that he did, because he didn't. He thought of her husband, and he thought of another drink. He also thought of the train he had to catch later.

He turned on the bedside light, pulling back a corner of the duvet. He checked the time – 4.15 a.m. – went to the toilet, stood over the bowl and released a long stream of Spanish-brandy-infused piss. He didn't feel so bad, because he knew he wasn't fully sober. He ran the cold water tap and drank greedily, took a capful of mouthwash, swished it around and spat it out.

He went back to bed. He took it as a signal that Mrs Claxton was still there, that she hadn't left. If she had wanted to, she'd had ample opportunity to do so. For some reason, she had chosen not to. His post-alcohol erection quivered as he placed a hand on her fleshy thigh, gave it a gentle squeeze.

'Your hand is cold,' she said. She didn't push it away. He took this as a signal too and pulled her to him.

Their love-making was short and hurried, completed quickly lest either of them changed their mind. And afterwards, lying together, her arm draped across his chest, she wanted to talk, wanted to find out about him on the inside, now that she had explored his body on the outside.

He tried to linger in his consciousness, fighting to stay awake. But his words slowed and slurred as he slipped into sleep, barely noticing as she sighed, withdrew her arm and left the bed. And then Beck fell into that great warm, black void of nothingness.

CHAPTER FORTY-THREE

History was like that. Neither dead nor alive. Like the Coliseum. Or the Great Wall of China. Or Stonehenge. The list went on. All of those existed, you could touch them, you could feel them. But all of those were dead. So, too, were the great civilisations. Those were all dead. But, at the same time, they lived. They lived because everything came from something, everything existed because of something else that had gone before it.

Many disagreed with this thesis. Something had to be either dead or alive, they said. There was no in between. It had to be one thing or the other. It was not possible for something to be both.

They just didn't get it. They had no insight. How could they think like that?

He had seen it himself. He had killed. And the urge to kill again was now greater than ever.

But there was something else. And it was this. He wanted recognition, some recognition, at least... No, not some, more than some. He wanted them to know, to know about him. *He really, really wanted that. Was it too much to ask? Damn it, he deserved that much, didn't he? He had waited so long. Well? Hadn't he?*

He caressed the knife in his pocket. He was looking forward to using this. He kept it for special occasions. Because she was different. The she-devil's memory was burned into his psyche. After all, it was she who had helped make him who, and what, he was. She was old now, and his only surprise was that she still lived. Which pleased him. Because it meant he would be the one to take her life away. There was an intimacy in that.

He passed through the town as a shadow, flittering from street to street, from alleyway to alleyway. It wasn't quite night. Lights glowed behind many of the windows he passed. But it wasn't day either. It was in between. That mysterious chasm. Between darkness and light. Between life and death. The lights glistened on the wet surfaces, the streets, the roads, the buildings. Voices and footsteps crackled through the silence, both fading, lost to the night. He felt a power. An exhilarating power. He could determine life and death. Within the furnace, down deep, where the embers glowed fiercest, his hatred burned. For her. Because she once had the power. To decide. What was in his 'best interests'. But how did she know? Taking his mother from him like that. Was that in his 'best interests'? No, was the answer. No, it fucking wasn't. He knew his hatred was incapable of giving him reason. But he didn't want reason. He wanted revenge.

He found the stone without difficulty. It was set in the gravel by the edge of the garden path. Underneath it, the spare key. He knew all her little secrets. The nearest light was from a lamp post on the narrow pavement, but at this distance it was only a glimmer, and he felt safe as he walked along the path to the front porch. He slipped the key into the door lock and gently twisted it, could feel the bolt sliding back. He pushed the door and it opened without a sound. He would expect nothing less from her; everything would work as it should do.

It was dark – he had to fumble his way ahead. There was no window in the front door and none along the hall. He took out the knife from his pocket, withdrew it from its sheath.

He was at the stairs now. He could feel the outline of the banister. And ahead, above him, a brushstroke of dim white light. Yes, she was old now, and would have to get up during the night to piss. The light would be left on so she could see her way to the bathroom.

He placed his hand on the handle of the first door, turned it.

He could see the bed, the outline in its centre that had to be the sleeping body of her. The mound in the centre of the bed was stirring now. Something else stirred, moving from the bed, at great speed, small and black and noisy. Heading right for him. And almost simultaneously he felt it, just above the ankle of his right leg, the sudden sharp pain. He looked down. The little bastard had sunk its teeth into his leg. He grimaced with the pain but kept his mouth shut. The useless, slobbering creature. He'd never thought it capable of this.

A shrill voice now, brittle and cutting, drowning out everything: 'Who's that? Who's there? My God! Who are you? I said who are you? What are you doing here? You! Is that you? Oh my God. It is you. What are you doing here?'

'Hello. You do remember me? I mean, really *remember me? You don't, do you?*'

'Boys like you are cowards at heart, aren't they?'

As if it was yesterday, but so long ago.

He raised his other foot, crashed it down onto the head of the dog. It didn't even cry out in pain. 'It would be nothing if you didn't. Talk to me. How are you?'

Eeny meeny miny moe, tittle tattle tock, I'm crazy and you don't know. Tittle tattle tock. Eeny meeny miny moe, tittle tattle tock, I'm crazy and you don't know. Tittle tattle tock...

And then the dam wall was breached and the water surged through as he raised his right foot again and brought his boot down onto the dog's back this time. It smashed like a wrecking ball into bone and sinew, disintegrating the tiny ribcage beneath, squashing internal organs like soft fruit. The dog released its grip on his leg with a short, soft whimper, and the animal became quiet and immediately dead. He looked down, could see the dog's head loll to one side, its pink little tongue protruding between two rows of gritted teeth.

A strange rasping sound came from her now. He took a step towards her, and the rasping sound became a wail; another step and the wail became a scream, and by the time he had crossed the few feet to her, she was screaming hysterically. The first stab wound silenced her, because the blade went through her throat and out the back of her neck. He stared at her, watching as her hands reached out to him, feebly clawing at the air. He touched the blood leaking out from around the blade with a finger and brought it to his nose, sniffed it, then pulled the knife from her neck and it came out with a loud popping sound like a finger plucked against a cheek inside a person's mouth. A geyser of blood erupted and splashed onto his clothes. He laughed, looking at it as he stabbed her again, and again, and again, and again. He continued to stab her long after she was dead.

CHAPTER FORTY-FOUR

Later, when he awoke for a second time, his first thought was that, despite his belief that he did not dream when he'd been drinking, he had after all been doing so. Because the tail end of something, an image that he couldn't define, slithered quickly across his mind and was gone. He lay there, wondering what it was, then attempted to judge the time by the amount of light filtering through the curtains. He guessed maybe eight o'clock. Either way, the train was long gone.

As he considered this, fear began to set in; he could feel it coiling around his lungs, pushing out his breath in short gasps. He sat up, opened the bedside locker drawer, took out the plastic bottle, used his teeth to unscrew it and popped two pills into his mouth. He lay down again and waited.

So, he had fucked up again. And he had no one to blame but himself.

If the phone had rung a moment earlier, he would have ignored it. But it didn't, it rang now. He glanced at the screen. Garda HQ. He took a deep breath, and for some reason, although he hadn't quite willed it, his hand reached out and picked it up.

Maria Mulcahy asked, 'Are you on the train?'

Beck processed this question and was confused. 'Um...' he began, but didn't progress any further.

'I'm very sorry, Mr Beck, but the Assistant Commissioner has had to cancel the meeting. He would like to apologise for not being in a position to have given you more notice.'

'Cancel the meeting, did you say?'

'Unfortunately, yes. I know this is very inconvenient for you. It's been rescheduled for tomorrow morning… By the way, where are you? You must almost be in Dublin by now.'

Beck looked at his watch for the first time. The time was 8.40 a.m. He'd been close.

'Yes, yes,' he lied. 'Almost.'

'Your expenses will be covered, of course.' Her tone was sympathetic. 'Perhaps you could make a day of it?'

'Yes,' Beck said. 'I don't think I have much choice now. And tomorrow, will it be the same time? It's Saturday, by the way.'

'Yes. I know. That's not a problem, is it, being a Saturday?'

'No, no problem. It's just senior management don't usually work on a Saturday, that's all.'

'I see. In any case, the Assistant Commissioner says 10 a.m. will be fine. Again, he sends his sincerest apologies.'

'Yes, okay,' Beck said, feigning annoyance and terminating the call.

He looked at the phone, turned it over in his hand. Had this really happened? He checked the call log to convince himself that it really had. *What now?* he wondered. Take the rest of the day off, remain hidden in the house, alone with his thoughts?

'You jammy bastard,' he said aloud and laughed, throwing back the duvet and placing his feet on the cold floor. He went into the bathroom, stepped into the shower and turned the water regulator all the way into the blue zone.

CHAPTER FORTY-FIVE

At one time, businesses would shut their doors on the approach of a funeral cortège, and would not open them again until it had passed, well passed. This tradition had all but disappeared now. But today was different. Today Tanya Frazzali was being buried. Beck had almost forgotten. Passing the closed shop doors now, he was reminded.

The recent rain had left the world sodden. The wind was blowing hard, and the dark clouds pushed across the sky like ocean swells. Beck buried his hands in his pockets and put his head down against the wind.

He turned onto Edmund Street, red-brick cottages lining either side. The cottages had been built by Edmund Kendrel, a substantial landlord, who had hoped to attract Italian craftsmen to his new enterprise of making riding boots from the hides of native Dexter cows, and which he hoped to export throughout the empire. He was a benevolent landlord, something evident in the fact that the street named after him continued to bear his name following the end of British rule and the creation of the Republic. Unfortunately, Edmund Kendrel had died before he could realise his vision, and his son Louis showed only as much interest as was required to sell off the estate piece by piece to pay for his mounting gambling debts. It dwindled from 7,300 acres to nothing in less than three years.

Beck reached the top of Edmund Street and came onto Bridge Walk. To his right he could see the first bridge, and a hearse with

wreaths piled high on its roof, slowly moving across on its way
to the cathedral, led by a garda motorcycle outrider. There were
hundreds of children following, most dressed in the uniform of St
Malachi's College. The sounds of their footsteps were carried on
the wind like an irregular drumbeat. Beck crossed the road and
stood by the river wall. He could see the funeral cortège trailing its
way back to Bridge Street. The river swirled with quick currents,
the crusts of yellow foam on top moving past, giving Beck an
indication of the water's speed.

He walked on, slowly. At the bridge he stopped and blessed
himself, stood with his hands clasped before him. Led by Father
Clifford, the mourners walked past, silent and sombre. It was the
biggest funeral Cross Beg had seen in years. He was about to cross
the road in the other direction and take a different route back to
the station when he saw Blake walking at the centre of the mourners. Looking at him now Beck realised how tall and powerfully
built the pharmacist was; he towered over those around him by a
good foot. Their eyes met. Both men stared at one another. And
then, as Beck watched, Blake did something Beck did not expect.
Blake smiled, a lopsided smile, a cold smile, a smile of someone
in an interview room who slouches back into their seat, whose
hands hang loose by their sides, whose expression says 'prove it'.
That smile.

Beck could hear the wind and feel it on his face and he could
hear the sounds of those footsteps like drums, fading now as they
passed and the cortège of cars following arrived at the bridge. And
Beck looked back at the last of the walking mourners and ahead
again to Norman Blake in the middle. He could not rid himself
of the image of that strange, lopsided smile.

CHAPTER FORTY-SIX

Debra Anne at DNA testing in Garda HQ had spent much time extracting samples from the preserved gall bladder tissue forwarded by… well, she wasn't quite sure who. The signature was practically illegible. A stickler as ever, she matched the reference numbers and discovered the sample had been forwarded by the state pathologist's office. Debra Anne was concerned because the sample displayed signs of degradation, and worried too that she may not be able to extract DNA. However, she diligently persevered and successfully extracted a segment. Next, she spent time amplifying the sample. Finally, when this was done, she was in a position to make comparisons. She tested more than one genetic marker from the fluid and hair samples taken from the young female murder victim in Cross Beg, because she needed to be certain, as certain as could be. And there was no doubt – well, there was always doubt, but it was less than 0.01 per cent. Both samples were from the same person. Next, when she compared the samples against the DNA extracted from the gall bladder tissue, again there was little doubt. Specifically, again, 0.01 per cent. Which meant that the certainty was 99.9 per cent. Whichever way you chose to look at it, the person whose gall bladder it was, was the person who had been with Tanya Frazzali.

And finally, Debra Anne did something else. She picked up the phone.

CHAPTER FORTY-SEVEN

Claire looked at Beck in surprise from behind her desk when he entered the Ops Room. He crossed the room and told her the meeting in Dublin had been cancelled at the last minute, and muttered vaguely a lie about having to change trains and travel back to Cross Beg.

'It was all a bloody inconvenience,' he said.

'But how did you get here so quickly? It's just after ten o'clock.'

'Developments?' he asked, changing the subject.

She looked at him.

'Developments. In the case. I presume there was a briefing.'

'Oh,' she said. 'Yes, a very short one. The results of Ned's autopsy.'

'Suicide?'

'Suicide,' she said.

Beck could see it now. An open investigation that was to all intents and purposes leading to an unsolved closed one. As he feared would happen. Doctors might bury their mistakes, but investigators, when there was nothing else to go on, placed theirs onto indefinite life support. When questions were asked later, as they inevitably would be, the stock answer would be taken down and provided: 'The investigation is still open and ongoing'. And in that statement, all bases were covered.

'What about the CCTV? Weir?'

'Tom? Yes, he's narrowed it down to three cars. The partial regs are from a Toyota, a Ford and an Audi. The car on the CCTV looks like an Audi, that's what he said. It drove along the road to Cool Wood but didn't actually pass it until an hour and a half later. So it had to have pulled in somewhere first.'

'I'd like to look at that CCTV. Maybe we could get it later today?'

'You want me to ring him now?'

Beck nodded, and just as she reached for her phone, it rang. She picked it up, 'Hello… Yes. That's correct. He's right here.' She passed the phone to Beck. 'It's for you.'

'Hello… Yes, it is. Hello, Debra Anne. Thank you, we've been waiting on those… I don't need to know the technical details, just the results, please.'

Claire watched Beck carefully. She could see his expression changing.

'Thank you,' he said, putting the phone down, staring at Claire.

'What is it?' she said.

'It's a match,' he said. 'It's him.'

CHAPTER FORTY-EIGHT

Nigel McBride had taken to biting his fingernails again. Karen watched her husband's reflection in the kitchen window while she cleared the debris from the lunch plates into the sink food-waste grinder.

'Want tea?' she asked, false cheeriness in her tone.

He appeared not to have heard, so she asked again. But then he answered, quick as a boxer's jab, and just as painful, more of a shout: 'No.'

She picked up a fork and threw it into the sink. He looked at her, pushing back his stool as he stood.

'I'm going back to work, at least I'll get some fucking peace.'

She wanted to shout back, but knew it wouldn't do any good. So she said, as calmly as she could, 'This isn't easy on anyone, you know, especially Melanie. Tanya was her best friend, for God's sake. Did you ever think of that? And it was me who went to the school on Monday. Me. It's always me. Why don't you go and talk to your daughter? Why don't you go and do that? Instead of running off to get' – she was unable to hide the contempt in her voice – '"a little fucking peace".'

He mumbled something under his breath; it sounded like 'bitch'. She said nothing, just stood there, watching him as he left the room, his angry footsteps fading along the marble hallway. There was a pause – she knew he was putting on his coat – then the front door slammed shut.

Karen leaned against the sink, the strength draining from her body. She buried her face in her hands, trying her best not to cry. She didn't want to cry. Not for him. Never again. She wondered once more why she was still with this man. For the kids was the answer, the same as it was for everybody else who'd married a bastard, she supposed. But why had she bothered in the first place? She had had no interest, she'd had to make herself interested. For what? For what Johnny McBride's son could give her: the big house, the big car, the ability to walk down the street with a swagger. To be someone. The big fish in the small pond. Ah, Jesus.

'Any dessert, Mum?'

The question irritated her. It irritated her that her son had become obese. Was his only comfort to be found in food? It was one thing for her to suffer, but must she inflict it on her children, too? Guilt softened her tone.

'There's frozen éclairs in the fridge, sweetheart. But they'll take too long to thaw out.'

'No they won't, Mum. Ever heard of a microwave?'

'That's disgusting. They'll just turn to goo.'

'That's okay. I like goo.'

She thought about that, an éclair turning to disgusting goo, her obese son slurping it up. What kind of a mother was she? She started to sob, a little at first, and then her whole body shook as she lost all control and it consumed her. In that moment she hated herself, because she knew she should be crying for Tanya. But she wasn't. She was crying for herself.

CHAPTER FORTY-NINE

Nigel pressed the starter button and the Audi growled to life. He drove quickly down the driveway to the electronic gates, pressed the onboard remote and waited while they slowly swung open. He drove out onto the road, turned left, heading into Cross Beg.

The loud shrill of his telephone via Bluetooth, the sound reverberating through the car. He wanted to ignore it, but pressed the answer button on the steering wheel console anyway. Convinced it was Karen, he barked, 'What?'

She didn't answer. What was it with that woman?

His finger toyed with the button that would end the call. He changed into sixth gear. One of the new electronic speed signs on the approach to the primary school up ahead flashed his speed in red: sixty-two, beside it the legal speed limit of thirty on permanent green display. He eased his foot off the accelerator pedal.

The voice on the other end of the line spoke. One he didn't recognise. The voice of a male.

'Nigel McBride,' it said.

'Yeees.'

'Pull over, McBride. We'll try and keep this as low-key as possible.'

He was immediately struck by the cold authority in the voice, and his being addressed simply as 'McBride'.

'Who's this?' he asked.

'We're right behind you.'

He glanced in the rear-view mirror. The garda car was almost on his bumper. He could see the faces of the two guards staring back at him from the front, looking right into his eyes. The blue lights flashed intermittently without sound. It felt as though an invisible horse had careered onto its forequarters and kicked him in the stomach. He opened and closed his mouth in quick succession, like a fish gulping for oxygen. His foot was off the accelerator, the car slowing, freewheeling. The Audi bounced against a kerb, jolting him. Nigel realised he wasn't breathing. He gulped for air again, a dry, croaking noise coming from his throat as he sucked it in. He felt woozy, like he was about to faint. He stomped on the brake pedal and the tyres squealed, digging into the tarmac. He was in the middle of the road now. In his head he could hear a voice, his own voice, screaming, Jesus, Jesus, Jesus, as the door opened and they hauled him from the car.

'What took you so long, McBride?' one of them said. 'Fucking us around, are ya?'

CHAPTER FIFTY

'You should have told me,' O'Reilly shouted. 'And aren't you supposed to be in Dublin anyway?'

Beck shifted in his seat, suppressing the impulse to do the same, to tell this moron to go fuck himself.

They had been summoned to Superintendent Wilde's office, who now sat behind his desk, O'Reilly next to him.

'Whose idea was it…?' O'Reilly growled.

'Take it easy, Gerry,' Superintendent Wilde said. 'That's not going to help…'

'… to collect samples for…' O'Reilly continued.

'Can you shut up? Jesus. Please.' Wilde pinched the bridge of his nose with an index and forefinger. He exhaled a long, loud breath. 'Okay, okay,' he said. 'Okay, okay.'

O'Reilly opened his mouth to say something.

'Gerry, please,' Wilde said. 'Yes, yes, they should have told you, should have told *me*… Anyway, I would never have thought it. Him.'

'Possibly,' Beck said.

'What the fuck…' O'Reilly forced the volume down. 'He's a close friend of mine. I've known that man for over twenty-five years.'

'Explain it to me, Beck,' Wilde said. 'Explain it. What?'

'I can't. The evidence is pointing his way. I was left with no alternative. It was made clear to me that he was not to be brought in without evidence. I got evidence.'

'You certainly did,' Wilde said. 'I won't go into the dubious legality of it here. By the way, I know him too. Everybody does.'

Beck felt a pain begin to press in along the sides of his head. He looked at O'Reilly, and said slowly, clearly, 'Listen to you. Instead of asking me questions, you should be answering them. From what I can see, you want a result – you don't care how you get it, just so long as you do. Samples weren't taken from Ned's body for comparisons, were they? No, so you were quite happy to have him blamed. Only someone who had got away with that in the past would think they could get away with it again now. So, please, don't growl at me or Detective Somers. Look in the mirror. Look at yourself.'

'Here...' O'Reilly began, getting to his feet, his fists clenched into tight balls by his sides. 'Think you can give me a sermon...?'

'Sit down, Gerry,' Wilde said. 'Beck, have you officially interviewed him yet?'

'No.'

'I'd like to interview him,' O'Reilly said. 'Let me do it.'

'You know him too well, Gerry, no, it might be a conflict.'

'I know everything that happens in this town,' O'Reilly said. 'This will ruin the man. Cross Beg will turn its back on him.'

Wilde looked at O'Reilly, an unexpected tone in his voice: 'You should have thought of that yourself then, shouldn't you?'

O'Reilly said nothing. His eyes narrowed as he stared at Wilde.

Wilde turned to Beck and Claire, indicated with his finger for them to leave.

'What was that about?' Beck asked when they were in the corridor outside.

'I think...' Claire began, and waited until they were at the end before continuing. 'O'Reilly is no angel himself. There was a rumour.'

'Go on.'

'I didn't mention it before now because I don't do rumours, generally.'

'Go on.'

'There was a rumour…'

'Jesus, Claire, there was a rumour. I get that part.'

'You remember last year, thereabouts, a report in the *Sunday Globe*?'

'The *Sunday Globe*,' Beck said, adding with a hint of sarcasm, 'It must be true.'

'An insider's report on the swingers scene in Dublin, accompanied by photos from a party, a thin black strip across the eyes of the partygoers to protect identities. Who can resist a photo like that on the front cover of a Sunday newspaper, eh?'

'I don't remember it,' Beck said.

'It referred to a mid-ranking member of An Garda Síochána. The rumour was the mid-ranking member was O'Reilly. Couldn't be proven, of course.'

'And could be a complete lie, too, I'll give him that. Actually, I do remember gossip about it. I didn't pay it any heed. In Dublin I had other things to worry about.'

'There's also another rumour.'

'Yes?'

'That he was having an affair with Nigel McBride's wife. That they all – the three of them, the McBrides and O'Reilly – liked to attend, ahem, parties.'

Beck grinned. 'You're kidding me? No, you're not, are you?'

'No, Beck, I'm not.'

CHAPTER FIFTY-ONE

McBride sat sideways in his chair, leaning on the table with his elbow, running his other hand through his jet-black hair. Designer stubble sprinkled a chin that had a prominent dimple at its centre, his skin was sallow and his green eyes flecked with yellow. They said that when the Spanish Armada sank off the west coast of Ireland some survivors remained whose forebears looked like McBride did now. Many people, sallow-skinned and black-haired, could be seen walking the streets of Galway city today who would not look out of place on the *calles* of Madrid, Seville or León.

McBride looked nervous, Beck noticed, even if he was trying his best to hide it. Beck said nothing, wanting to see how McBride reacted to silence.

But Claire spoke. She said casually, trying to avoid any discomfort this silence generated, when Beck was trying to exploit it, 'We need to ask you a few questions, Mr McBride.'

He smiled, a forced smile, the corners of his mouth turning up, the lines creasing along the sides of his eyes, but Beck could see the strain underneath. 'What?' McBride said. 'You're staring at me.'

'Me?' Beck said.

'Yes.'

'No. I'm not.'

'What is this about?' McBride asked, like he had better things to do; a parry, Beck knew. He was trying to sidestep.

So that's the way he wants to play it, Beck thought. 'Where were you,' Beck asked, 'last Sunday evening?'

Beck watched McBride carefully. Despite his swarthy complexion, he seemed to have gone suddenly very pale. In the couple of seconds it took for him to speak, Beck knew the man was deciding whether or not to tell the truth. And Beck could tell even before he spoke that he had decided on a little of both, in the way he leaned forward, placed his other elbow on the table and buried his face in his hands.

'Oh God,' he whimpered. 'Oh God, oh God.' He rubbed his eyes and Beck could hear the squelching sound they made. When he took them away again his eyes were red and moist. His skin seemed to hang from his face and he looked old and grey, as if he was allowing them to see him now, as he really was, without the mask. Those eyes looked at Beck, hollow and scared.

'Is there something you need to tell us?' Beck prompted.

'This got all out of hand,' McBride began, his arms on the desk now, his head lowered. 'I mean, oh Christ, it all got completely out of hand.'

Beck glanced at Claire, held her gaze. She understood. Neither of them spoke.

'Tanya is a friend of my daughter's,' McBride continued after a pause. 'You know that, don't you? You spoke to her at the school.' He raised his head and looked at the ceiling, said, 'Oh God, this is a nightmare.'

'For you, that is,' Claire said. 'Meanwhile, Tanya is dead.'

'Did you kill her?' Beck asked simply, leaning forward so that mere inches separated his face from McBride's.

'No,' McBride answered immediately, looking at Beck, staring into his eyes. 'I swear to God. I did not kill Tanya. I wouldn't do such a thing. Tanya. I... I really liked her.'

'Spare me the bullshit,' Claire said. 'She was a kid. A kid!'

'I want you to tell me exactly what happened that night,' Beck said, sitting back.

McBride looked down slowly at his hands, then up again at Beck.

'There'd been a rugby match. Cross Beg Trampers against Galway Natives. It'd rained for the entire game. I was drenched. So I had to go home to change. I didn't want to go home, because that would mean explaining why I had to go back out again.' He paused. 'I had to go back out again. I was meeting Tanya.'

Beck nodded.

'So I told my wife I was meeting friends in O'Callaghan's, and in case she asked around to find out whether or not I'd really been there, I went to the pub and spent about an hour in company.'

Beck asked, 'You said your wife might ask around. Why? Was she suspicious of you?'

McBride nodded. 'It was mutual.'

'Can you elaborate?'

'What can I say? We've both been unfaithful to one another in the past. The problem is, we married too young. Karen, my wife, became pregnant while we were both in our final year at secondary school.' He glanced at Claire. 'You've been in Cross Beg long enough. No doubt you've heard the rumours. About me, that is. About us.'

'It's irrelevant,' Beck said. 'You were saying…'

'I was saying,' McBride went on, his voice low. 'O'Callaghan's was packed, I slipped away sometime after ten o'clock. I drove to Cool Wood. I was late, and…'

'Stop right there,' Beck said. 'You say you drove to Cool Wood. There were no tyre marks in the car park. An Audi car, partial reg matching yours, was observed on CCTV driving towards Cool Wood, but it didn't pass until well over an hour and a half later. Can you explain that?'

'I parked the car in the outhouse of the Richardsons' old place, it's an empty property on my sale list. I had to walk along the road from there to get to the wood, so I ran. I didn't want anyone to see me.'

'Why the wood?' Claire asked. 'If the property was empty, you could have gone there.'

McBride sat back in his chair, folded his arms. 'What's that got to do with anything?'

'It seems like an obvious question to me,' Claire said.

'Because,' McBride said, 'the forest is something separate, distinct, distant, it's not a part of my life. The property was, is, part of my life, it's my job. I didn't want any overlap between the two. The truth was...' McBride suddenly fell silent.

'The truth was,' Beck prodded, not allowing him any time to think about it.

'I'd had enough of Tanya. The novelty had worn off. The reality had set in. Here was this teenage girl desperate for a fairy-tale romance, pestering me to leave my family, telling me she wanted to have my babies. It was crazy. I wanted out. No, I didn't want to meet her anywhere except in the wood. But that doesn't mean I wanted to kill her, or that I did kill her.'

'Jesus,' Claire said under her breath. 'Did you take pictures of her, by the way? Do you have pictures in your possession of her now? You know what pictures I mean.'

McBride looked away, pursed his lips.

'Listen,' Beck said, 'I appreciate your honesty so far. Really. Forget about the pictures for now, okay? So, you parked your car at the Richardsons' old place. You ran to Cool Wood. What then?'

'She was waiting for me. I'd wondered if she would. I was over an hour late, after all. A part of me hoped she wouldn't be there. But she was. She'd waited. In the woods. Alone.' He looked at Claire. 'I felt like a right bastard, if that makes you feel any better. She was angry with me, really angry. I knew I had to end it. I just had to.'

'And did you?' Claire asked.

McBride looked away again. 'No. I decided not to, not that night. I'd let it cool for a while first, make it easier on her.'

'For fuck's sake,' Claire muttered.

'Continue,' Beck said.

'She didn't want me to leave when I was getting ready to go. She clung to me. So we just lay there, together, for a while.'

'On what?' Beck said. 'When you say you lay there. What did you lie on?'

'A tarpaulin. I kept it in the hollow of a tree.'

'Isn't that a bit cold, uncomfortable?'

'We used our' – McBride dropped his eyes – 'jackets.'

'Is that tarpaulin still there?' It was Beck.

'As far as I know.'

'We may need you to show us, later.'

McBride nodded.

'Go on,' Beck said.

'I left around eleven twenty, walked back to my car.' McBride fell silent again.

'And Tanya,' Claire said. 'Did you ever wonder how she was supposed to get home at that hour, in the dark?'

'Tanya always took the shortcut. It's only ten minutes away. It was a good night. Bright.'

Claire couldn't contain herself any longer. 'Ah, spare me.' Her voice was loud.

Beck was thinking, from a distance, in dim light, that McBride could pass for Johnny Cash.

McBride watched him. 'Tell me you don't think I killed her,' he said.

Beck knew McBride was starting to think of self-preservation now. 'I can't tell you that. On the contrary, the evidence points to you, Mr McBride.'

McBride's voice cracked. 'I was open and honest with you. I hid nothing. And by the way, it was Tanya who did the running after me. She came on to me, you know, in the beginning.'

'Really,' Beck said. 'How so?'

A look crossed McBride's face. 'I can't say any more, you understand. I've said enough. I need my solicitor.'

CHAPTER FIFTY-TWO

The house on Bog Road gave no sign of what lay behind its doors. The postman and been and gone, dropped three envelopes through the letter box and hurried on his way again. The two ladies standing on the doorstep now would not be so quick to leave, however. The rain had petered out to a light drizzle, but the sky was still dark and the wind like a great rumbling beast.

Mrs Fiona Hogan and Mrs Charlotte Cummins were supposed to be making final preparations for next week's coffee morning in aid of the National Association of Carers in Ireland, along with Imelda, who was meant to oversee the group responsible for cake baking, which last year had brought in more money than all the other activities combined. Except Imelda hadn't shown up this morning, and Imelda hated not showing up for anything. If she absolutely couldn't help it she would always ring first and notify somebody. No one had heard anything from her since yesterday, and Imelda's friends worried, because they were at an age now where death occupied a permanent seat at their dinner table. They had come round to check, to satisfy themselves that all was well.

But they didn't know what to do now, because they had never really considered anything being wrong, never imagined Imelda not answering the door when they called. They looked at one another now. They hadn't thought of this. And so they waited, and they hoped that she would soon come and open the door and everything would be as it was supposed to be. They liked having things the way they were supposed to be. And as they waited and it became apparent that no, Imelda was not going to come and answer the door today, Mrs Cummins, who was by far the pluckier of the two, knelt down and opened the letter box, peered in. The familiar hallway revealed itself as it should, everything in order. She straightened and went to the front windows, Mrs Hogan trailing behind, cupped her hands and looked in. Nothing to arouse her suspicions here either.

'Maybe she's gone to visit someone, or something,' Mrs Hogan offered, both hands clasped around the straps of her handbag. She wasn't happy with this at all.

Her friend shook her head and said with great certainty, 'No. Her car is still here. And she wouldn't, anyway. Not Imelda. No. You mean just take off? Not possible.'

They stood for a moment considering. Then Mrs Cummins said, 'This way,' and led the way from the front of the house along the footpath at the side, to the back of the property. They stood in the small neat garden here and looked up at the window where they knew her bedroom to be. The curtains were drawn.

'Something's not right,' Mrs Cummins said. 'I can't even hear the dog.'

Mrs Hogan looked very worried now. 'What should we do?'

'Call the police,' Mrs Cummins said without hesitation, rummaging in her pocket for her mobile phone. It was her first mobile phone, a gift from her daughter three Christmases ago. She didn't carry a handbag.

'Is that not a bit drastic?' Mrs Hogan said, not wanting to make a fuss. She never liked to make a fuss, still unable to contemplate anything having really happened to her friend, because in her world, nothing ever happened that wasn't supposed to happen, even death. 'I mean, I'm sure she's fine. Let's wait a little longer.'

'No,' Mrs Cummins was adamant. 'I'm not so certain everything is fine. I'm not certain at all.' She pressed '9' three times and put the phone to her ear.

CHAPTER FIFTY-THREE

Sometimes a 999 call to the guards in Cross Beg did not result in an immediate response. The station cars were often tied up with other call-outs, and a crew might have to travel from a different station within the district or sometimes from a different district altogether to get to the scene of an emergency. This all took time, and slow 999 response times were a hot political topic locally. But that wasn't the case now.

Because of Tanya Frazzali's murder, more than a dozen patrol cars were in or about the town, and ninety seconds after Mrs Cummins had made her call, a marked patrol car turned onto Bog Road and pulled up in front of Imelda Jean Butler's house. Despite the prompt response time, the two gardai in it seemed in no hurry to get out of their car and go to the house. Minutes passed before they emerged from the vehicle and made their way along the garden path to the front door, talking to each other as they went, one laughing, motioning with his foot as he kicked an invisible football. Mrs Cummins scowled, and Mrs Hogan forced a smile.

'And the bedroom curtains are drawn, are they?' the smaller of the two gardai asked without any introduction. He had fair hair and bad skin.

'Yes,' Mrs Cummins said. 'You can have a look yourself. Come on, I'll show you. It's round the back.'

The guards didn't move. They had picked up on Mrs Cummins' natural sense of authority and didn't like it. The older of the two, tall with thin shoulders and white sideburns, said, 'We'd better go round the back, Des, and have a look,' as if by saying it he was maintaining control.

They followed Mrs Cummins down the path at the side of the house to the back garden. Mrs Cummins pointed to the window.

'That's it right there. See? The curtains are drawn.'

The fair-haired guard bent down and picked up a couple of loose pebbles and threw them up at the window. They tinkled against the glass and fell back down to earth.

'Imelda has very good hearing,' Mrs Cummins said. 'We knocked on the door. Nothing. Something is wrong, I'm telling you.'

'We'll have to force the door,' the older guard said. 'Des, put your shoulder to it and see if it gives.'

The young guard went to the door, pressed his shoulder gently against it, testing it. He could tell it was old. He readied himself, positioned one foot as an anchor, and rammed his shoulder against the wooden panel. It took two more attempts before there was a splintering sound and the panel gave. The guard reached in and turned the latch.

'Look at her door,' Mrs Hogan said. 'My God. Did they have to do that?'

'Stay outside, please,' the young guard said, stepping into the hallway. The two guards walked into the kitchen, looked around briefly, came out again into the hall, went through all the ground-floor rooms. Finally, they climbed the stairs. On the landing they paused, looking at the closed doors across from them.

'That should be her bedroom,' the older guard said, pointing to the door on the left. He moved over to it and knocked twice.

'Hello? Mrs Butler. Are you in there? This is the guards.' He put his hand on the doorknob and turned it slowly, pushed it open.

The smell was like a toilet that hadn't been flushed in weeks; he saw the body lying across the bed, and about it and on the floor – as if someone had splashed a can of red paint – was blood, but turning black now, thickening.

The younger guard took a step forward but the older guard caught him by the arm. 'No. Don't do that. It's a murder scene now.'

The younger guard had not thought of that. He had not fully processed the sights before him. A suicide, possibly, or a freakish accident, but not murder. In any case, it was too late, as his foot came down on something soft with a distinct crunching sound. He looked, saw that his boot was planted firmly into the centre of a squashed dog. Beside it, where the head should have been, nothing but tooth splinters and splattered brains.

'Holy fuck,' he swore, as he jerked his foot up.

CHAPTER FIFTY-FOUR

Beck was in the ops room, standing next to Claire's desk, by the window, looking out on to the street below. McBride's solicitor had arrived and was interviewing his client in the Prisoner Consultation Room in the holding area. It was unlikely that McBride could be held beyond twenty-four hours. A file was being prepared for the Director of Public Prosecutions, so his detention would be suspended while the case against him was prepared. He would also have to surrender his passport. There was not enough to detain him for the murder of Tanya Frazzali, but he would be charged with the crime of statutory rape.

From where he was standing, Beck could hear the sound of voices coming over the radio in the Comms Room, tinny and full of static. He was not listening, not as such, more like processing, similar to an automatic monitoring system programmed to pick up on keywords. Beck picked up on keywords now: 'victim', 'dead', 'cordoned off'.

He went quickly across the Ops Room, stood in the Comms Room door, saw the green light illuminated on the dispatch table as the dispatcher notified all units... 'Bog Road in Cross Beg, body of female, multiple stab wounds, found inside property. Note, house can be located by presence of marked unit parked outside. All units with exception of priority attend.'

The blue and white chequered crime scene tape fluttered in the wind. They were the first detectives to arrive. Two uniformed guards stood on the pavement outside the tape. Other guards milled about along the pavement, a half-dozen marked cars haphazardly parked on the roadway, roof racks turning and headlamps blinking, like a scene from a TV crime drama. The two guards in front of the crime scene tape were the first responders. Beck was pleased the older one had the presence of mind to seal the crime scene. No one would enter until the Technical Bureau arrived. Beck learned the older guard was Joe Burke, who, on approaching him now, displayed the calm demeanour of a seasoned old-timer. He explained to Beck and Claire how he had found the body.

'Good work,' Beck said, but the old guard seemed impervious to praise.

Beck saw an unmarked Hyundai pull up and O'Reilly and Wilde get out. O'Reilly's shoulders were hunched and his face expressionless. He walked straight over to Beck.

'You,' he said, jabbing a finger. 'I don't want you here. You've done enough for one day. Just fuck off.'

Wilde had stopped further behind, was talking to a uniformed guard. He glanced at Beck once, then looked away.

Beck knew you had to pick your fights – your battles – call it what you will. You decided which were worth it and which were not. And very few were worth it, and even though this wasn't one of them, Beck found himself stretching to his full height; if he could, he would have pawed the ground like a buck deer. Instinctively, O'Reilly squared up too in reply.

'You're an arsehole,' Beck spat. 'You know that? Who the fuck do you think you are anyway? Arsehole.'

O'Reilly pointed, spittle forming in the corners of his mouth. 'Sherlock fucking Holmes himself, is it? Ha! Your problem, Beck, is you think you're better than everybody else. You think you can look down your nose at us, at me…'

Around them, everything stopped; faces turned to watch. No one spoke.

'That's enough!' It was Superintendent Wilde now, striding up and stepping between them. They were so close he had to push them apart. 'Beck. Go back to the station. Please.'

Beck opened his mouth to object.

'Beck! There's little can be done here, anyway. For now.' The superintendent glared at him.

Beck bowed his head, turning, began walking away.

'You come with me,' O'Reilly said to Claire, before Wilde could say another word. Wilde placed his hands on his hips, looking about. He pointed at something, and a uniformed garda turned to look. O'Reilly glanced quickly at Beck, then back again.

Although it was mid-afternoon, the light was murky. Motorists turned their headlamps on. As Beck walked away, he could feel it, intangible but real, permeating everything: fear.

CHAPTER FIFTY-FIVE

Beck went home, packed an overnight bag and made the five o'clock train to Dublin with minutes to spare. He passed the journey brooding about O'Reilly. The inspector's petty grievances were getting in the way of professional objectivity. He was like poison ivy, spreading a sense of stinging irritation everywhere he went. Just past Athlone, Beck rang Claire. She answered immediately.

'Beck. How you feeling? You have grounds there. He humiliated you.'

'He humiliated me?'

'Yes.'

Beck waved an arm through the air, almost hitting the person sitting next to him. He turned towards the window. 'I don't think so. He annoyed me, got my goat up, yes. But he's not capable of humiliating me. Humiliation is in the eye of the beholder. No, he did not humiliate me. Anything I should know?'

There was a pause. Beck listened to the gentle clickety-clack of the iron wheels on the rails. 'It was quite brutal,' she said. 'I mean, there was a lot of blood.'

'You were in there?'

'Yes. I went back.'

Beck could see, reflected in the carriage window, the person sitting next to him, a middle-aged man with a high forehead, wearing glasses. He saw his eyes slide towards him now.

'We'll talk later,' Beck said, and hung up. He closed his eyes, and nodded off for the remainder of the journey.

Beck turned the key and went into the house. It was literally like stepping into a fridge. In fact, it was colder in the house than it was outside. With it came the musty smell of damp.

Beck went straight to the oil burner switch in the kitchen and turned it on, heard the whoosh as the oil ignited.

His house was in the Dublin suburb of Ranelagh Village. He'd bought it over twenty years before. Or rather, he'd nominally bought the front door knocker, the rest being given over to a mortgage that stretched off to infinity. At the time he had been thinking of getting married but had been finding it difficult to move beyond the theory stage and on to the practical and to actually do it. When his fiancée at the time, a soft, kind-hearted nurse named Valarie who was simply too sweet for a man like Beck, eventually realised the idea of marriage to him was never going to be anything other than that – an idea – she finished the relationship and moved on. She had surprised him with her steely resolve. But by then, the house had been purchased, and without her contribution, the mortgage became a major strain on his income as a young uniformed garda. But fast-forward and now, because of Dublin property prices, the house had increased in value tenfold, and Beck found himself, technically speaking, a millionaire. However, in the land of the blind the one-eyed man is king, and so Beck would never see the monetary benefit of this. Because to sell the property and live in Dublin would mean having to buy another, and he'd be back to where he had started again. Unless he actually did retire and move to Spain as, according to Gumbell, he'd been talking about doing in O'Callaghan's the other evening. A simple stone house with a terracotta slate roof, an olive grove out back and wine on tap in a barrel. He also thought of sunburn and flies, sweat dripping into his eyes and that he'd probably be dead within a year.

He knew he would have to make a decision about this place soon. Rent or sell? And in that was the answer as to whether he would remain in Cross Beg or not. The only upside to remaining was that property prices were considerably less in Cross Beg. With a million, he could probably purchase the entire Main Street.

He went through the house. Everything was in order. He should be grateful; it had not been burgled. Or maybe it had and he just hadn't noticed yet, because the burglars had left again without taking anything, not interested in the paltry pickings on offer. And the alarm hadn't gone off because Beck didn't have an alarm. What he had was a two-box dummy alarm system purchased from Lidl, fitted to the front and back walls and with blinking green and red lights. It was solar-powered, so he never had to worry about batteries.

Beck waited for the central heating to melt away the chill of the house. He sat in the living room with its one settee, one armchair and a bookcase crammed with old Sunday newspapers but no books. He kept his coat on, watching the wisps of condensation puff from his mouth and nose each time he exhaled.

The shrill sound of his phone cracked the silence. He took it from his pocket, looked at the screen, saw it was a private number and answered. The feeling that came from knowing it had to be her, that she had rung, even if she would not speak, made him feel like a giddy teenager.

He listened, but it took a moment to realise that there was sound, and to understand what it was. It was the sound of someone crying.

'Who is this?' he said.

The crying softened, and he heard a long, sniffling sound. A voice spoke softly.

'I waited for you. You never came home. Where are you?' The edges of the words slurred.

'Mrs Claxton? Is that you?'

'Mrs Claxton, is that you? Mrs Claxton, you say! Do you even know my first name? I'll save you the trouble, will I? It's Sheila! Did you even know that? Check the lease if you need reminding next time.'

'Mrs... Sheila. I know your first name. I don't need to check the lease. I'm in Dublin. I have a meeting in the morning.'

'Are you with someone? Is that it?'

Beck silently groaned. 'No, Sheila, no, I'm not. I'll be back in Cross Beg tomorrow. I'll see you then, okay?'

'I've had a little too much sherry, Mr Beck.'

'It's Finnegan.'

'You told me no one ever calls you that. That's a funny name, by the way.'

'Finn for short. I don't mind.'

'You also told me no one calls you that either.'

'I can see you tomorrow, Sheila. I need to go now. I have an early meeting, like I say.'

'Well,' she said, 'You can fuck off then. Don't let me keep you.'

The phone line went dead.

Beck didn't have too much time to think about it. The phone rang again almost immediately. A private number. Mrs Claxton ringing back? He hesitated before answering, then waited... For a long time there was the low hiss of a digital vacuum. Beck did not speak. And the line went dead again.

CHAPTER FIFTY-SIX

Beck did not sleep well, not enough to fall beneath the layers of his subconscious, to go down deep to where *they* waited. He tossed and turned throughout the night, unable to resist thinking of the woman whose memory filled this room. Like a dog unable to resist a bone, he kept going back, gnawing at that memory. He could almost hear her voice in the darkness, could almost feel her body next to his. But he knew that he was fooling himself, because he only wanted her, only really, really wanted her, when he could not have her.

When the morning light finally crept into the room, lingering, as if sensing the mood, deciding whether to stay or leave again, he was grateful that the night had passed.

There was no food in the house, so once he'd showered and dressed, he left and walked down to the village. Beck did not know the surname of Sammy, only that he was a Christian, from the city of Fes in Morocco, hence the name over the door: 'Fes Café'. Sammy was giving change to an attractive woman at the cash register. He was too busy with her to notice Beck. His eyes were still on the woman as she turned and walked to the door. Finally he looked at Beck, and a wide smile crossed his bearded face.

'My friend, where have you been? I have missed you.' He walked down and leaned over the counter, reaching over and taking one of Beck's hands with both of his. He whispered, 'Did you see that woman? My God. The most beautiful woman I have seen all day, I tell you.'

'It's only eight thirty, Sammy.'

Sammy's smile broadened. 'Yes, I know. It will be a good day, I tell you. So, where have you been? Please tell me.'

'I have been away.'

'You are back now. To stay?'

'No,' Beck said. The two people behind him shifted restlessly. It was a Saturday, and Sammy's staff did not start their shifts until 10 a.m. Beck ordered a sausage sandwich on brown and a large black coffee.

Sammy grimaced, reaching for the bread, 'I tell you. I have twelve types of bagel, six hams, pancakes with Greek yogurt, mixed berries, sweet jam and Harcha from my own city. People love my food. And you, you always order sausage sandwich.' He shook his head.

Beck sat at the window counter and gazed out. Everything was the same but different: his home, this café, this city. All the same, but different. Because he was no longer part of it.

Something had changed. Imperceptible yet real. He realised now this was not home. This had never been home. Because Beck didn't have a home. The thought depressed him slightly. Okay, made him feel a little sorry for himself. Was it too much to ask, he wondered? To want to belong? To want to be loved? Because Beck ran from both. And sometimes he needed both. Desperately. He knew that. But still, it made no difference. It didn't stop him running.

On the wall next to the window was a framed photograph of a desert, orange sun in the background, sand dunes stark and angular and beautiful in the foreground. Beck looked at it. Across the bottom were words written in Arabic, beneath them the English translation: *He who follows the crow will be led to the corpses of dogs.*

Beck stared, slightly shocked at its malevolence in such benign surroundings. Why had Sammy put it there? He'd often heard him say that to appreciate beauty one first had to know ugliness;

to experience joy one first had to feel sadness. Beck thought of crows. He thought of Cross Beg. He thought that all crows looked alike. So how was it possible to tell who was the killer in a town already full of crows?

He wanted to change the inscription to one that read: To follow the crow one must first become a hawk.

CHAPTER FIFTY-SEVEN

Beck alighted from the taxi at the security barrier of Garda HQ, presented his identity card to the guard at the gate house. The guard ticked his name off a list on his clipboard.

Garda HQ, also known as The Depot, was a sprawling affair on the edge of the Dublin metropolitan region, situated in the largest public park in Europe, the Phoenix Park. It was built during the early 1840s, and the original stone facade had remained unchanged since that time.

The Assistant Commissioner, Finbar Sullivan, opened the office door himself when Beck knocked. He was in civilian clothes: sneakers, cargo pants and sweatshirt. Beck had only ever met the Assistant Commissioner on a couple of occasions. He had the build of a heavyweight boxer; indeed, the Assistant Commissioner had boxed for many years in tournaments all over the world with the Garda Boxing Club. His nose was a little off-kilter and a scar ran down the side of his cheek. He looked more like a criminal than a police officer. His grey hair was tightly shaved on a head that sat on a squat, powerful neck.

'Beck. Come in.'

There were two others in the office, and, like Sullivan, they were in civilian clothes. One he recognised as Chief Superintendent William Healy, a small, wide man with large black spectacles, the commander of Garda Internal Affairs.

'You know William,' Sullivan said, indicating the other person. 'This is Superintendent Will Leahy, from Corporate Affairs, who is also a trained lawyer, by the way. Take a seat, Beck.'

The office was similar to the office of Superintendent Wilde in Cross Beg, exuding that same sense of history: Georgian windows, marble surround fireplace with brass centrepiece, a similar big antique desk with a leather inlay. In a glass case over the fireplace, an old Dublin Metropolitan Police helmet was housed.

The Assistant Commissioner sat behind his desk, tented his hands beneath his chin. He observed Beck for a long time before he finally gave a weak smile and spoke. 'You have been exonerated fully from any responsibility in the death of officer Jason Geraghty. I want to begin by telling you that right away.'

Beck heard those words and felt as if he had been released from a decompression chamber. He crawled from that decompression chamber now, and sat in his chair, holding himself straight, as if the weight of a thousand tonnes had just been lifted from his shoulders.

'We gathered a lot of evidence,' the Assistant Commissioner went on. 'You were unfortunate for a number of reasons, Beck. Primarily because it was you. You know what I mean?'

'You mean, because I'm…' He searched for a word, and smiled, because he couldn't find one.

'Erratic, I'd call it,' Chief Superintendent Healy said.

In other words, Beck thought, *someone perfectly placed to take the blame.*

'Unfortunately, Garda Geraghty was not all that he seemed,' Sullivan said. 'He was having problems, money problems. He did a good job giving the impression that he was a reliable and committed member of the force, that all was well in his life, but gamblers are very cunning, I've always found.'

'Gambler?' Beck said.

'Yes. He owed money, fifty thousand euro, and that's what we know of. He'd also remortgaged his house, his family home, I'd like to emphasise. No, he wasn't what we thought he was at all. He killed himself, Beck.'

'He what?'

'He killed himself. But that is, and will remain, unofficial. For his family's sake. His life insurance policy was worth half a million. The only people who know about this are in this room, and there it will stay.'

'Which is why we need you to sign this.' It was Superintendent Leahy. He slid a sheet of paper and pen across the desk towards Beck.

Beck picked the paper up, looked at it. It was a legal document. He read the first line in the stream of tightly packed legal text, took up the pen and signed it. He slid the paper and pen back across the desk to Leahy. They looked at him, surprised he had signed without comment.

'How?' Beck asked.

Sullivan scratched his head. 'Officer Geraghty's weapon, as you know, was a nine-millimetre Sig Sauer P226. It was discharged three times. The weapon retrieved from Byrne's body was a Czech CZ revolver. However, Byrne was struck only once – a direct shot to the centre of his forehead. Geraghty was a sharpshooter. He'd received specialist military sniper training at the Curragh, so he didn't miss. Once maybe, but never twice. The other two nine-millimetre bullets fired from his weapon were pulled from the wall to the right of Byrne's body. Why? To scare Byrne enough to loose off his magazine, we think.

'The way we've established it,' the Assistant Commissioner went on, 'is that officer Geraghty confronted Byrne as he came down the hallway. Byrne was at the top of the stairs. Geraghty approached, weapon drawn, we have confirmation of this from CCTV in the doorway. The CCTV doesn't extend to the end of the hall – privacy matters to do with another business on the first floor. We can see Geraghty with his weapon, shouting, animated, even agitated, I'd call it. We availed ourselves of the services of a lip-reader. What he's saying is, "Shoot, you fucker, or I shoot you, go on, shoot you fucker, SHOOT!"'

'Officer Geraghty was hit five times, in the torso, chest and neck. Random shots, Byrne just blasted away. Geraghty didn't die immediately. He put one in Byrne's head first, one expert shot, killing what he thought was both Byrne and his secret. A desperate scenario devised by a desperate gambler. But it worked.'

Beck wondered about something. 'The CZ is a standard revolver, isn't it?'

The Assistant Commissioner nodded. 'It is.'

Beck thought of his dream, the clicking sound, that of a revolver chamber turning. 'And that's the way it happened,' he said.

Sullivan nodded, raising his eyebrows. 'Fuck, Beck, you don't make it easy. There were empty cans in the boot of your car. What were you thinking?'

'If I may,' Superintendent Leahy peered down at Beck. 'None of this actually happened. It couldn't have happened because we can't let it happen. Regardless of circumstances, a commanding officer intoxicated, an armed commanding officer, over a firearm's unit... Fuck sake, no, we can't let that out. None of this happened.'

'I wasn't drunk,' Beck said, but wished as soon as he said it that he hadn't.

'Tell me you didn't say that, Beck,' Sullivan said.

'He did.' It was Leahy.

The Assistant Commissioner sat back in his chair and closed his eyes. When he opened them again he looked at Beck with grim intent. 'Yes, this organisation is inefficient at times. Yes, we can be lazy. Yes, we can be wasteful of resources. Yes, we are often accused of taking only serious crime seriously. Beck, what can I say? But you produce, like a good cow, you keep on giving. I don't want to alienate you so much that you walk away. With the advent of Pulse, we can produce spreadsheets on everything, as you know. Your homicide success rate is 96 per cent. X-factor territory, Beck.'

'But,' Beck said, 'I can't sing for shit.'

The four men laughed, a sign of the enduring camaraderie that all men in uniform shared.

The Assistant Commissioner became serious again. 'By the way, Beck, you are hereby restored to the rank of inspector. We'd like you to return to Pearse Street, too. How do you feel about that?'

Inside his head a voice went 'Yes!' He had to stop himself from jumping to his feet and punching the air.

'I think that would be good,' he said in a forced calm demeanour. 'I'd probably like that, yes.'

'Only not just yet,' Sullivan continued. 'You have business to attend to in Cross Beg. How is that investigation going?'

Beck gave a brief summary of it.

'I spoke with Superintendent Wilde this morning,' the Assistant Commissioner said, 'before you arrived. Is it manageable, Beck? Or is it getting out of hand?'

'A very good question,' Beck said after a moment.

Superintendent Leahy coughed. 'Don't we have a round of golf to play, gentlemen?'

He was a lawyer, Beck reminded himself. This conversation was making him feel uncomfortable.

CHAPTER FIFTY-EIGHT

In the taxi back to Ranelagh, Beck suddenly changed his mind, told the driver to turn around and gave him new directions. The driver shrugged and performed a U-turn in the middle of traffic, stirring up a hornet's nest of flashing lights and blaring horns. Beck told him to drive slowly past the house, and when he saw there was only one car in the driveway – a small Fiat – he told him to pull in further along the street and wait. Beck got out and lit a cigarette, walked slowly along the pavement, furiously smoking before tossing it into the gutter, and turned into the driveway. He walked with purpose to the front door and rang the bell.

Part of him hoped it wouldn't be answered, that he would have no choice but to turn round and walk away again. But a part of him, much bigger by far, wanted to see her, wanted to hear her voice, wanted to feel her eyes on him again.

The door opened and she was standing there. She had no make-up on; her skin was clear and fresh. It didn't look like she was struggling without him. She looked remarkably well.

'Natalia.'

She took a sharp intake of breath, like a swimmer breaking for air.

Beck cleared his throat, and delivered a line from the top ten of the corniest lines ever. 'I was just passing.'

She folded her arms tightly across her chest. A reflex action: protection, safety; leave me alone.

'This is not a good idea. Why are you here?'

'Like I said. Really. I was passing.'

A flicker of a smile. 'Goodbye, Beck.'

The door began to close.

'I know you've been ringing me.' Beck was aware of desperation in his voice, like a hormonal teenager, and he was angry with himself for showing it. There was nothing worse.

Clunk! The door closed, and Beck was looking at a gleaming brass knocker. He felt like grasping it, and banging, banging, banging until the whole world could hear him and she had to answer.

He turned away slowly and started back down the drive. But he could feel something, and knew what it was. It was her eyes, on his back, staring right into him.

He reached the top of the drive and was about to turn onto the street outside.

'Beck.'

He turned.

The door was open, and she was standing there.

He walked to her. Followed her into the house. Into the living room. Where she sat. Legs crossed. Tightly. Arms too. A fortress. Looking at him, her eyes peering out as if behind peepholes. Physically, there was nothing that he did not love about this woman. Just the very sight of her made him tingle, made him start to get hard. She had something. It wasn't beauty. Because she was pretty rather than beautiful. But it was…

Something.

'You've been ringing me,' he repeated.

She hadn't offered him a seat. He was perched on the armrest of a settee. There was a family photograph on a shelf behind her. He tried not to look at it.

It was the first time he had been in this house. He thought it a little old-fashioned. The carpets, the dark-wood furniture. It was not what he imagined. He considered her more… daring.

'I'm sorry,' she said.

She ran a hand through her long hair. She had on a loose dress, no hint of the body beneath it that drove him wild.

'You know how it is,' she added. Again, she fell silent.

'No. Know how what is?'

She turned her head away, staring out the window into the back garden. Beck could see a pond, a jet of water rising from the centre.

Not what he imagined at all.

Was this her house? Or his? The chief superintendent was always one to exert his authority. And that, Beck knew, extended to his marriage. He knew that was why – part of the reason why – she had sought an affair. An escape. He didn't care. Then or now. He knew what he wanted. Which suited them both just fine.

'Seems a bit odd,' he said, 'when you say you don't want anything to do with me.'

Her head snapped round to look at him.

'Wrong,' she said. 'I *can't* have anything to do with you. There's a difference.'

'So... You ring to what? Tease me? And yourself?'

She smiled, the little crease lines beside her eyes filling with folds of flesh. He loved that smile.

'Maybe?' she said.

Silence descended between them.

'Why not *not* tease?' he said.

'What does that mean? Not *not* tease?' The smile again. 'I think you better go, Beck. He'll be home very soon.'

He'll – she was not bothering to use his first name.

Still, Beck did not move.

She turned towards the window again.

'I won't ring you again. Promise. Now go.'

CHAPTER FIFTY-NINE

The train arrived in Cross Beg. As Beck walked along the platform he saw her standing at the end. He nodded as he drew near, confused about whether to stop briefly and say hello, or just keep walking.

'I took a chance,' Mrs Claxton said. 'That you'd be on the train. Can we talk?'

'Um... yes, but I... Yes, we can talk.'

'I can give you a lift. You going back to the house?'

'Yes. I am. Thanks.'

Mrs Claxton made small talk as she drove, cutting off any hint of silence before it could take hold. Beck sat back, content to gaze out the window. At the house he laid his bag on the kitchen floor and they sat at the table. He wanted her to leave again as quickly as possible. He could see the all too familiar signs because he usually suffered from them himself: the bloodshot eyes, the rattled nerves, the inability to sit still. She had the mother of all hangovers.

'I don't mean to be clingy.' She gave a nervous giggle, like she was still a little under the influence. 'I'm not a lovelorn teenager, I'm of a certain age, after all. I just want to know where I stand, that's all. In this relationship.'

'Relationship.' Beck repeated it like he'd just been presented with an outlandish restaurant bill.

'Yes... darling.'

Beck stood, went and picked up his bag. 'Mrs Claxton...'

'It's Sheila.'

'… Mrs Claxton. I have to get to the garda station. Please. We can talk about this later. I must go.'

She got to her feet slowly, came and stood inches from him. 'Only if you promise to see me later. Promise me that. We can discuss it then.' She lingered.

Beck looked at her in silence. When he sensed she was about to lean in, he picked up his bag. 'Yes. We can talk later. Now, I really must get going.'

She paused, her eyes searching his. Without a word she turned and left the room. Beck waited for the sound of the front door closing before going quickly up the stairs to his bedroom. He took his old uniform from the bag. It was crumpled and smelt of mould. He debated whether to wear it or not, a part of him wanting to show the world his newly restored authority. But he hung it up and closed the wardrobe door.

CHAPTER SIXTY

'Look, Beck, maybe we got off on the wrong foot, okay? And congratulations, by the way. Inspector Beck.' O'Reilly was driving his own car, a grey, mud-splattered Volkswagen Passat. They were on their way to the murder scene on Bog Road. 'You know how it is,' he continued, 'when you're of higher rank, everybody hates you. I'll admit, I could have been more civil... You'll need an office, by the way.'

Beck looked out the window, uncomfortable with O'Reilly's new-found affability.

'No,' Beck answered. 'I'll float about, the way I have been doing. I like it that way.'

'Fine,' O'Reilly said with a wide, false smile. 'The body was removed late last night, by the way.'

'Autopsy?'

'Not yet. The deputy state pathologist is still at the scene.'

'Nigel McBride was released from custody?'

'A little after eight this morning. He was held overnight.'

The silence between them became thick and heavy.

'An exact time of death will be hard to measure,' O'Reilly said.

'He was a friend of yours, wasn't he?' Beck asked.

'Well... We played football together one time. We knew each other, yes.'

O'Reilly glanced over at him, the old O'Reilly, peeking out from underneath his sudden false guise of geniality. 'What you need to know about a town like this is that everybody who thinks they matter are friends of people who think they matter, until they don't matter, get it?'

And Beck had an image of McBride languishing in a prison cell while O'Reilly climbed the next rung on his career ladder and the next step on the stairs in McBride's house to shag his wife.

'It's in the DPP's hands now,' Beck said. 'Either way, he's going to get prison time.'

O'Reilly's false smile disappeared, as if he was reading Beck's thoughts.

CHAPTER SIXTY-ONE

There was a sole guard with a clipboard outside the scene on Bog Road. O'Reilly and Beck pulled on crime scene suits from the back of the Technical Bureau van. O'Reilly remained at the door of the house talking to a technician who was using a blue light on the skirting board just inside. Beck continued, found Dr Price at the end of the hallway, giving instructions to an assistant, a breathing mask hanging loose around her neck. Beck recognised the deputy state pathologist by the way Gumbell had described her: small and mousy with short hair and bottle-lensed glasses.

'Dr Price?'

'Who're you?' Her eyes were wide and curious.

'Ser... Inspector Finnegan Beck.'

'Gumbell told me all about you.' Her tone was that of a mother being introduced to her daughter's new wayward boyfriend.

'A couple of questions?' Beck said.

'Yes, but be quick. I'm busy.'

'Time of death?'

'I would roughly estimate between 10.30 p.m. and 1 a.m. That's Thursday night into Friday morning.'

'Would it be possible,' Beck began, 'to tell anything about the stature of the person who did this? Is that possible?'

'Yes, somewhat,' Dr Price answered. 'By the way, we lifted a bloodstained fingerprint impression from the lampshade by the bed. Other surfaces had been cleaned, but this print was captured on the fabric of the shade and is perfectly intact. It had been on the side facing the curtain, so presumably the killer didn't notice it. It's been uploaded to the system. There's no match.'

Who was this person? A phantom?

'It was missed earlier, the print, I mean?' Beck said.

'Looks like it. My technical team found it.'

'It was the Scene of Crime officer from Galway who dusted the place first,' O'Reilly said, coming down the hall, preventing any blame from sticking to himself. 'He went through the place while we waited for forensics to arrive from Dublin.' He looked at Beck. 'He was in the area.'

'No one is saying anything,' Beck said. 'It was a correct call to make.'

'About what you asked,' Dr Price said. 'There are multiple wounds to the torso, too many to count here. Some, in the middle of the chest area' – she indicated with her hand – 'display a ripping effect, consistent with the killer tugging on the handle in an upward motion in extracting the blade. This tells me he was standing over her, leaning in, or stretching, like this.' She played out the motion, bending forward and thrusting an imaginary knife through the air. Beck felt she was working it out for herself too. 'A smaller person would have been unable to do this. They would have been unable to lean over the body, they would have had to maybe crouch on the bed in order to get into a position to stab the victim. In that scenario, the stab wounds would be from above, the incisions cleaner. Which is not the case here. In this instance, it's likely the person was leaning forward, and in order to extract the blade, like I say, pulled forward and up, because he wasn't directly above the victim, he was to the front and side. Therefore, the killer was tall, I have no doubt, oh, and very athletic. It took quite a lot of force to do what he did.'

'Thank you, doctor.'

'I can show you. The body. Demonstrate. It may make more sense.'

'That's okay. You just did.'

CHAPTER SIXTY-TWO

The big house was silent. Karen McBride sat on the edge of the armchair by the empty fireplace, staring into it, her hands knitted together. She'd been crying, but now it took too much effort to even do that, for she was tired, so tired. So she sat there, not moving. She felt that if she sat for long enough, and didn't move, then somehow, some way, this might all pass by, move to another realm and leave her and her family alone.

But that would not happen. She knew that. She could not turn back the clock, could not go to a time before this terrible thing had occurred.

They say he might have killed her, too.

She thought about that: that he might have *killed* her.

He'd had sex with her. He'd put his penis into her. Put his penis into a girl who was young enough to be his daughter, who was the best friend of his daughter. Had done things to that child that no man should do to any child. He had done all that. Her husband. The father of her children.

Still, she did not move.

The silence had a sound all of its own. She could hear it. She could hear it louder than anything she had ever heard in her life before.

Still, she did not move.

Melanie had screamed earlier. When she'd arrived home from school. A long, visceral scream. That's where she'd heard about it, at school, the poor child – that her father had been arrested. Her daughter had heard about it even before she had. And then she'd run all the way home, left her bag and coat behind and arrived, hysterical, to the house. The school had rung ahead, thankfully, told her what had happened. And that's how she had found out, too, from the school, in a roundabout way.

Melanie had screamed at her, demanding to know how could she have married an animal like him. Blaming her, but not yet able to blame him. Screaming about how the children of an animal turned out to be animals too. Screaming that she and her brother were the spawn of evil, the offspring of the devil.

She would have to check on Melanie later. When she got up from this chair, that is. Paul was in his room too, and the house was completely silent. But Melanie was the one she worried about. Her daughter was fragile, she'd always known that, delicate, like a flower petal. More so since the death of Tanya.

And now…

Jesus, and now…

She wanted to move, to get up and check. But she couldn't; she couldn't move, just couldn't.

In her room, Melanie lay on her bed, a slow Justin Bieber song playing on the stereo, the speaker lights changing from soft green to yellow to red. The curtains were drawn and the room's lights were off, but the shifting lights from the speakers gave the room a mystical aura. She coasted on her high, carried on its jet stream, way up, soaring and diving, feeling the wind on her face. She touched her cheek and smiled, turned her head and looked about, as if seeing everything for the first time. She reached down and picked up the empty blister packs of Xanax and Diazepam on the floor by the bed, raised her arm and dropped them onto her chest, watching them fall. The trouble with Xanax was that when you got high you could never be sure how many you'd taken; it was never possible to remember. She reached in under her pillow. There were four Xanax tablets hidden there. She popped them into her mouth one by one and swallowed, turned her face towards the ceiling, feeling nothing. Nothing at all.

CHAPTER SIXTY-THREE

There were twenty investigators in the Ops Room. Beck had called everyone back. He detected grumpiness and a lethargy of movement as they milled about, searching out seats and sitting down. When the room had settled, Beck saw the confusion on their faces. They looked at him standing alongside Wilde and O'Reilly at the top of the room. Wilde had pulled in his beloved whiteboard, while Beck had arranged a small table next to it.

Beck addressed the assembly. 'Good evening, people. I know it's been a long day. I don't want to keep you any longer than I need to. Just a few items to go through, then you can go, get some well-earned rest and we start this thing afresh in the morning. Okay?'

He surveyed the faces. No one spoke.

'Right,' he continued. 'I won't go into the ins and outs of this, but I've been restored to my previous rank of inspector. Has anyone ever heard of a murder book?'

Heads shook.

'I have created a murder book on Pulse. Anything anyone has done up to this point I want put into that book, properly dated and with a shoulder number, so I know who put it there. I don't need to tell anyone that this case is not straightforward. If we are to include Ned Donohue, we now have three murders on our hands. In the space of one week. This doesn't look like it's going to stop either.'

A hand went up.

'Yes,' Beck said. 'Introduce yourself, by the way.'

'Michael McCarthy, on temporary assignment from Athlone. You think Ned is a victim too?'

Beck nodded. 'I do.'

'And what about Nigel McBride?' McCarthy asked. 'There's a feeling now that he's our man.'

'Is there? And maybe he is,' Beck said. 'But it's doubtful. Consider for now that he's not. A print lifted from Bog Road was not his. I don't want anyone putting him into their back pocket for the murder of Tanya Frazzali, knowing that if all else fails they can pull him out. That won't work.'

People shifted about on their chairs.

'Instead I want people to pursue this thought for a moment,' Beck said. 'That Tanya Frazzali was not killed by McBride. When Ned Donohue claimed to have seen someone kill her, believe it. Ned was then killed by this same person, and it was made to look like a suicide. Not as difficult as it may sound, if you think about it. The killer comes across Ned by the river, possibly followed him there, simply pushed him into the water. We have another victim now, of course: Imelda Butler.'

Beck paused, looked about the room. He'd got their attention. 'What's running through this is the apparent randomness of it all. And also something else. The increasing violence. Imelda Butler was viciously murdered. The modus operandi appears to have changed. The killer is becoming increasingly erratic. Something I want to bring to people's attention… Claire?'

Claire Somers had been sitting quietly at her desk. She stood now and strode to the top of the room, a laptop tucked under her arm. She put the computer down onto the table Beck had placed beside the whiteboard and plugged a mini-projector into a USB port. She asked for someone to lower the lights, and as these dimmed two enlarged images appeared side by side on the wall at the top of the room. One was of Norman Blake, in the crowd at Tanya Frazzali's funeral, the other a grainy CCTV still image of the bridge attacker of Nina Sokolov. Claire looked to Beck, who nodded to her.

'Inspector Beck asked me yesterday to prepare these PowerPoint shots.' She quickly outlined the background to the images, and continued, 'If we take both images and...' She pressed a couple of keys and one image merged onto the top of the other, becoming an almost exact fit. 'We can see that both individuals share the same features. In fact, we can say it is very likely this is one and the same person.'

'Does everyone agree with that?' Beck asked the room.

'Well, I don't.' It was Inspector O'Reilly. He pointed. 'See there? The face profile is a bit off. And the arms. The differences are subtle, granted, but differences between people are subtle anyway.'

Beck looked. He was right, of course. But still, many similarities remained.

'Can anyone put a name to the images?' Beck asked.

There was a murmuring in the room, but no one felt brave enough to say it out loud.

Beck nodded to Claire again, and a third image appeared on screen, a head-and-shoulders shot. She duplicated the image and reduced it in size, superimposed it onto the other two.

Beck could see Superintendent Wilde's mouth open as he stared at the face looking down at him from the wall.

'We need a warrant,' he said. 'Right now.'

CHAPTER SIXTY-FOUR

'Mr Blake.'

The shop assistant, Rebecca, the prettier of the two, popped her head round the drugs storeroom door, lips coated in glistening ruby-red lipstick. He tried not to look at those luscious apples of temptation because lately he had begun to realise he was forming a habit of staring at them.

'A customer to see you. I brought her to the consultation room.'

'What, now?' It was almost closing time.

The consultation room was what his mother used to call the pantry. He'd had it converted, capitalising on a health service grant initiative designed to relieve pressure on doctors' surgeries. People were now encouraged to see their local pharmacist instead, to seek advice and buy the latest expensive non-prescription remedies.

'I'll be there in a minute.'

He took the boxes he had come for and went back out into the dispensary, put these away into their relevant cabinets, stepped out from behind the dispensary counter and opened the door to the consultation room, which was covered in smoked glass for privacy. And smelt it immediately, the pungent aroma of soap and, what was that? Peach body wash? It overpowered all other aromas, that of the expensive perfumes and colognes from the fragrance section, the biscuity medicine smell that always seemed to hang in the air everywhere in the shop. All now gone. His nose twitched. It was almost enough to make him gag.

When he saw her he got a sudden sick, hollow feeling in the pit of his belly. She was sitting on one of the two low stools – there wasn't enough room for proper chairs – wearing a loose, light grey tracksuit, hood up, legs crossed, one knee cupped tightly in both hands. He noticed her fingernails, alternating pink and red, a sprinkling of sparkle.

'Melanie.' He was forcing himself not to shout. 'I told you not to come here. I told you. I told you all not to fucking come here.'

Melanie pouted. 'You heard about my father? My life is crap right now. I need something. And you're going to give it to me.'

She bit her lower lip, sat back, leaning against the wall, then came forward again, uncupped her hands from around her knee, placed them under her thighs.

'I don't know,' he said. 'I can't give you something just like that. We have arrangements in place.' Blake didn't like this. Didn't like this one bit. Darren Murphy was supposed to take care of this stuff now. Blake himself was never meant to get involved. Never.

'You're high, aren't you?' he said. 'Look at you. Jesus!'

Melanie looked at him, felt something she had never felt before: an exhilarating rush, better than any bungee jump, better than any roller coaster ride, better than any drift around the Tesco car park in Ballinasloe in Sean Murphy's Subaru after midnight. It was better than *anything*. It was power. A power she'd never felt before.

'You'll do as I say,' she said, slurring her words, staring at him, her bravado disguising the fact that she feared all the same that he might suddenly slap her across the face and send her on her way.

But that's not what he did. Blake rubbed his eyes wearily with two big chubby fingers and left the consultation room. He came back with one box of 20 mg Xanax and one box of 30 mg Diazepam.

'You'll pay for these as normal,' he said. 'Tell Rebecca that a prescription will follow.'

'No, I won't pay,' Melanie said. She laughed. 'Because I have no money. All I have is my black lace panties.'

His face reddened.

'Why not?' she said, enjoying his reaction. 'Don't you like young girls, too? My father does. Creep. Are you a creep as well?'

But then her smile disappeared and she looked like she might cry.

Blake wanted her out of here as quickly as possible.

She began fumbling with the box of Xanax, tearing it open, pulling out a blister pack, squeezing a couple of capsules from the foil wrapping.

'Not here,' he said. 'Jesus. Not here.'

She enjoyed his reaction; it took her mind off things.

'Why not?' she said, popping both capsules into her mouth.

Blake looked on helplessly, said nothing. *Yes*, she thought. *This is it, control.* That did something for her. Weird, or what? But it did *something* for her. She shivered, but it wasn't the cold, it was the thought of it. He was old enough to be her father.

The sound of a commotion outside on the shop floor got their attention. Blake stood, pushed open the door of the consultation room enough to see out. And looked right into the eyes of the big policeman, the one who'd been in the other day for paracetamol, the one he'd seen at Tanya's funeral. The big policeman wasn't alone either – there was a half-dozen uniformed officers with him.

Blake did something his rational mind told him was useless, but he went ahead and did it anyway. He closed the consultation room door and hoped they would all just go away.

But immediately the door swung open again, almost striking him in the face, and the big policeman entered.

'I'll have those,' Beck said, swiping the two boxes from Melanie's hands as she tried to push them down inside her tracksuit bottoms.

Melanie glared.

'Hello again, Melanie,' Beck said.

'They're not mine. I just picked them up.'

Beck held the warrant out for Blake to see. 'This is a warrant to search your premises. Is there anything you'd like to tell us about before we begin?'

Blake's shoulders crumpled as he reached out, steadying himself against a wall.

'My wife. She has MS. If I could ask, please, don't disturb her. I'll show you everything.'

'Where is she?'

'In her room. Sleeping.'

'We still need to search every room.'

'Please.'

Beck nodded. 'We can leave it till last, then.'

'It's this way,' Blake said.

'What? What's this way?'

'What you're looking for. Someone's tipped you off, haven't they? I'm relieved, in a way. I can't take this any longer.'

'What we're looking for,' Beck said. 'Yes, lead the way.'

A uniform was left with Melanie while another cleared the shop and locked the doors. Beck followed Blake into the living area, up the stairs to the first floor. Blake took a key from his pocket, opened a door and threw it open, stepped aside.

Beck heard the hum of ventilators, shading his eyes against the harsh white light spilling out of the room. With it came the smell. He stood in the doorway and peered in, looking at a miniature forest of swaying cannabis plants.

But that wasn't all.

CHAPTER SIXTY-FIVE

O'Reilly had not been part of the search team, but he came straight over when he was informed of the positive result. Beck led him through the property. He looked dazed, like he couldn't keep up with the speed of events. Which was probably true. Beck guessed he'd had to deal with more in the past week than in his entire career.

There were three rooms, and the plants were already being pulled from their pots, numbered and placed into evidence bags.

'How many?' O'Reilly asked.

'Three rooms,' Beck said. 'I'd guess about two hundred and twenty plants.'

'That many? And there was something else, is that right?'

'Yes, there was.'

They went back down the stairs. Beck led the way into the basement, a uniform standing at the bottom. The basement was a large rectangular space, support pillars running down either side. At one end two long trestle tables had been placed end to end. Various buckets were scattered on the floor next to each, the buckets lined with plastic bags containing a white powder. On one of the tables was a Bunsen burner and various glass jars and tubes.

'I believe it's a factory,' Beck said.

'Doesn't look like any factory I've ever seen,' O'Reilly replied.

'For the manufacture of methamphetamine.'

'Methamphetamine.' O'Reilly could hardly pronounce the word. 'You can't be serious.'

'Unfortunately I am. Looks like that to me.'

O'Reilly said nothing, looking about the room. 'Right under our noses. I never… I mean. Why? Has he said?'

'No. He hasn't been interviewed yet.'

O'Reilly looked at Beck, fisted his hand and held it in the air. As they bumped fists, Beck thought it was the silliest thing he had done in a long while, which was saying something.

The curtains were pulled in Blake's wife's room, and a night light glowed on a table next to a medical bed with its sides pulled up. There was a smell of talcum powder and bleach, and sickness. The body shape underneath the blanket could have been that of a child. Blake leaned over the bed and looked down at his wife. The shape beneath the blankets stirred.

'Are you alright, darling?' he said softly. His wife said something indiscernible in a weak, dry voice. 'It's okay,' he soothed. 'I'm just showing these people around. It's nothing to worry about.'

Blake straightened, turned and walked over to Beck. 'She's soiled,' he said. 'She needs to be changed. I'm the only one who can do it. Could we have some privacy?'

'I'm sorry,' Beck said. 'That's not possible. You're under arrest. I need to remain with you.'

'What will happen? To my wife? Who's going to care for her?'

'I imagine social services.'

'What have I done?' Blake muttered, as if to himself. 'Oh, God. What have I done?'

In the silence of the room he undressed her with practised efficiency, cleaned her with a soft cotton flannel, placed on her a fresh nappy and nightdress and pulled the blankets up loosely about her chin. He kissed her forehead and raised the sides of the bed again. They clicked into place.

Beck stood in a corner of the room, waiting. Blake came to him and he led him out. O'Reilly ordered two uniforms to take the prisoner to the station. As he was led away, his hulking frame between two guards, Blake paused briefly in the doorway to the street outside. Beck watched, wondering if he was about to turn and say something. The guards on either side stiffened. But he bowed his head, said nothing, continued to walk away.

CHAPTER SIXTY-SIX

In Interview Room One at Cross Beg station, after he'd been given the cup of coffee he'd asked for and which he now left untouched on the table in front of him, Blake began to talk. Beside him was Harold Gray, his solicitor, who Beck insisted on having present, and on the other side of the table, Beck, O'Reilly and Wilde.

Blake began by talking about his lonely existence, of the years spent caring for his wife, of feeling utterly trapped, of having no one to talk to.

'No one knows what it's like,' he whined on. 'No one. People asked about my wife. How she was. In the beginning, that is, but then gradually, as the years passed, they didn't bother any more, except maybe the odd time, like an afterthought. But really, I knew that they couldn't care less. It was then I came to realise that ultimately people don't care about anybody else but themselves. That was quite a revelation to me because I'd never thought about it like that before, I always looked for the good in people. They act as if they do care, but they don't, not really, it's just all about them, once you scratch the surface a little bit, even when they themselves think it's not, if that makes any sense.

'You know, they come into my pharmacy complaining about, I don't know, athlete's foot or something, or wanting to lose weight, like nothing else matters in the whole world. I'd think if they wanted to lose weight they should stop eating so much and get some exercise. They buy multivitamins and supplements, organic coffee and sugar alternatives, colonic irrigation products, probiotics with billions of active cells in every capsule. No need for any of it. And don't get me started on "Made in California". If "Made in California" is printed on the label, the land of the permanently young, the never dead, the Botox and supplement waifs in the land of the unfat, it's "gimme gimme gimme", don't care what it is, they just want it anyway. It's all a sad joke, enough to drive a man insane. Meanwhile, the really sick ones, the ill people like my wife, they slowly die, forgotten about.'

So. Blake was angry, Beck decided. But angry enough to kill?

'I tried alcohol,' Blake went on, and Beck's ears pricked up. 'But every time I got drunk I was sick for three days afterwards. Not sick like I was puking in the toilet, you understand, but sick depressed, not wanting to do anything, just wanting to hide.'

Then drink again, Beck thought. Problem solved.

'I tried drugs next. After all, I was surrounded by them. But that didn't work either, because sometimes I got high preparing prescriptions, and a couple of times I got it wrong. I knew it was only a matter of time before I killed someone, and I didn't want to do that. So I stopped.'

The three police officers exchanged glances.

'It started with a lottery scratch card. I won a hundred euro. Amazing how quickly it escalated after that. You know what the biggest buzz of all was? The losing. That's what. Isn't that mad? The more I lost, the... how can I put this, the *happier* I became. Happy in my misery is how I heard it once described. It completely obliterated every other feeling I had, which is what I wanted. I knew then. That gambling was for me. That I'd found my escape. And boy, did I find it.'

Beck thought of Jason Geraghty, lying dead on the stairs leading to the number one Thai restaurant in Dublin.

'It's funny how these people can sniff an opportunity,' he went on. 'When I became desperate, really desperate, I seriously contemplated robbing a bank. I didn't care. I quite liked the idea of being an outlaw. But I couldn't do it. I could, I mean, I was capable of it. But what would happen to Mary? It was then that they came to me, like they could sense the best time to move in for the kill, just as a wild animal would. They knew I was already supplying prescription pills. Yes, I was. Amazing what you'll do for money when you have to. You'll do anything.

'That got out of hand, the prescription drug thing. I'm amazed you, the gardai, didn't know about it. I had schoolkids literally queuing outside my door sometimes, during their lunch hour. I tried to stop it, but they wouldn't listen. Anyway. They came to me. They said they'd take all my problems away. They'd look after it. And they did. Overnight, the queues disappeared. They would give me the orders and I'd fill them. All I had to do was... do what they told me. And I did. It worked. I was so preoccupied with the new arrangement that I didn't gamble. I didn't have the headspace, I was shitting myself with the worry of this new thing instead. You know, I have to say, I'm glad I've been caught. Really. Because in the end it all became too much. They wanted me to do more and more.' Blake lowered his eyes. 'But Mary, what's going to happen to her?'

'You refer to those people as they,' O'Reilly said. 'Who are "they"?'

Blake's solicitor leaned in, whispered something in his ear.

'No comment,' Blake replied.

Beck didn't care about who those people were or were not. There was only one thing he wanted to know.

'Did you murder Tanya Frazzali?'

Wilde and O'Reilly turned, but before Mr Gray could say anything, Blake had spoken. 'You think I'd do something like that?'

'You tell me,' Beck said.

'I'm not a murderer. I didn't kill anyone.'

'Did you supply her? Was Tanya one of your customers?' Beck pressed.

'No comment,' Mr Gray said quickly, but Blake raised his hand to silence him.

'Yes. She was. A few Xanax pills every weekend. That was it. She was a good kid. I think she was just trying to fit in.'

'Do you have any idea who might have killed her?'

Blake bowed his head. 'No.'

'I would like to consult with my client before you pursue any further line of enquiry,' Gray said. 'I've literally just arrived, there's been no preliminary.'

Wilde nodded, raised his hand to Beck, pressed the recorder off.

CHAPTER SIXTY-SEVEN

He could smell Mrs Claxton when he got home – she was in the air, a mixture of perfume and something else, lavender maybe. But it was her smell. He went through the rooms, finally to the bedroom, where it was most pungent, where he imagined she had lingered. It didn't disturb him that she had been here. He listened, could hear nothing through the walls from next door. He lit a cigarette and sat in the living room, smoking and playing over details of the case in his mind, his thoughts wandering to Spanish brandy, cold cans of lager and drunken escapades. But he didn't *feel* like a drink. *Be grateful for small mercies*, he told himself.

As he smoked, he felt the tiredness begin to crawl through his body. By the time he threw the cigarette butt into the empty fire grate, it was all he could do to get up, make his way into the hall and climb the stairs. In the bathroom he looked at the dark rings beneath his eyes. Perhaps he could take a holiday when this was all over, an all-inclusive week-long break somewhere in the Costas? He went to bed thinking of this, of twinkling water tickling his feet, of hot sand and cold beers under beach umbrellas. He knew he was fooling himself – he didn't really intend to go – but still he wondered, and hoped that happy thoughts might mean that tonight they would not come for him, they would leave him in peace, hidden in their lairs buried deep within himself.

They did not leave him alone, of course. They came; one by one they filed up from below, stretching and waking, chattering amongst themselves, eager to resume where they had left off, eager to display their annoyance at having been neglected for so long.

In his sleep he talked and muttered and shouted, raised his hands and sliced them through the air as if trying to swat an imaginary fly. Finally he awoke with a jolt, with a feeling that someone had been watching him. The room was still, the sound of the wind outside like the breathing of a giant. He lay there, his own breathing quick and shallow, the bedclothes hot with sweat. He pulled back the duvet, the cold air on his flesh bringing him instantly awake. He glanced at his watch on the bedside locker – just gone 2.30 a.m. He lay back on the bed, and listened as his breathing calmed and became more regular.

A sound.

Beck listened.

Like grains of sand falling, fading.

He sat up quickly, resting on one elbow, and looked about the room. He saw it just as it reached a corner, disappearing into a crack in the skirting board. A cockroach, a great big cockroach. Beck had never seen a cockroach in the house before. He'd heard mice scurrying about in the attic when he'd first moved in, yes, but nothing since Mrs Claxton had called in the exterminators.

The feeling came to Beck slowly. It was nothing more than that, a feeling. But Beck was familiar with feelings, with respecting and listening to them, and understood that he had to be patient, to wait until he knew what it was they were trying to tell him.

He lay on his side, very still, his chin hanging over the edge of the bed. Whatever it was, it was from below, somewhere down there.

Beck pushed himself further forward on the bed, his face now resting along the side of it. His hand lowered and he coiled a finger around the edge of the duvet, began to hoist it up as he slowly peered underneath the bed...

Oh shit!

Mrs Claxton's wide, frozen eyes stared back at him, grey flesh, lips twisted with terrible torment. But it was the eyes, as if they were silently screaming, beseeching him to come and help her, to rescue her. But he could not. She was past all that now.

CHAPTER SIXTY-EIGHT

Beck stood in the kitchen with the night sergeant, Eddie Connor. Beck could tell by the sergeant's demeanour that he wasn't sure how to deal with him. He also knew by the suspicious glances he threw his way that he was weighing up the odds of the killer being the man who was now standing opposite him.

'Won't be long,' Connor said. 'Superintendent Wilde's on his way.' And with an air of authority: 'Take a seat, you're making me nervous standing there.'

Beck sat down, said, 'It looks like she was strangled. I'd say she's been dead a good few hours. I was at the station before I came here. Before that I was on an operation with a half-dozen others. Before that I was in Dublin. Just saying, Connor.'

And he remembered. Mrs Claxton at the railway station. He pondered this as Connor threw another dubious look his way. He said nothing.

Sergeant Connor had red eyes and the pasty skin of the night shift worker. He licked his dry lips. 'I never said it was you.' But his tone was unconvinced.

At 3.10 a.m. Superintendent Wilde arrived. He stood in the kitchen in a tracksuit, hands on hips, observing Beck. 'I'm trying to get my head around this. I'm having difficulty. How did the body of Sheila Claxton get under your bed? My wife played bridge with the woman. This is some shock, I can tell you.'

'Yes, it is,' Beck said. 'Believe me, I don't know how her body got under my bed. I didn't kill her. She was my landlady. She had a key.'

'Your relationship was strictly professional, was it?' Wilde asked.

'Yes,' Beck lied. It wouldn't serve Mrs Claxton's reputation if he were to reveal the truth. Her memory would be nothing more than a titter behind a raised hand for years to come.

'You're a suspect, of course,' Wilde said. 'Of sorts. But I wouldn't worry too much about it. I imagine you'll be quickly eliminated.' He looked at his watch. 'They won't get here until morning, of course.'

'Dr Price,' Beck said. 'She's already in Cross Beg.'

'No, she's not. She went back to Dublin late yesterday evening. There's nobody around except us.'

'And Inspector O'Reilly?'

'No answer from his phone when I rang. I didn't expect one, mind. He's not on call. Can't be on call all the time, you know? The door to Mrs Claxton's house next door was open, by the way, there's signs of a struggle in the hallway. We didn't go in – leaving that to forensics. Why her? Why leave her body here? Your house, was it locked?'

'Of course,' Beck said. 'But she had a key, like I said.'

'Perhaps she came looking for help,' Wilde said. 'But it's too early to make any assumptions.'

Beck had mixed emotions. He did not want to attempt to rationalise it, because rationality did not apply. Mrs Claxton, he told himself, was dead because some crazy fucker had killed her, not because of any association he had with her. It was the killer who was responsible, not Beck, and not Mrs Claxton. But why had somebody apparently gone to a great deal of trouble to place her body underneath his bed? There was also something else. A sadness. And grief. But more than anything, anger.

'There's nothing can be done until morning now, anyway,' Wilde said then. 'The scene is secure, there'll be people here all night. You need rest, Beck. We both do. You can't stay here, not for a while … If you ever want to stay here again, that is. No, come with me. I insist.'

CHAPTER SIXTY-NINE

They know me now. Or should I say, they know of me. I'm not a one-off. They know something has awakened, something they can't understand, something cleverer than any of them. Something they can't stop. I am invisible. No one sees me. I go where I please. I kill who I please. The hotshot, the one from Dublin, the one called Beck. He has noticed me. Oh yes, he has noticed me. I left her under his bed. I particularly enjoyed that. I realise that I no longer care about life and death. I only care about death.

I've been doing this a long time. A very long time. They don't know how long. They don't know anything.

The one called Beck. How good is he really? I know something for certain. That he is not good enough.

CHAPTER SEVENTY

Mrs Wilde had the quiet acceptance that comes with being a senior policeman's wife. She was accustomed to middle-of-the-night telephone calls, struggling to keep dinners warm for hours on end and sleeping with one eye open, unable to relax until finally she heard the sound of her husband's key in the door.

So she was not surprised when she came downstairs to the living room and found her husband with Beck. Beck fell quiet when she came into the room, until Wilde announced, 'You can relax, Beck. Vera can be trusted. We've been married thirty years. I tell her everything. Otherwise I'd crack up.'

Beck looked at Wilde's wife, this tall woman who carried herself with a quiet reserve, who moved lightly without much sound. She disappeared for a moment and was back again with a plate of sandwiches under cling film on a tray, pre-prepared and waiting for a moment just like this. Beck said he wasn't hungry, but she watched as a succession of sandwiches quickly disappeared into his mouth anyway.

'You knew Mrs Claxton,' he said, swallowing, realising suddenly that if both women were friends, then she might have told this woman about him.

'We were in the same bridge club, yes,' Vera said. 'But Sheila was a very quiet woman. Kept things to herself. She didn't have many friends, not really. I don't know anything about her private life, no one did.' Vera looked at Beck, and her expression changed. 'Andrew says she was found in your house.'

'It was her house,' Beck answered. 'I merely rented it.'

He could tell what she was thinking. So too could her husband.

'Vera, don't put two and two together and come up with five. We believe the poor woman had been dead for hours. Beck here was at the station, and before that he was in Dublin.'

She gave a nervous smile. 'Of course. With all that's been going on lately, my nerves are beginning to get a little frayed. Someone out there is… Shocking when you think about it.'

'I was thinking,' Wilde said to his wife. 'Perhaps you could get away for a few days? Stay with your sister down in County Cork.'

'What, Andrew? You don't mean someone might… Oh my God.'

Wilde placed his big arm around his wife. 'It just occurred to me. It'll only be for a little while. As a precaution.' He kissed her cheek, got to his feet. 'In the meantime, Beck, let me show you to your room. It's not long until morning. Come on.'

CHAPTER SEVENTY-ONE

When daylight broke, so too did the story. Though it had been there all along, in newspapers and TV reports, it had been subdued, done with the unspoken understanding that, regarding Tanya Frazzali at least, the killer had likely known his victim. It was a crime of passion – no one really had anything to worry about; it was only a matter of time before the killer was caught and brought to justice. Killers were usually caught and brought to justice quickly; homicide detection rates in Ireland were amongst the highest in Europe.

But suddenly that had all changed. The murderer had not been caught. Instead, the morning radio news programme on the national broadcaster RTE led with the story of yet another murder victim in Cross Beg. The story also ran on Sky News and the BBC TV news. The late city editions of some of the print newspapers had it, too. One tabloid headline screamed: 'Butchered: Latest Victim of Serial Killer'. There was no mention that, actually, it was unknown as yet how the victim had died, or that the body had been discovered in the home and under the bed – *under the bed* – of a serving police officer. But soon it would be public knowledge.

At 7.45 a.m., even before the arrival of the Garda Technical Bureau's big-panel van, a TV satellite truck arrived in Cross Beg, pulled in against the kerb a short distance down from the garda station. The front passenger door opened and a man in a crisp blue suit got out. He ran a hand through his hair and checked himself in the door mirror. He had fifteen minutes before he was due on air, the first live TV report from Cross Beg since this had all started.

Some of his coverage would be fed to the twenty-four-hour news channels, which would run segments of it on a loop. Serial killing was good for news ratings, good for business.

CHAPTER SEVENTY-TWO

Eleanor Murphy, retired schoolteacher, stood at the top of the beach, known locally as Haven's Cove, next to the sand dunes, and called out, 'Mozart, Mozart.'

When there was no response, she called out again, louder this time, a sense of growing concern taking hold, the sound flittering about on the wind. 'Mozart. Mozart.'

She decided, as punishment for Mozart's disobedience, that he would go without his dinner today.

'Mozart. Mozart. Come here, boy. Now!'

Mozart heard her. He'd heard her the first time, cocked his head and contemplated, then went back to the business at hand.

Eleanor Murphy took a step up into the dunes now, muttering under her breath, feeling as she used to feel when one of those little shits she once taught tested her patience. A short, sharp slap across Mozart's snout was in order, for sure. At the very least. That would teach him. The brat.

A gust of wind stirred the sand up into her face. She blinked as the grains entered her eyes and stung them, cursing under her breath. That bloody dog. She was becoming angry now, really angry.

'MOZART! Where are you? MOZART!'

She stepped into the dunes, following the trail that wound between them. It went in a loop pattern, emerging on to the beach a little further on. And there, a short distance in, she observed the tail of Mozart, high in the air, on the other side of a dune next to the beach, as he dug furiously in the sand.

'MOZART, there you...' she said, rounding the side of the dune, her voice trailing off as it was lost to the wind. She stopped, noticed the blotches of what looked like fragments of brown fabric, and how two pieces were joined together by a single button. It had been a jacket one time, although most of it had rotted away by now. Mozart sent a stream of sand back between his hind legs as he continued to dig, obscuring her view. She stepped closer, could see a strip of something white, below it two hollow circles through which the sand disturbed by Mozart filtered through, as if in an hourglass. On the edge of this strip of white she could see a patch of black, dull and viscous. As Mozart cleared away more sand, she determined the patch of black to be hair.

And with it came the realisation of what she was looking at. For the first time in the almost four years since she'd had him, Eleanor Murphy forgot about Mozart, ran screaming from the beach.

CHAPTER SEVENTY-THREE

Inspector Andy Mahony was one of two technical team officers sitting next to the driver on the bench seat of the big Mercedes van. The driver had turned off the satnav when it insisted Haven Cove was part of an archipelago off the northern coast of Alaska. Mahony used a book map instead to provide directions. His map-reading skills were excellent, and soon the big van was travelling along the rutted beach track to Haven Cove.

Except Mahony had made an error, which he noticed now. This was a double call, and somehow he had placed Haven Cove ahead of Railway Road. At the latter, the body of a female had been found, under a bed of all places. That was the priority, and not, he checked his notes again, skeletal remains found by a dog walker, buried on a beach. But too late. They had arrived.

At the end of the track a marked patrol car was parked. The technical van pulled in alongside it, the front wheel mounting the dunes. Mahony got out and stretched, felt the cold, biting sea wind on his face.

'Tape off the area,' he told his sergeant as they walked into the dunes. He could see that part of it had collapsed onto the beach, exposing the bones underneath. 'Clear the surface sand, enough to see what's what, if all the bones are there or not. Don't be fussy, won't make any difference now. While you do that, I'll go over to this Railway Road. You follow when you're ready. As quick as you can, now.'

His telephone rang. It was Dr Gumbell. He knew he was ringing from Beck's house, where the body had been found under the bed, to find out where the hell he was. Mahony acted like he hadn't heard it.

CHAPTER SEVENTY-FOUR

Claire Somers pulled the Focus onto the soft sand along the edge of the track to make way for the marked patrol car approaching at speed. Beck recognised Mahony, the technical officer, sitting in the front passenger seat. He didn't notice Beck, but stared ahead, his face grim.

As Claire attempted to move off again, the wheels of the Focus spun. She deftly changed up a gear, pressed on the accelerator and the Focus gently gained traction as she brought it back onto the track.

The tide was turning, the grey cold water running in from the sea just yards from the dunes. Beck could tell by the dark patches that the water had, moments earlier, reached the dunes themselves. In time, had they not been discovered, the bones would have been carried out to sea and lost to the bottom of the ocean, possibly forever.

A solitary uniformed guard stood in the dunes, wearing a fleece jacket zipped to the neck, a clipboard held under one elbow, both hands in his pockets.

Beck knew the critical work in this instance would take place in both a pathology lab and on a computer keyboard. It would be down to specialists, a forensic anthropologist, an odontologist and possibly an entomologist to officially determine the identity of the remains and cause of death. But Beck knew that sometimes the dead could speak for themselves too in the evidence they left behind. Because of this, identifying the dead, in some instances, was easier than identifying the living.

Beck noted the crime scene tape loosely tied to clumps of rushes in a meandering rectangle.

'Wilde and O'Reilly aren't here,' Claire said.

Beck grunted. The priority was the murder scene on Railway Road. Which made him think of poor Mrs Claxton. He was trying to block out the reality of his brief relationship with her, and that the crime scene was his home. He simply referred to it now as 'Railway Road', and would not mention Mrs Claxton with any other term but 'murder victim'.

They walked into the dunes and stepped over the crime scene tape. The guard noted the time and wrote their names onto his sheet. Two Scene of Crime technicians had already mapped out with yellow tape an area in the sand in a block body shape, long and narrow, and were clearing sand away with surprising speed, placing it into clear plastic bags, to be stored for analysis later. Already the upper torso and head were visible.

'Anything you can tell us? Male or female?'

'Male,' one of the technicians said without looking up. 'Been here a long time, too.'

Beck thought about that. It was unlikely the sand they were bagging would be of much value then.

'How long do you think?' Beck asked. 'Roughly.'

'Years. That's roughly enough. Can't pin it down any better than that. Not yet.'

Beck pointed. 'Looks like he was wearing a tweed jacket. Is that right? And is that hair? Black?'

The technician nodded again. 'Sand is an excellent preservative. Partly because it soaks up moisture so effectively. Probably the reason the particles of clothing and hair have remained. But nothing is that good. It's been a long time.'

'If you were to hazard a guess,' Claire asked, 'what age would you say?'

The technician straightened, creasing his face in concentration. 'The bone formation tells me probably a teenager, late teens, maybe seventeen, eighteen, nineteen tops. And that black hair. Curly and thick, another reason why some of it lasted. But we really need to get it on the table.'

'How tall was he?' asked Beck.

'He was tall. And lanky. We're talking six foot, easy, here. We'll know more when we get him on the table, like I say.'

Beck nodded, turned to Claire. 'Let's get back to the station. We've enough to get on with our own digging now.'

CHAPTER SEVENTY-FIVE

Beck's phone rang. He took it from his pocket and answered.

'Beck. You are not to return to the station, got that? Not today. Not tomorrow. Maybe not ever. You hear me?'

The old O'Reilly was back, reinvigorated by the sniff of opportunity in the air, and the self-righteousness that went with it.

'I hear you. But why?'

'Haven't you seen the headlines? The story's already online. You are a murder suspect. Go have a look. Superintendent Wilde is in full agreement with me, by the way.'

'Where will I go in the meantime? Disneyland?'

'I don't care where you go, smart arse,' O'Reilly growled, and hung up.

'What was that about?' Claire asked.

She brought the Focus to a stop at the end of the beach track, looked both ways as she moved onto the main road. Beck was about to answer when an SUV rounded the bend ahead, travelling fast, too fast. Claire cursed, stabbed the accelerator, and as she reached the correct side of the road, the SUV shot past and turned off onto the beach track. Beck saw it had blacked-out windows. Claire watched in the rear-view mirror as its brake lights glowed and it came to a sudden stop, throwing up mounds of damp sand. Then it started to reverse along the track, swung violently back onto the road, wobbling like a boat caught in rough surf. It began approaching fast in the rear-view mirror. Claire pressed the accelerator again, but this time the six-year-old Focus with a quarter of a million miles on the clock objected. Although the needle slowly began to climb, the engine started to make a low rumbling noise that increased in tandem with the climbing needle. At seventy miles an hour the noise was deafening and she eased her foot back and held her speed steady.

'Right,' Beck said, looking over his shoulder. 'He's breaking the speed limit now. Put on the blues and we'll pull him over.'

The blue lights inside the rear window swirled to life as Beck lowered his window, motioning with his arm for the SUV to pull over. It indicated immediately and followed the Focus onto the hard shoulder where both vehicles came to a stop.

Beck got out and stomped over to the driver's door. As he drew level with it – an explosion of white light. Again. And again. He covered his eyes with both hands, hearing the whoosh and chirping sound of the camera flash each time it activated.

Claire's voice then, high-pitched. He thought to himself, almost smiling, because she'd hate him for thinking it, that her voice sounded so girly. 'Put that camera away. Now!'

Beck leaned against the SUV, his eyes shut tight, waiting for the snowstorm to clear. As he slowly opened his eyes again, the driver crystallised into view. He was young; goatee beard, sideburns, a prominent square chin. Next to him was another man – similar age, clean-cut, holding a Canon camera in his lap, like a harmless pet that couldn't possibly have bitten anybody.

'Sorry about that,' the passenger said. 'Really. The camera motor got stuck. It happens sometimes. Really, really sorry about that. Okay?' But his voice sounded like a verbal smirk. On the SUV dash, next to a large yellow sticker with the word 'Press' in thick black lettering, Beck could see the evening edition of the *Dublin News*, with a similarly lettered headline: 'Murder Victim Found in Cop's House'.

'Bit of advice,' Beck said. 'Fuck off.'

The driver smirked now. 'You want to say something? Promise we'll run it exactly as you give it to us.'

Beck walked back to the Focus, opened the passenger door and looked over at Claire, still standing beside the SUV.

'Come on,' he called.

They were almost at the station when he spoke again. 'Drive past and pull in.'

Reporters were on the street outside the station along with a couple of TV news crews. Beck turned his head and sat low in his seat as they drove by. He took a deep breath and slammed an open fist onto the dashboard in frustration. Claire jumped.

'Jesus, that's not going to help anything,' she said.

'All missing persons cases,' he said, 'over the last fifty or so years have been uploaded to Pulse nationally, did you know that? Accompanied by photographs. Have a look. It has to be in there somewhere.'

'And where will you be?'

Beck thought about that. 'The Hibernian. I'll book a room for a couple of nights.'

'You can stay with us, it's no trouble.'

'Thanks, I appreciate that, really, but The Hibernian should be fine.'

'Well, if you have a problem, let me know.'

'I will,' and, after a pause, 'who's the oldest guard you can think of who served in Cross Beg and is still around? Know anyone?'

Claire didn't have to think about it for long. 'Jim Molyneaux. He was a sergeant here for donkey's years. He's in St Brendan's Nursing Home now, on Bridge Walk.'

'Change of plan. Can you drop me there instead?'

Claire didn't ask any questions, just swung the wheel and pulled out again from the kerb.

CHAPTER SEVENTY-SIX

The nurse with the name tag 'Jacinta' who Beck had stopped in the foyer to ask where he could find Jim Molyneaux was in a hurry. 'Day room,' she replied, slowing down but not stopping. 'By the window.'

A female resident was at the front door Beck had just come through, fumbling with the handle, mumbling to herself. Beck knew that to exit, a second handle higher up had to be pulled at the same time. She looked at Beck. 'Can you open this? I need to collect the children, you see. Himself will be home soon and I've nothing ready.' She looked about, then back to the door, then back to Beck. 'Who are you? Seamus, is it, the coal man?' Finally she looked at the door again, before shuffling slowly away along a corridor.

Beck thought of his dreams. Would the lines between his reality and his dreams one day merge so that his life became a living nightmare? Would he have the courage to seek escape, to end it, before that happened? Many said they would, but yet they drifted on, and drifted over, until it was too late and they were lost.

The day room was large and bright, residents sitting about on high-back armchairs, some watching a loud television in a corner, others looking at newspapers and magazines, and some just looking at their hands. Only one was sitting by the bay window looking out on to the road and across it to the river.

He turned the moment Beck walked into the room.

It was immediately evident in Jim Molyneaux's eyes that there was no problem with merging realities here. His body, however, was ravaged by age, the skin puckered and creased like old leather, the back slumped, even if there was still a full head of white hair on top of it. As Beck approached, he smiled, the smile of someone emerging from the woods and seeing his first human in days.

'Sergeant Molyneaux?' Beck asked.

'I haven't been called that in a long, long time.'

If Beck had closed his eyes, he would not have placed the voice into such a feeble body. It was strong, with the cheerful sing-along rhythm of the southern counties. He was dressed in blue pyjama bottoms and a T-shirt. It was warm in the day room.

'You look like a cop,' Molyneaux added.

'Inspector Finnegan Beck,' said Beck, offering his hand.

They shook and Beck pulled up a chair and sat down.

'Inspectors, the bane of my life.' Molyneaux's face crumpled into an exaggerated frown.

'Maybe you could help me with something?' Beck asked.

'And maybe you could help me with something, too. Go and get my wheelchair from my room. Number seven' – he nodded his head – 'just down there. Take me out for a bit. Can you do that? I'll need a coat, too.' He lowered his voice. 'In the top drawer by the bed, at the back, there's a packet of fags and a lighter. Now, good lad, can you look after all that?'

Beck nodded. 'I can look after all that.'

Molyneaux's room was clean, functional, *sterile*. A bottle of blackcurrant squash sat on the bed tray, but no other signs were evident that anyone occupied this space. An overcoat and a couple of shirts hung in the wardrobe, some socks and underwear on the shelves. Beck took the overcoat, found the pack of cigarettes as instructed and returned to the day room. He helped the old sergeant with his coat and placed the cigarettes and lighter into a pocket. They left, Beck pushing the wheelchair across the road outside and along the path by the riverbank. They stopped at a bench and Beck sat down. They lit up, and Molyneaux coughed once and spat onto the ground.

'Apologies, my wife detested my spitting.'

'That's okay.'

'It is a disgusting habit, especially if you have to watch it. Not the same when you do it yourself… like a lot of things, I suppose.'

Beck inhaled. 'You have family?'

'I don't know, maybe.'

Beck looked surprised, said nothing.

'My wife died five years ago,' Molyneaux explained. 'That's when I came here. Frank, our son, died at nineteen in a car accident. I have a brother in New York. I don't care much about him. So you see, it's gone full circle. I'm back where I started. On my own. But that's not why you're here, is it? To talk about any family I possibly might or might not have?'

'I came here to ask you something. A body was found at a beach, a place called Haven Cove…'

'I know the place,' Molyneaux said.

'… a skeleton, actually. Looks like it'd been there a long time, maybe thirty years.'

Molyneaux was quiet, staring at the river, holding his cigarette between two fingers, resting his thumb against his chin. He was listening.

'A male,' Beck continued. 'Young, tall, remnants of a brown tweed jacket on his torso, some hair still preserved, black and curly, the way it was described.'

Molyneaux took a long draw on his cigarette, and when he spoke, the words tumbled out with the thick stream of smoke. 'Young Jimmy Reidy. Has to be.'

It took Beck a moment to realise he was standing there with his mouth open.

*

Sergeant Molyneaux was driving the area patrol car, a Chrysler Avenger, up Main Street on that wet and stormy night; in the passenger seat beside him was Garda Patrick Donnelly, a gruff Leitrim man who spoke only if he absolutely had to. They were returning to the station, looking forward to taking off their heavy greatcoats and drinking steaming mugs of tea and, if the telephone didn't ring, getting some shut-eye.

It was the middle of the night shift, November 1984. The song of the moment, I Feel For You by Chaka Khan.

The windscreen wipers juddered across the glass, partially clearing away the rain, Molyneaux concentrating on the road ahead. Suddenly, Donnelly shouted 'Stop', and before the car had come to a halt he was out and running into an alley. Molyneaux cut the engine and was about to follow, but Donnelly shouted over his shoulder for him to stay where he was. The sounds of dustbin lids overturning followed, and a prolonged and loud 'Aaaggghhh'. Then Donnelly emerged with two young fellas in headlocks. 'Look what I found,' he said, like a farmer having just trapped two rats in his feed store.

Donnelly told Molyneaux that he'd been looking out the window when he'd seen a flicker of light from inside the alley, enough for him to make out Reidy in the flame of a match setting fire to some newspapers and trying to push these through what turned out to be a smashed window at the back of a newsagent's.

Donnelly threw the prisoners into the rear of the Avenger and sat in between them, a rare smile on his face, passed the time on the way back to the station playing 'slap-a-boo'; each time he shouted 'slap', the prisoner had to respond with 'boo', immediately. If he didn't, and even if he did, Donnelly would slap him viciously around the head. And the prisoner wasn't allowed to protect himself. That was against the rules. If he did, Molyneaux would hit him twice as hard. And Molyneaux remembered Donnelly kept telling Reidy he looked like a white black man with his big afro hair. The rest of the shift Donnelly spent going in and out of their cell, making them crawl about on their hands and knees, barking like dogs, as he shouted out commands like 'Sit' and 'Give me the paw', kicking them throughout. No one worried about leaving marks on prisoners back then. You could do that sort of thing, he told Beck when he caught that look on his face; in fact, it was expected, by both prisoners and commanding officers.

As dawn broke and thoughts were turning to home, Donnelly finally rang their parents. Damages were paid to the newsagent's and that was the end of it. The end of it for that particular night, that was. But in another way, it was only the beginning.

'They kept us busy,' Molyneaux said. 'Two little bastards, they were.'

It couldn't be proven, of course, that they were responsible for what followed: the spate of small unexplained fires, the broken shop windows, the dead animals hanging from lamp posts, cats mostly, but also a small dog once or twice, sometimes with its throat slit, sometimes a limb missing, sometimes a head. There was no CCTV back then, nor any willingness to divert scarce resources into a full-scale investigation. As long as no one was being killed or injured, it was ignored.

But Molyneaux wasn't so sure that was the case, that no one was being killed. He thought they might be, but in ways that didn't raise suspicion.

'I don't need to remind you,' he said to Beck, 'that suicide was a taboo subject back then.'

And it was. For years the church forbade the burial of victims in consecrated ground. A collective shame built up around it, and suicides were rarely – very rarely – recorded accurately. Unless it was absolutely necessary, could not be classified as anything else, well, then and only then did it go down for what it was: suicide. And yet, even against that criterion, it was impossible to ignore. Suicides were on the rise in Cross Beg, suicide by drowning that was, because there were no others.

Molyneaux said he was suspicious about it all. But Beck wondered if that was only because it was after the fact.

But then it stopped.

Everything.

The unexplained fires, the broken windows, the dead animals hanging from lamp posts. And the suicides. And something else. Reidy and his pal had disappeared. Just like that, too. They were reported missing, but not much effort was put into finding them. The belief was that they had scarpered off to London or America. It happened a lot back then. And good riddance, if that was the case. Because no one really cared.

Molyneaux wrapped his collar tightly around his neck. He suddenly looked pale and tired. 'I'd like to go back in now.'

'Of course,' Beck said. 'One more thing. What about their parents?'

'Reidy was the son of a teacher. Respectable family. Another reason why no one wanted to bother them, the parents that is. And that tweed jacket you mentioned, I don't think I ever saw him wearing anything else, always seemed to have it on, winter or summer. Perhaps he had more than one, I don't know.'

'You didn't say much about the other fella,' Beck said. 'Who was he?'

Molyneaux fell silent, but after a moment continued, his voice rising. 'I saved the best till last. Oh yes, the other fella, ah, the other fella, that's a good one. He didn't have a father. Not an easy thing for his mother back then to stay in a small town like this when she was up the duff. But stay she did. So people had plenty to gossip about, and started putting two and two together, especially as the kid grew up and the resemblance became clear.'

'Resemblance to who?'

Molyneaux gave a throaty laugh. 'To the local priest. A young curate, they say he was the dad. His name was Father Matthew Clifford. Right enough, the woman had worked in the presbytery for a time, as a housekeeper, so there was plenty of fuel for gossip there. She left abruptly, around about the same time

Father Clifford was sent off on the missions. That's what got people thinking. Botswana, they say, or was it the Congo?' The throaty laugh once more. 'You couldn't get much further than either of those places, now could you?'

Beck stood, gripping the handles of the wheelchair. 'The young fella. Was he named after his father?'

'Of course not. He was given his mother's name, Farmer. Benedict Farmer, it's a religious thing.'

'Tell me about it,' Beck muttered.

'What was that?'

'Nothing.' Beck began pushing the wheelchair. 'And his mother? What was her name?'

'Angela. Good-looking woman, too. There was a history there, though.'

'History?'

'Ya, the nerves they call it. Mental illness. I know she was in and out of the psych ward at times. There was one occasion we had to go to her house, where she was holding Benedict out the top-floor window, dangling him by the legs. We sectioned her for that for a while. A social worker was involved with the case. I'll tell you something interesting, will I?'

Molyneaux paused.

'Go on,' Beck said, softly.

'Imelda Butler. That was her name. The one who's been murdered.'

Beck imagined a piece of jigsaw clicking into place.

'It is her, isn't it?' Molyneaux asked.

'I can't say,' Beck replied. 'Not at this time. You know the drill.'

'If it's her immediate family you're worried about,' the old sergeant said, 'I can save you time. She doesn't have any. A crabby auld spinster was what she was. And the young fella hated her. He was cute enough not to do anything about it. She was a State employee, after all. We were told to keep an eye on her. But if it was him... which, of course, it can't be. Because he's dead. Has to be. Fellas like him are like white phosphorus, cause mayhem but burn out quick.'

'Yes,' Beck said. 'But if it was him?'

'Well, he'd be pretty fucking mad by now, wouldn't he? All that pent-up anger and hatred. He'd do quite a job on her, I'd say... But there's no one with that name in the town, is there? I check sometimes. Old habits die hard. Anyway, back to my story. Angela got married in the end. To a local man, name Willie Kelly, worked in Shreever's Builders' Providers, long gone now. They had a daughter, Margaret. Not sure what happened to her. Think she went to America. Willie himself died of a heart attack – he was only forty-seven years old. You know, I never thought Reidy was the evil one. He was more a follower. It was Farmer who was the real bad egg. And did you know?'

'Did I know?'

'That he's back. Not Farmer. Like I said, I think he must be long dead. But himself, Father Clifford, the boy's dad, suitably atoned for his sins after his years on the missions in Africa. Nobody remembers him now of course, except old codgers like me, hanging onto life with both feet in the grave, so he probably thinks it's all forgotten.'

'I met him,' Beck said. 'I met Father Clifford.'

'He was only a young fella back then, when he got her pregnant. So he's not as old as you'd think. It's like when you meet a schoolteacher from when you were a kid. You expect them to be ancient. But they're not, because they weren't much older than you were to begin with. Same thing here. He's not even sixty, I'd say, not old for a priest at all. Comes in here every Sunday.' The throaty laugh. 'Maybe you should talk to him.'

'Maybe I should,' Beck said, stopping at the zebra crossing. 'And Angela, is she still alive?'

'Nah, she's been dead a few years now. You'd never guess?'

Beck started to cross the road.

'You mean…'

'Yes, drowned in the river, poor woman.' He raised an eyebrow. 'They say she fell in, of course.'

And then it came, the throaty laugh again.

CHAPTER SEVENTY-SEVEN

Beck was still thinking about what Molyneaux had said when he approached the reception desk in The Hibernian Hotel and enquired with the man standing behind it about a room for the night. Beck recognised him too as being the barman from the other evening when he'd been drinking here with Gumbell. But Beck was too absorbed in his own thoughts to fully notice that he wasn't responding, that he was merely standing there, looking at him; gaping at him was the term. When he heard him say 'Just a minute', and saw him disappear through a door into a back office, Beck was pulled back into the present, his mind focusing on the matter at hand. Then he re-emerged, along with an older, bespectacled man, dressed in a knitted sweater and chinos which Beck deemed too casual for a member of general staff. He surmised this man to be either the owner or manager. Beck also noted the thick gold watch on his wrist.

'Hello,' the man said, but there was no smile. 'Maurice Tynan. I'm the owner of The Hibernian. You were looking for accommodation, I believe.'

'There's a problem,' Beck said, but it wasn't put as a question.

The man fidgeted with a pen held between his fingers. 'To be honest...' he began.

Which always annoyed Beck, because it meant that anything else was not honest.

'Yes,' Beck said. 'To be honest, what?'

'There's no need for tones.'

Beck knew it would suit him if he had a tone, to blame him for what he guessed was to come.

'You were saying,' Beck said. 'About being honest.'

'We're full,' the owner announced. 'We have no rooms. Sorry.'

Beck decided to get into character. He looked at them both, but neither held his gaze. He leaned on the counter. The owner took a step back, swallowed once. Beck waited, then, one, two, three, ACTION:

'BOO!'

Beck was lighting a cigarette on the street outside when Superintendent Wilde rang.

'Where've you been, Beck?' Wilde asked as Beck turned into an alley. Beck was beginning to understand how Ned must have felt.

'Didn't you know?' Beck said. 'The instructions were clear. Do not return to the station.'

A weak ray of sunlight washed the top half of the buildings on one side of him. The bottom half of the alleyway never received any sun, and the air was permanently cold and damp.

'Yes, yes, that's all changed now,' Wilde said.

'It has?'

'The press office has taken control. They want you back here. A press conference is scheduled for five o'clock, and they want you at it. If you're not, it will raise all sorts of questions. Look, Beck, no one is seriously considering the notion that you killed your landlady, except the press, that is.'

'That's reassuring.'

Beck could hear an intake of breath at the other end.

'How are you... coping, that is?'

'By not thinking about it,' Beck replied.

'Beck, listen, you and your landlady. I mean, she wasn't a bad-looking woman, all things considered, did you and...'

'I have something to do,' Beck said abruptly. 'I'll be there by five thirty.'

'It's five o'clock, Beck, it's five o'—'

Beck finished the call, took a last draw on his cigarette and emerged onto Bridge Walk.

CHAPTER SEVENTY-EIGHT

The life of a sperm cell. Fighting its way upstream like a spawning salmon, programmed for one thing and one thing only: to reach its destination and spark life. If it's lucky, that is, if it's very, very, very lucky indeed. Because millions of other sperm have the very same objective. And only one can survive. Only one! The rest die, to be soaked up on wads of tissue paper and flushed down the toilet.

So arbitrary.

He remembered he'd been thinking this the day he'd held his breath, watching through the keyhole of their bedroom. Fleeting images: his stepfather's narrow back, his mother, sitting on the edge of the bed, wearing the long white nightdress he'd seen hanging from the washing line countless times.

Crept to his bedroom. Made too much noise. Her voice following him down the hall, asking was he alright, why wasn't he in bed?

Said nothing. A door opening, footsteps, stopping outside his bedroom.

'What is it, Benedict?'

Said nothing.

The doorknob turning.

Got ready, time like a concertina, opening out, a brief second becoming an eternity, contracting, an eternity gone in one second. She rattled at the lock and then he heard her footsteps retreat back down the corridor. Then the sound of her bedroom door closing. After this, sometimes, he could hear the creaking of bedsprings. Slowly at first.

Then faster, faster, faster. He would cover his ears and chant the words to block the sounds out: 'Your time will come. You will die. Your time will come. You will die...'

CHAPTER SEVENTY-NINE

The cathedral, The Cathedral of St Jude and Malachy, to give it its full title, was by far the largest building in Cross Beg, a huge neoclassical grey stone structure built in the mid-1800s.

'I was in the vicinity,' Beck said to the dour young priest sitting in the parish office opposite. It was dimly lit with heavy dark wooden furniture, a reception desk in one corner, a carpeted floor. There was no one else present but himself and the priest. 'I thought I'd enquire on the off chance that Father Clifford might be about.'

The dour young priest did not question him, it no doubt being normal for people to call in unannounced seeking the parish priest. He smiled, and the dourness temporarily disappeared from his face. 'The Father wasn't feeling well earlier. I think he is somewhere about in the cathedral. Or the presbytery. The presbytery is right there.' He pointed.

Beck followed his outstretched hand and could see through the glass panel in the door a square brick house on the other side of a low hill at the back of the cathedral. The house took him by surprise; he'd never seen it before, hidden as it was by both the cathedral and the hill.

'Thank you,' he said and left, walked across the car park and entered the cathedral through one of the vaulted side doors. It was silent inside, like cold static energy you could almost touch. Amongst the rows of pews were lone figures bent in prayer. The light filtered through the stained-glass windows and gave a surreal otherworldliness to the place, which was the whole point, really,

Beck considered. He hadn't been in a church in years, not even for funerals, which he didn't see the point of. He'd been an altar boy for a time, and he remembered climbing creaky stairs that twisted their way inside the spire to the bell tower, the floor littered with the carcasses of dead birds that had squeezed through broken air vents and were unable to get out again.

Someone coughed, and the sound pierced the silence and rumbled through the expanse of the cathedral. Beck did not linger. He left again, making his way to the presbytery, passing the well-tended flower beds to the front door where he pressed the doorbell. No one answered. He was about to press it a second time when a window above him opened and a face appeared, looking down at him.

'Father Clifford, sorry to trouble you,' Beck said, peering up.

'Yes?'

'I was hoping to have a word.'

'Yes. I'm in bed, though. The flu. If you still want to come up, feel free, push the door and come through.'

Beck did and stepped into the hallway; there was a frayed floral carpet, a large mirror in a heavy wooden frame, edges faded with age, and the musty smell of damp in the air. He went up the wide stairs. 'In here,' a voice called, and Beck saw a door slightly open.

The curtains were drawn, a lamp on a bedside table throwing off a feeble light. Father Clifford was partially sitting up in bed, his head resting against some pillows. A collection of medicine bottles were scattered on the table next to him. Father Clifford coughed and pulled the blankets tighter around him.

'I'm sorry,' Beck said. 'This is a mistake. I can come again another time.'

'No, no. You're here now. You're the police officer I met at Frazzali's the other day, aren't you?'

'Detective Inspector Finnegan Beck.'

'A policeman. Yes. What do you want?' The priest coughed again.

Beck stood awkwardly, feeling the intrusiveness of his presence in the room. There was no chair.

'What do you want?' Father Clifford repeated. 'Bring a stool in from the bathroom and sit down. It's next door.'

'I was speaking with a retired sergeant,' Beck said when he was sitting. 'About an historical crime. Remains found at a local beach.'

Beck noticed the change immediately. The priest's hands, which had been resting on the outside of the drab grey blanket, twitched and came together, squeezing against each other tight.

He was younger than Beck had imagined, his black hair streaked with grey, combed back on his high, steep forehead, with skin that was almost boyishly fresh, and small, thoughtful eyes that suddenly carried a heavy pain.

The priest dropped his head onto his chest.

'I see,' he said. 'Remains were found, were they?'

'Yes,' Beck said. 'They were.'

'And... what did he tell you, the sergeant?'

Beck was uncomfortable on the small stool, his legs spread before him, his upper body angled forward to relieve the pressure on his neck.

'That the body, the remains, are probably going to be those of Jimmy Reidy.'

The priest was quiet, and rock still. He even seemed to have stopped breathing. In a low whisper he repeated, 'Jimmy Reidy,' and louder, 'you know then, don't you? Yes, you do.'

Beck said nothing.

'You know that I have a son.'

'The way I heard it, it was merely a rumour.'

'Humph. I have a son. I gave in to temptation, the devil got his reward.'

The priest rested his head into his pillows, staring at the ceiling, the knuckles of his right hand pressing into his neck. At that moment he looked very old. He lowered his eyes, focusing on Beck.

'It breaks my heart to say it. Yes, I have a son. And I abandoned him. And his mother, too. I deserve to be punished for what I have done.'

The priest closed his eyes and blessed himself quickly.

'Have you heard from your son?' Beck asked.

'I have gotten letters and emails. Splurges of vile filth and hate. The product of a sick, deranged mind. They have worn me down. Look at me. They have made me ill. To think that someone could hate so much. I was in the Congo, you know, The Republic of the Congo… for over thirty years. Every day was a scene from a dystopian horror, life cheaper than a matchstick. But it was easier than reading those words of his, to put up with that. I went to the capital Kinshasa more than once, to see my superior. I always felt my son was close by. I felt he was watching me. And it frightened me. I wanted to be sent somewhere far, far away, further away than Kinshasa, to the furthest reaches of the earth. But they told me I was suffering from the delusions of stress and guilt. It was why they allowed me to return back here. But he is still close by. I know he is. And yet I wonder, am I deluded?'

The priest bowed his head again, and tottered on the verge of tears.

'When you say your son is close by,' Beck said, 'where specifically? Would you know?'

The priest knotted the blanket in his hands, pulling it down for the first time. His hands flew to his neck.

'Sergeant Molyneaux told me of his strange behaviour all those years ago,' Beck said.

'It was a dreadful time. And dreadful times have returned, have they not? But now they are much worse.'

'Do you think your son could be…?'

'Responsible? For the spate of murders? Yes, I do. It breaks my heart to say it. But it is possible.'

'Why didn't you come forward and inform us before now?'

'And say what? That my son is responsible? A son who hasn't been seen in the best part of thirty years? When I have no evidence? They told me it was delusions caused by stress the first time. I haven't forgotten that, by the way.'

Beck wondered. Was this the fanciful tale of a tormented soul? Or was there some truth to it? He didn't know. He just didn't know.

'Why do you shake your head?'

'Was I?' Beck hadn't realised that he had.

'Yes… You don't believe me, do you?'

Beck looked at the priest, noted the way his small blue eyes seemed to radiate with what little light there was in the room.

'I don't know what the truth is. But I intend to find out.'

CHAPTER EIGHTY

No one had told Beck. He went through the station's front door to find the foyer filled with press. They surrounded him immediately. A hand wrapped itself around his wrist and yanked him away into the public office. She seemed far too petite to have the strength to have just done that.

'Victoria Plaistow, Press Office, we need to speak.' Her voice was smoky. She had sunglasses pushed up onto her coiffured blonde hair, and wore a tight pink dress under an expensive-looking leather coat tied loosely at the waist.

Beck finally spoke. 'Are you actually a guard?'

'No. I'm from Ogliby, Hegarty and O'Mara, public relations consultants. Listen up. The conference will be held in the foyer. Sorry we couldn't get word to you in time. They wanted to hold it in the Ops Room. I couldn't believe it. They'd go through every desk in there. Nothing would be private. So it's the foyer. Beck…'

'Yes.'

'Answer their questions but don't elaborate. They will want to question you. You've seen the headlines. The top brass at Phoenix Park are concerned. This is your chance to put an end to it, okay? Before we go out there, honestly, is there any reason you know of why that woman was found under your bed?'

'No.'

'Good. I'll be right behind you.' She reached out to open the door of the public office.

'Wait,' Beck said.

'What?'

'Give me a minute. I'm not ready.'

'You're ready.' She handed him a sheet of paper.

'What's this?'

'Your statement.' Her hand was on his back now, pushing him towards the door.

The TV camera lights stung his eyes. He lowered them, stared at the statement in his hands. An eruption of voices around him, excited and agitated, one louder than the other, all asking different questions and all at the same time.

Victoria Plaistow's voice behind him: 'Give the inspector a moment, please. Please. Let the inspector speak.'

Beck began: 'My name is Inspector Finnegan Beck. In the early hours of this morning I awoke in my home to find the body of a female underneath my bed. This female was my landlady, Mrs Sheila Claxton. I rented the property from her. I do not know how she got there or who might have done this. I am not responsible. Speculation that I am does nothing but divert attention away from the investigation into the multiple murders in Cross Beg. I am as shocked by her death as anyone else, more so because, as I said, she was my landlady. I am not the killer. I repeat: I am not the killer. The state pathologist, Dr Derek Gumbell, has now confirmed that time of death was at least six hours prior to my finding the body. Please note that for the preceding thirty-six hours I was not in my home in Cross Beg. I was in Dublin attending a work-related meeting and had stayed in the city the night before. I travelled back to Cross Beg after this meeting and went directly to Cross Beg Garda Station, where I remained on duty until 11.37 p.m. last night. This is the logging-off time on my computer. I did not have an opportunity to kill Mrs Sheila Claxton, even if I had wanted to. I did not want to kill Sheila Claxton, and I did not kill Sheila Claxton. End of statement. Thank you.'

The reporters began shouting out a flurry of questions, but Victoria Plaistow stepped in and led Beck back towards the Ops Room. Behind him, he could hear Superintendent Wilde speaking. 'Any operational questions concerning the investigation can be directed to me now. Inspector Beck will not be taking any questions. He is returning immediately to the active investigation. Yes, you, Bobby, go ahead…'

'Perhaps you could somehow lend the same efficiency to this investigation,' Beck said when they were in the public office.

Victoria Plaistow smiled. She was a life-size Barbie doll straight out of the box. He could see the duty sergeant had his chair turned towards her.

'I'm sure you know better than anyone else what you're doing,' she replied.

The fact was, Beck didn't, not really. He knew that floundering investigations depended on information supplied to push them over the line, most often tip-offs from members of the public. Results of investigations from legwork, despite advancements in forensics and the increasing sophistication of available tools, ran a very distant second to plain old information supplied, and also, good luck.

CHAPTER EIGHTY-ONE

The glass of red wine Lucy had poured remained untouched. Their apartment was in the Claddagh, the oldest part of Galway city. The kitchen area they were sitting in was separated from the living area beyond it by a low partition wall. From where Beck was sitting, he could see into it: the TV in one corner, a brown leather settee and a matching armchair, framed photographs on the wall, group photographs of smiling faces, family probably. A section of wall beside it was taken up by a large framed print of Vincent van Gogh's *The Starry Night*.

'I worry,' Lucy said. 'How do you know he's not going to come for me?' Her eyes widened. 'I mean, he could.'

To hell with it, Beck thought, and reached for the wine. He took a polite sip, tasted the delicious tangy afterglow as it went down his throat, forced himself to put the glass back onto the table.

'I don't think he's going to come here or anything, babes,' Claire said. 'Don't worry about it.'

'But I *do* worry about it. I feel so… vulnerable.'

Claire reached across and squeezed her wife's hand, stroked the back of it. Beck noted the dynamic between the two.

'Don't worry,' she said again, 'it's going to be alright.'

'If you're sure,' Lucy said, and looked at Beck.

He got the feeling she wished he wasn't there.

'I'm sure,' Claire repeated.

Which was a lie, because no one could be sure of anything.

'Make certain everything is locked,' Lucy said. 'And don't forget the windows.'

'I won't. I'll look after everything,' Claire said. 'I promise.'

Lucy stood. 'I'm going to bed. Please don't be long, Claire.' Her voice took on a distinct formality. 'Good night, Inspector Beck.' She turned to leave, but paused, looked back over her shoulder. 'See, I'm more sensitive that I first appear, aren't I? Quite fragile, really.' She looked at Claire. 'Thank you for looking after me, darling.'

'She is quite fragile,' Claire said when they were alone.

Beck thought: *So is the Spanish flu virus.*

'But no one is what they appear on the outside,' Claire added. And looking into Beck's eyes: 'Are they?'

Beck rubbed his eyebrows between two fingers, feeling suddenly very tired. 'Thank you again. For putting me up for the night.'

Claire waved her hand in an 'it's no problem' gesture, said, 'Why did he come back? Father Clifford.'

'I never asked him that. He's a tortured man, if you ask me. He feels great guilt, running away the way he did; he feels responsible. I don't think he can forgive himself. Maybe his feelings towards his son are an expression of his guilt. The story seems so far out, I doubt if he exists anywhere other than in his mind. But the person we're looking for is real. He's out there somewhere. And we need to find him.' Beck took a deep breath. 'Some years ago I participated in an FBI international law enforcement programme…'

'I have to ask, Beck,' Claire said. 'But where did it all go wrong for you?'

'… I spent a very cold winter attending classes at the FBI headquarters in Washington DC. I remember a module on serial killers. To cut a long story short, serial killers, most of them anyway, want to get caught. But because they believe they're too smart, they often think they *can't* get caught, so they reach out, as it were, to speed matters along, to help investigators out, because no one is as smart as they are, or so they think. But here's the thing: despite all this, they still believe they *won't* get caught, even when they're nudging the police to find them. And this dichotomy, this yin and yang, somehow makes an appeal to their inner rational self and sometimes, before they can actually be caught, they realise that "oh shit, maybe the cops are smarter than I think after all", and they stop. So they disappear, sometimes forever. It's a self-fulfilling prophecy. Think Jack the Ripper.'

'Did you actually say Jack the Ripper?'

'Just to contextualise the debate,' Beck said.

'This may make more sense in the morning.'

'It may do.'

She stood. 'I'm going to bed. Good night, Beck.'

'Good night.'

He remained for a while, thinking things over, and as he stood, his telephone rang. He looked at the screen, hesitated, then: 'Gumbell. It's late.'

'Yes, old boy, it is.' The words were slurred.

'I was just about to go to bed.'

'I tried ringing earlier, *hic*. I thought you were staying here. Where are you? Want to have a drink?'

'I'm not staying at the hotel. They wouldn't allow me. They thought I stabbed that poor woman to death.'

'Yes. I heard about your spot of bother. Come down anyway.'

Beck closed his eyes tightly, opened them again. Of all people he should, but did not, have the patience required to listen to a drunk person's dribble.

'What did you learn?' he asked.

Gumbell was smoking. He could hear the undercurrent in his breath as it carried the smoke, then the long wispy sound of the exhale. There were no outdoor sounds, traffic and suchlike. Was Gumbell smoking somewhere inside the hotel?

'I've learned that m-mindfulness and positive thinking and everything else they tell me to practise is but an ink drop compared to the beauty of the prose I'm writing.'

Beck wondered: *Is that how I sound when I'm pissed?*

'The poor woman was strangled, Beck. Not like young Tanya Frazzali, the other victim – the pressure was constant. He didn't play around, hic.'

'You need to go to bed. I will talk to you in the morning.'

'I am in bed. Thought I'd go down to the bar again if you were there, seemed like a good idea.'

'It's not. Go to sleep.' Beck hung up.

He went into the spare bedroom Claire had prepared for him, took off his shoes, lay on top of the bed in his clothes and feel instantly asleep.

CHAPTER EIGHTY-TWO

She was sitting on a chair in a bedroom. Her head hurt, and the curtains were drawn. Soft light was coming from a floor lamp in the corner of the room. There were two single beds, a duvet on each with brown and purple floral patterns.

Melanie closed her eyes, remembering. She had run from her house, from her mother, from him. She hadn't wanted to be there. Hadn't wanted to be in the same house as him. She had gone through the empty streets of this town. She had walked and walked, trying to rid herself of the image of him, her so-called father. Finally, she had gone down to the river, walked through the high, dead grass, sat there listening to the sounds of the rushing water.

She had one blister pack. Would it be enough? One by one she took out and swallowed each pill, then lay back, listening to the water, its sound quickly fading, as she began to be carried off, taken to that tranquil place, that place of peace, where nothing could ever hurt her again, and from where she hoped she would never return.

A couple of hours later she moved, tried to sit forward, not feeling so well, her head heavy, feeling like she might vomit. She couldn't move. She wanted to move, she willed herself to move. But she couldn't. *Why can't I fucking move?* There was no wind on her face, no tickly brush of grass against her body. *Where the fuck am I?* She was sitting. In a chair. Again she tried to move. But something was holding her back. In the grey light of the room she saw the rope that bound her wrists to the armrest. Her stomach lurched as if a hidden trapdoor had given way inside her as she realised: I'm tied to the fucking chair.

Melanie tried to make sense of it. *Is this home? Is this a hospital? Is this a joke?* She looked about the room. *No. This is not home. This is not a hospital. Where the fuck am I?*

And why am I tied to this fucking chair?

Then she forgot about the dull pain in her head, forgot about wanting to vomit; everything else was pushed to the side by one overriding emotion: fear.

She pulled against the rope. But it was useless. She tried to move her legs. But that was also useless. She was hog-tied.

The sound of her breathing, loud and desperate. Melanie could sense someone standing behind her, as a cold liquid sensation underneath her made her realise she was pissing herself. The urine dribbled down the legs of the chair and formed a puddle on the floor.

'You mustn't be so frightened, Melanie.'

The voice was soft, yet it seemed to fill the room, to bounce off the walls, the floor, and finally bounced around inside her ears. She shuddered, literally felt a cold, creeping sensation at the back of her neck, moving to the top of her head now, stroking her hair. It was a hand.

'If you scream, I will have to gag you. Don't scream, Melanie.'

Melanie's mouth opened; a whimpering sound emerged. 'Pleeease. Pleeease. Don't hurt me.'

He walked out from behind her now, crossed the room to the curtains, the floor lamp throwing his shadow onto the wall. He turned and looked at her. His eyes bore into her. Small, cold eyes, like a snake's.

He looked familiar.

The collar of his black shirt was open, the end of the white tab inside hanging loose.

'P-p-priest,' she stuttered. 'You're the priest?'

He laughed, a low, squeaking sound.

'No, child,' he said. 'I am not a priest. But my father was. He was a naughty priest. A bit like your father, I suppose. You poor girl. It must be very traumatic for you. I understand, really I do. I was made a bastard, you see. I don't have a father.' He laughed again. 'Now I do have a father. Of course I do. Everyone has a father. Or I did. Until I… well, you don't need to know about that, do you? Or maybe you do. I shall tell you anyway. Melanie. I believe there is too much fuss made around this whole business of killing. Don't you agree? Or the "Secret Slaughter", as the Vikings called it, as opposed to "slaying", which they lauded, and were very good at indeed. But really, I don't see the problem. If I don't like somebody, and even if I do, well, I just kill them. Poof! They're gone! It's really that simple. And if you take a few elementary precautions, you can literally get away with it, with murder.' He laughed. 'I mean, who's to catch me? The police? I don't think so.' But then he thought of Beck, and his smile disappeared.

'Anyway. I made my father disappear. Around about two years ago. You can put two and two together, I'm sure, Melanie. He never died officially, of course, my father, and yet he has ceased to live. Nor is he missing. I had arranged to meet him when he came back to Ireland. He had returned to take over as parish priest here in Cross Beg. We'd kept in touch over the years, even while he was in Africa. It is important that a father and son should stay in touch, don't you agree? But I wanted some stability, I wanted to settle down, as it were. And he owed me, oh yes, he owed me big time. And when he returned it all worked out much better than I ever could have imagined. We looked like twins, you see, which helped. Quite clever to choreograph such a sequence of dance steps, if I say so myself, too. But I did. Then when he was gone, I myself attended at the missionary headquarters in Maynooth in place of my father. No one had any suspicions about my identity, not for a minute. Indeed, I was given a cheque for five thousand euro for charitable undertakings in my new parish of Cross Beg. So, you see, my father is between life and death. Neither dead. Nor alive. That is a condition I always strove to achieve, and now, in a way, I have. I am a person who doesn't exist. Who is dead. And yet I am alive. Isn't that fascinating? I mean, isn't that just *fascinating*?'

Despite her dreadful fear, a memory sparked inside Melanie, of a TV programme, a girl, somewhere in America, explaining how she had survived a kidnapping ordeal. 'I had to become his friend,' she'd told the camera. 'I figured he wasn't going to kill me if I became his friend.'

'I'd like to do the same to my father,' she said now, surprised at how calm her voice was. Because she had realised in this moment that she didn't want to die. She wanted to live. Oh yes, she wanted to live. More than anything else, she wanted to live. And she would do whatever it took to make sure she did. 'Maybe you could teach me?'

He passed her, holding something in his hands. She saw it was a mobile phone.

And then she noticed the glittery pink sticker in a corner. *Oh, Jesus!* The phone was Tanya's.

'Yes,' he said softly, 'this is Tanya's. But don't be frightened. I just like to keep… things, that's all. I often saw them in the forest, you know. Tanya showed no moral responsibility. Nor did your father. His punishment will come. All in good time, my dear.'

Oh, Jesus!

She heard his footsteps walk behind her, retreating to the end of the room. There was a rustling sound, like he was searching for something.

'Yes,' he said, his footsteps approaching again. He came round to the front once more, his head lowered. She saw there was something covering his face. He knelt down before her, then raised his head slowly. She screamed, a short scream, high-pitched and sharp. He was wearing a mask, a grotesque caricature of a bird.

'You like it,' he said, holding her chin by the tip of a finger, his eyes darting about inside the small cut-outs that allowed him to see. 'It's a crow. I bought it at an Africa Day event in Dublin last year. What a great day that was. And such respect for a man of the cloth. I was immediately drawn to it. Because this is a town of crows, you see, they're everywhere… Have you ever seen a dead crow, by the way? No, neither have I. And yet they're everywhere. So you see, they are neither dead nor alive, Melanie, isn't that strange? Don't you find it fascinating? I know I do.'

CHAPTER EIGHTY-THREE

Beck dreamed. Of the classroom, with its high windows that allowed the sunlight in but hid the world outside, removed it, made it something separate, alien. Of the teacher, the one they called the Scarecrow. Brother Pius was his name, with long, stringy hair, a stooped posture, small cold eyes, always dressed in a black soutane and black leather shoes, old and cracked, and which made a squeaking noise each time he moved about. The Scarecrow, with foraging hands that liked to crawl about beneath desks, sweeping his cane across the continents on the pull-down map that covered half of the blackboard, coming to rest on Africa. The class was silent. The Scarecrow stepped forward, approaching Beck, who was sitting in the front row.

'Kinshasa,' he snarled, 'is not in the Republic of the Congo, you meandering idiot. It is the capital of the Democratic Republic of the Congo. The capital of the Republic of the Congo – a totally separate country – is Brazzaville. What is the capital of the Republic of the Congo? Brazzaville! Brazzaville! Brazzaville! You idiot. Did I really teach you to be this thick? And why would anybody hold a blanket around their neck unless they didn't want you to see it – their neck, that is! I may be evil, Beck, but you are one stupid fucker. And I know too about covering tracks, don't I? Because I covered my own for long enough, didn't I? It takes one to know one, after all.'

The Scarecrow raised a bony hand and slapped Beck across the face.

*

Beck awoke suddenly, his eyes snapping open, reaching up to touch his cheek where the Scarecrow had slapped him.

He played over in his mind the image of Father Clifford rubbing his neck with the knuckles of his hand. Trying to take the edge from an itch. It was hard not to scratch when you really needed to. Because wounds as they heal itched like crazy. And Tanya Frazzali had cut her killer with the nails of three fingers. Three long nails. That would itch.

A missionary priest, a true missionary priest, could not make a mistake like that. It wasn't possible. For Father Clifford to say Kinshasa was the capital of the Republic of the Congo, was like Beck saying Belfast was the capital of the Republic of Ireland? Impossible.

So what, then?

The sound of the rain falling on the window. It always seemed to rain when he visited Galway. In fact, he couldn't think of a solitary time he had come to the City of the Tribes when it hadn't rained.

He sat up, looked at his watch: 2.35 a.m.

CHAPTER EIGHTY-FOUR

The Meteorological Office had predicted the low centre of pressure from the north had been lurking out in the Atlantic, where it had sat, warm air swirling about it, building winds to 78 knots, or almost 90 miles an hour. The satellite photographs revealed the weather system static, the equilibrium of conditions dictating that it would likely sit on the water and blow itself out. But that was not what happened. It began to move.

CHAPTER EIGHTY-FIVE

Beck knew all too well that night shifts made the body colder, more sluggish, fuzzed the thoughts into candy floss. He watched the night sergeant, Connor, yawn and give an involuntary shiver, dancing back and forth on each foot to keep warm, the wind whipping the collar of his hi-vis jacket about his face. They were parked at the bottom of Main Street, at the junction with Bridge Street, standing on the pavement next to the public order van. The Ford Transit, its windows and doors covered with wire mesh, had been sent over from Galway. As it was every weekend.

Claire had been quiet leaving the station, sitting in the back of the crew cab. Twice her phone had rung, each time Lucy demanding that she return home immediately and look after her. Finally, Claire had tossed the phone into the door well and ignored it.

Beck did not pass comment.

'The heater's broken,' Sergeant Connor said. 'Turn on the engine and it blows out cold air, can't be switched off. What I have to put up with.'

The night was brooding, the sky low and heavy. They stood in silence for a long time, watching the street lights illuminating the black glistening pavements.

'Why am I here?' Connor asked with all the enthusiasm of an inmate of a Siberian Gulag starting another shift down the coal mines.

And Beck couldn't tell him. Because even in modern Ireland, to arrest someone, especially a priest, on suspicion of murder was not something to be done without verifiable proof. And Beck didn't have that. Beck had nothing, nothing but his dreams.

Claire folded her arms. She wasn't comfortable with this herself. Beck stood perfectly still, looking at the shafts of light stretching down from the lamp post up ahead.

The radio crackled. 'Smithy, where are you? Come in Garda Smith.'

Sergeant Connor pressed the talk button on the radio as he unclipped it from his jacket tunic. 'He still not returned from that shout?'

'No, Skipper, he hasn't.'

'How long's it been now?'

'An hour, more.'

'Smithy,' the sergeant said into the mouthpiece, 'come in now. SMITHY! WAKE UP! Are you asleep? Skipper here, Sergeant Connor. Come in, for Christ sake.'

Connor held the radio in his hand, pressed the talk switch again, heard the crackling of static. There was silence as he released the button, clipping the radio back onto his tunic. 'He answered a call about a public disturbance. Some fella shouting in the street. Should only have taken a minute...'

'He went alone?' Beck asked.

Connor was silent for a moment. 'Yes,' he said then. 'It was nothing. He was just going to move the fella on. Tell him to go home and sleep it off. The usual. Get them all the time, can't double crew for a shout like that.'

Connor said it like he was trying to convince Beck.

Beck continued staring at the street lamp, at the way the shadows swung back and forth through the beam of light. And realised that shadows didn't normally have a length of rope attached, nor did they have...

He stepped slowly forward. He could see now what it was. Beneath the light, the rope was tied around a neck, the other end slung over scaffolding on one side of a shop door, slicing into the neck, rimming it with blood, the head cast downward to the ground. There was a gash in a corner of the forehead, blood covering the side of the face. The body had the posture of a gingerbread man, the legs and arms slightly angled, moving back and forth. A gingerbread man dressed in the uniform of a guard.

Beck didn't say anything right away.

Connor turned his tired eyes towards him, slowly following his gaze.

Claire was too busy thinking of Lucy, guilty at having left her alone, irritated that her wife was so damned needy, to notice anything.

Beck walked forward, stood directly beneath the lamp post, staring at the body in front of him hanging from the scaffolding pole a few feet above the ground. The wide, dead eyes gazed back at Beck.

Connor's eyes finally made out what Beck was staring at. 'Ah, Christ,' he said. 'Ah Christ. Ah Christ.'

The sergeant rushed forward, waving his hands in the air in that desperate way of people who don't know what to do. There was nothing to do. Not for Garda Smith. Not now.

Behind them, no one saw the figure dart into the alleyway. The wind, pushing from the west towards them, carried on it the faint echo of footsteps running between the buildings. Beck heard those footsteps, turned and walked to the mouth of the alley, peered in. At the end, a fleeting glimpse, a glint in the street light, moving from the alley, disappearing on to the street at the other end. He sprinted into the alley after it.

Claire saw him go, was about to follow, but hesitated. Something at the very edge of her vision. She turned away from the alley, watched as the orange glow crept over the brow of the hill by the cathedral. Like a sunrise.

'Fire!' she screamed. 'Fire! The presbytery's on fire.'

*

Beck emerged onto the street at the other end of the alley. He stood there, holding his breath, listening. And saw it again, a glimpse of a yeti, a giant, a hulking great shape flitting between the shadows of the buildings, moving towards the river. He started after it again, regretting every cigarette he had ever smoked, every hangover he had ever endured. His legs felt wooden and heavy, but he pushed himself on. He crossed Main Street onto Bridge Street and reached the river wall. He stopped. His lungs were on fire now, his heart jackhammering inside his ribcage. There was a rattling, wheezing sound each time he sucked in air. He knew he was bending the needle, pushing it way, way into the red zone. It seemed like an eternity, but in fact was less than a minute, before the needle dropped out of the red zone and he regained his breath.

There it was again, captured in the weak pools of light from the street lamps, moving along the riverbank now, moving slowly, as if goading him to follow. Beck slipped from the street through the gap in the wall and down towards the river. He cursed himself for not having brought a torch.

It started to rain, sudden and vicious. Beck moved forward, the ground soggy and slippery underfoot. The rain stung his face, dripped into his eyes, the world becoming a black smudge.

*

Two patrol cars were already pulling up at the end of the driveway to the presbytery when Claire swung the Focus into the cathedral car park. The fire brigade had not yet arrived. Cross Beg's fire brigade was mostly volunteer. It would take a little time for these men – and they were all men – to get up from their warm beds, dress, travel to the station, change into their personal protective equipment and start up the fire engines.

Claire stood with Sergeant Connor just outside the gates. The entire top floor of the house was ablaze, but the ground floor, strangely, was as yet untouched. Already the flames were licking just above the front door; it was possible to see the fire creeping down the wall, like a beast from hell, a deep, low, hungry rumbling noise coming from it as the wind's churning air currents whipped it up into a greater frenzy.

'Someone's in there!' It was Connor, pointing, his face alive in the light of the dancing flames.

At the centre window on the top floor, behind the cascade of falling rain, an outline, a silhouette, squat and wide. What was it? Claire squinted, discerned the backrest of a chair, and it was enough for her brain to find the missing link and realise that it was someone sitting in a chair. As she watched, the chair began to move, shaking from side to side, then back and forth. And Claire understood: this person was not sitting in the chair, this person was tied to it, and they were trying to escape. And at that moment the window pane popped, shards of glass slicing through the air and onto the grass below, smashing onto the tarmac of the drive. And with it the sound of the desperate voice escaping: *'Heeeeelp!'*

*

Beck stumbled ahead, his eyes half closed against the rain that was pummelling him, with nothing, no buildings or tree lines to weaken its intensity. He was disorientated, as if he'd woken up in a darkened room half drunk, groping about for a light switch or door handle, anything to corral the darkness and reassure him he had not fallen into a black hole. He had no idea where he was on the riverbank.

He took a step forward, but as his foot came down he knew he had travelled too far. There was nothing there; he was right on the edge of the riverbank. He brought his foot back up, vulnerable and off balance, and it was then that he felt his arms being pressed in on either side of him, and he was being turned around and around, spun like a top, then released. And now he was falling backward. In that instant before he hit the water, he twisted like a cat, his legs in front of him, his upper body contorting into an exaggerated 'C' shape. Beck was not trying to stop himself from falling; it was too late for that. He was just trying to take the bastard who had pushed him down too. He hit the water, felt the coldness like a punch to the solar plexus, the water flooding his nostrils and mouth, his arms flailing about through the air. He felt something with one hand, not knowing what it was, and his other hand, as it followed, reached out and wrapped itself around it too and held on with the desperate determination of a drowning man. And as Beck held on, what he was holding gave way and he was swept away with it. He still held it in his hand, but it began to spasm now, jerking furiously, hitting him in the side of his face, again, and again, and again. And Beck felt the hot liquid on his face that was his blood and he understood what was happening. Someone was kicking him in the face.

*

The other windows were popping now, too, a series of crackling sounds with the w*hoosh* as the pent-up energy from the fire was released, like air brakes on an out- of-control juggernaut.

Claire looked on, her mind a roller coaster but her body rigid, stuck to the spot. A voice inside her screamed Move! Do something! For God's sake. You have to do something.

But she did not move; she did not know what to do.

And like a force propelling her, she turned and began running towards the public order van a little way behind, the beginnings of a vague idea forming in her head. 'The keys? Are they in it? The fucking keys. Are they in it?'

Connor looked back at her. His hands began moving to his pockets, began to rummage about looking for them. But she was at the van now, opening the driver's door, leaning in. Saw the key. In the ignition. Sat in. Turned it. Felt the cold blast of air from the heater as the engine started like an unexpected embrace.

Beck released it, pushed it away, this thing kicking him in the face. But it came back again. He watched it splash into the water next to his ear. It rose from the water again, but Beck grabbed it before it could come down a second time. He pulled on it and used it to leverage himself through the water, clawing at the body beneath him, ignoring the flaying hands until his weight pushed against it, forcing it under the water. Still he did not let it go as he felt it pushing and squirming beneath him. He felt the hornet's nest of pain on his face for merely a moment before his mind cast the pain aside, too busy with the business of surviving to consider anything else. He held onto the body for as long as possible, until it stopped moving. Then he released it, and almost immediately a dark shape rose from beneath the water next to him, and he could see the pale, dead face of Father Clifford, frozen eyes staring into his. He was midstream, where the currents were most powerful, within the miniature whirlpools of water. He saw the body of Father Clifford tumble through a white top and into a trough of water. It did not come out again. Beck was carried along, the currents pulling him under, dragging him down as if yanked on a chain, then *pop*, it released him again, and he swam frantically what he thought was up, until he broke the surface, sucking air into his seared lungs before the ice-cold tentacles reached out again, gripping him, pulling him down, down…

The Scarecrow was laughing, bent over double, hands on knees, looking up at him every so often before quickly turning away again, as if the sight of Beck fighting for his life was too much of a pleasure to bear.

Beck stopped fighting. He was too tired now. He did nothing, was simply swept along. He had given up.

Behind the Scarecrow, Beck could see all the way down, down into the depths where the Old Duffer, the others, the misfits, the ogres, the dead, were coming out to watch. It was the dead who were the most interested, Jason Geraghty amongst them, standing at the back, his clothes blackened by the scorch marks where he had been shot, and smeared red with his blood. They had opened their door wide, the dead, waiting for him to come and join them.

Beck was swept along, surprised at how easy it was. How easy it was to die.

He was almost there now, where the water was no longer cold, but instead warm and still. He was almost there.

But then he saw her: Natalia.

He opened his mouth, but there was no air now in his lungs, nothing to disturb the water, not even a single bubble. All that moved were his lips as he mouthed the words 'I love you'. His legs and arms began to kick about in a wild rage.

*

The engine howled as Claire drove the public order van towards the burning building, the inferno up ahead filling the windscreen. The heat was like putting your head into the open door of a burning stove. It was almost unbearable... *almost.*

When it seemed she was about to journey into the very flames themselves, Claire whipped the steering wheel to the right. The front wheels clawed at the melting tarmac, the rear wheels sliding the car wide in an arc, and then she stamped her foot on the brake pedal and the van lurched to a stop, side on to the fire. She opened the door, taking off her jacket and covering her face as she clambered out.

Was this too little, too late?

She screamed towards the window: 'Topple! Lean forward. Topple! Now, for God's sake. Topple!'

But her voice seemed lost to the roar of the fire. Whoever was up there was going to die anyway, she thought. Even if they did topple, that didn't mean they'd survive… *Ah fuck, I don't know.*

Anyway, it was too late, she suddenly decided. The fire was curling through the windows now, and Claire could smell something, like the acrid stench of singeing hair. Then realised that was what it was. Singeing hair. Her singeing hair.

Just a little longer, she told herself. *Just a little longer.*

And then, as if in slow motion, the shape moved, joined with the flames, becoming one with them, but only briefly, before separating, falling from the flames, falling from the window, turning over as it went, falling through the air.

Voomp! It landed on the roof of the van, the metal crumpling beneath it, and by its sound, Claire thought – Claire *hoped* – it was the back of the chair that had taken the impact, because if it was the front… *Jesus, please let it be the back.*

Claire became aware of people coming to her, running, led by Sergeant Connor. The chair and its occupant were sliding from the roof of the van; hands reached out, strong, powerful hands, grasping it, catching it before it impacted with the ground, starting to carry it away, swiftly away, Claire behind, running from the flames that crackled and roared like a beast seeking to devour them.

*

Anger had propelled him, had given him the reserve of energy he needed and held him, sustained him just long enough – a second maybe, but enough to keep life in his veins until he bobbed to the surface on the turning current and he could gulp at the precious air, literally breathe life into his body then wait to go back down again, knowing that he would not survive this time. But he did not go down again. Instead, Beck was on the other side of the churning water, in the river estuary, where the water stretched out between wide banks on its approach to the sea, where it was calm, where the wind could no longer funnel between the narrow banks and whip the water into a frenzy.

Beck stretched his body and did not move, for there was nothing more for him to give. He closed his eyes and allowed himself to simply be carried along on the gentle current, heading towards the shore.

CHAPTER EIGHTY-SIX

There was a warmth in the air, the sky a canopy of blue stretching from one end of the world to the other. The weathered old buildings along the crooked streets in the centre of town, those stooped and grey buildings with their black slate roofs latticed in green moss, seemed to stretch before the yellow-washed sun.

But there was a silence. Everywhere. Even the traffic seemed to move quietly, without sound. It was as if an enemy had gone through the town, leaving behind the stillness of death.

And shock too.

It would take time, a long time, for Cross Beg to recover.

Beck was sitting on the edge of the bed in his room at the County Hospital, looking for his missing slipper. He'd woken during the night without any recollection of how he had arrived here, content to lie still and quiet in the half-light – for hospital rooms were never truly dark – feeling grateful that he was simply alive. This morning his nurse had informed him that heavy doses of morphine had been administered, which explained the Zen-like calm he had experienced.

He'd like to try that again.

Where was the ruddy slipper? He gave up, walked to the door, stretched his arm out towards the handle when the door swung open and Claire Somers was standing there. Her flesh, on her hands and face, where the flesh had been exposed to the intense heat, was tenderised and red, her hands covered in dry dressing.

'They only just told me,' she said. 'That you were… Jesus, your face.'

She was in a dress. It was the first time he'd seen her in a dress. Even if the dress was a hospital gown.

Beck had forgotten about his face, because there was no pain. He went to the sink next to the door and looked in the mirror over it. One eye was ringed in black like a panda bear's, his jaw yellow and purple with flashes of red where the skin had broken, his right cheek swollen like a bowl.

'And you?' he said, turning to her, the words lopsided. He felt like he had a tennis ball in his mouth.

'Minor burns.'

Her hair looked like a Brillo pad. He was about to say that her burns didn't look all that minor to him, but decided against it.

They had both survived. That is what mattered.

CHAPTER EIGHTY-SEVEN

The book he'd been reading was resting on his chest when Beck opened his eyes. It was dark now. A sliver of light came under the door from the corridor outside. He reached up and turned on the switch over his bed. The morphine had worn off. His face hurt, his legs hurt, his arms hurt. Everything hurt. He became aware of somebody in the room. He turned his head. Natalia was sitting there. He blinked. It really was her.

'I had to see you,' she said. Her hand reached out and sought his, held it gently, the flesh warm, soft, so soft. She'd been crying. 'I didn't know what to… You're alive. Thank God. You're alive.'

'I didn't expect to see you. You came.'

'I love you, Beck. You know that. I never stopped loving you.'

He said nothing. They looked at one another, silently staring into one another's hearts.

'I want to kiss you,' she said. 'But I can't.'

'You can.'

'Very gently.'

She leaned forward. He could smell her perfume, like fresh flowers. Her lips found his. It stung a little, but he moved against them, forgetting the discomfort. The moment their lips touched, he felt a warm, quivering sensation. Then she sat back. 'I don't think we should.'

'I think we should.'

She smiled.

'Are you staying overnight?'

She shook her head. 'I'm driving back. I want to be back by ten.'

'Or do you *have* to be back by ten?'

'I had to see you. He doesn't know I've gone anywhere.'

Beck looked away, took his hand from hers. There was a new feeling now, a hollow, empty, cold feeling.

'Please, Beck.'

'Why do you do this?'

'Do what?' There was hurt in her tone.

'This. Give with one hand, but take away with the other.'

'That's not fair. Really.'

Beck said nothing for a minute. 'Thank you for coming,' he replied slowly.

'Please, Beck…'

'I mean it. Thank you for coming.'

He could hear the sound of her breathing. She stood, holding her small handbag in both hands in front of her. Her nails were perfectly painted. She turned, and he watched her go, noting the high heels and the perfect legs, the curve of the hips inside the tight dress.

As the door closed he picked up his book and threw it on the floor.

The Aftermath…

Series of brutal killings leaves Cross Beg reeling
By Lucy Grimes

One small town. One crazed killer. One devastating secret. One church's sanctity violated. No, this is not the blurb to a Hollywood blockbuster. This is what happened in Cross Beg, Galway. And it happened last week. Our reporter Lucy Grimes tells it like it is. She tells the *real* story. It begins right here…

As funerals continue this week for the victims of the gruesome series of murders in the sleepy south Galway town of Cross Beg, the question on everyone's lips is this: how was it possible?

I first met the person everyone thought of as Father Matthew Clifford when he returned to Cross Beg almost two years ago now. A tall, imposing man, with cold, piercing eyes, he claimed he'd spent more than thirty years as a missionary priest at various locations in the Republic of the Congo. The rumour he'd been sent there after getting local girl Angela Farmer pregnant was long forgotten. The nineteen-year-old Farmer had been employed as a part-time housekeeper in the presbytery at the time when Father Clifford, a curate, had lived there. It was the talk of Cross Beg back then.

I never liked Father Clifford. I felt there was something not quite right about him. Call it intuition. And my feelings have been vindicated. A statement issued by Inspector Gerald O'Reilly of Cross Beg Gardai identified the primary suspect in the spate of killings as Mr Benedict Farmer, Father Clifford's and Angela Farmer's illegitimate son.

Evidence supporting this was found in the ruins of Cross Beg presbytery, namely a passport in Benedict Farmer's name. Sources state that a victim – who cannot be named for legal reasons and who is recovering in hospital – revealed to gardai that Farmer admitted killing Father Clifford and impersonating him. When contacted this week, there was no one available to comment at either the diocesan office in Galway or the headquarters of the Missionary African Fathers in Maynooth.

Detective Inspector Finnegan Beck and Detective Garda Claire Somers were hailed as heroes for their actions in the ordeal. They both remain in hospital today following the dramatic events of Sunday night. Events that began with the gruesome discovery of the body of Garda Justin Smith hanging from scaffolding at a shop front, and the unnamed victim being persuaded by Detective Somers to jump from a burning window. Detective Inspector Beck gave chase to Farmer and followed him down to the Brown Water River where, in an ensuing struggle, they both fell in.

It is believed that Benedict Farmer died in the struggle, though his body, at time of going to press, has not yet been recovered. An extensive search by gardai and volunteers continues.

Inspector Gerald O'Reilly of Cross Beg gardai told this reporter that officers Beck and Somers were merely doing their jobs. He went on to praise the determined efforts of the dedicated task force led by himself and Superintendent Andrew Wilde, which was, he said, responsible for 'flushing' the culprit into the open, and so bringing to an end the spree of killings. He said that the Garda Síochána was a dedicated and proud force of officers, and that it would be unfair to single out any member for special attention. 'This was a team effort,' he said. 'People were merely doing their duty.'

What We Don't Know...

I spent all day Monday this week trawling through official death records in the HSE offices in Galway. I wanted to follow up on something I had heard people in Cross Beg talk about for years. It was this: a dramatic increase in suicide rates in the town during the early 1980s. This was at a time when suicide rates were being massaged downward, when it was considered almost a national humiliation that any suicide should take place in the country at all. Yet, despite this, between January 1982 and January 1984, nine people ended their lives by suicide in Cross Beg, mainly by throwing themselves into the Brown Water River. This figure dropped to zero in the year following Benedict Farmer leaving the town. And in the last two years, the rate had started to creep up again. Coincidence? We may never know. Because it seems that the death of Benedict Farmer took more than his life – it also took his secrets.

Detailed report and analysis by our team of reporters on the ground in Cross Beg: pages 4, 5, 7 and 8.

EPILOGUE

Four weeks had passed. Farmer's body was snagged in the propeller of a boat in the estuary of the Brown Water River, not far from Haven Bay. It was bloated and rotting and mutilated, but bore the remnants of a priest's cassock matching the one Farmer was last seen in. A DNA sample was extracted and matched a sample taken from a niece of Angela Farmer, who was tracked to Galway city where she lives. The body, or what remained of it, was buried alongside his mother and her husband, Willie Kelly. The funeral took place early on a Monday morning before Cross Beg had fully shaken itself awake. A howling gale blew in from the sea as the last shovel of dirt was thrown onto his grave, the sky a swirl of black. There was a low and constant rumble of thunder – with it bolts of lightning, pulses that fizzled and glowed, rupturing the black sky and striking the earth, where, instead of impacting the ground, they seemed to disappear beneath it.

People later talked about it in hushed tones. They said something evil had returned to where it had come from that day: Hell.

Beck, standing at the graveside, the lone mourner, would laugh about this when he heard it. His mind had no place for such nonsense. People sought explanations for the inexplicable in any way they could.

But the truth was that Benedict Farmer, lying in his grave, would never be forgotten. Dead most certainly, but he would always live on in the minds of people, certainly for a generation, but maybe, in some way, forever.

He would, Beck mused, probably have quite liked that.

A LETTER FROM MICHAEL

I want to say a huge thank you for choosing to read *Where She Lies*. If you did enjoy it, and want to keep up to date with all my latest releases, just sign up at the following link. Your email address will never be shared, and you can unsubscribe at any time.

www.bookouture.com/michael-scanlon

Every cloud has a silver lining is a phrase that is so true to me, never more so than now with the publication of my debut novel. I always wanted to be a writer, and by that I mean I always wanted to write stories that people would want to read. And all my life I've been doing this, but most of my work, short stories and long, complete and not-so-complete novels, remained hidden in the bottom of wardrobes and lockers. I never felt I was good enough.

But in 2014, I became gravely ill while on holiday in Spain. I spent three months in hospital in Tarragona with (what remains) a mystery illness, hovering between life and death. For the following two years I was in and out of hospital. Throughout this period, once the initial symptoms subsided, I wrote. And I read. I read and I wrote more than I have ever done in my life. It kept me sane, it literally stopped me from falling into a black hole of depression. And out of a very dark period in my life something good has come, as I braved sending my work to an editor again. It took over three years and a life-threatening illness to finally get round to it. And boy, am I glad I did! And another silver lining: I don't worry or fret like I used to. I simply do the best I can.

Finnegan Beck is a character who is very close to my heart, too. As a civilian employee of An Garda Síochána, I know the pressures that officers work under. I also know of the commitment they give, which often goes far beyond the call of duty. For Beck, flawed as he is, his job, essentially, is his life, although he would never admit it. I hope you'll spend more time with Beck in my subsequent novels, getting to know him better. There is a lot to know.

I hope you loved *Where She Lies*, and if you did, I would be very grateful if you could write a review. I'd love to hear what you think, and it makes such a difference helping new readers to discover one of my books for the first time.

I would love to hear from you, too, and am on Twitter if you'd like to reach out!

Thanks,
Michael

 @MScanlonAuthor

ACKNOWLEDGEMENTS

First, I would like to thank you, the reader, for taking the time to read this book. Equally, I would like to thank Isobel Akenhead and Bookouture for spotting something in my writing and taking a chance on me. I hope to live up to expectations. Truly, thank you.

To Eileen, my wife, for always being there, and my beautiful daughter, Sarah; words will never be enough. To Breda Jennings, Rosemary Flaherty and Marian Nagle, all crime book enthusiasts who gave me honest feedback and allowed me to alter course when required.

Again, to Isobel Akenhead, also Rachel Rowlands and Jenny Page, for their hard work and invaluable expertise during the editing process. And to Noelle Holten and Alexandra Holmes. Thank you all.

To my civilian colleagues at An Garda Síochána, especially Declan, Ruth and Michelle. To Patrick Feeney, a man with a heart as big as his musical talent. To Dr Dustin Portilla at Hospital Universitari de Tarragona Joan XXIII, Spain, and Natalia Higuera Haines, Tarragona, Spain – truly, there are angels who walk amongst us.

To Dr Luke O'Donnell at University Hospital, Castlebar, and my GP, Dr William Brunker. To the kindness of strangers and the goodness of the human spirit. When I needed both, I found them in abundance.

To the writers who have influenced me and whose brilliance has intimidated me in equal measure. I hope I've found my own voice now.

Made in the USA
Columbia, SC
26 August 2021